Demons and Shadows

DEMONS
and
SHADOWS

The Ghostly Best Stories of
ROBERT WESTALL

FARRAR, STRAUS AND GIROUX

NEW YORK

Copyright © 1993 by the Estate of Robert Westall
All rights reserved
Published simultaneously in Canada by HarperCollins*CanadaLtd*
Printed in the United States of America
Designed by Debbie Glasserman
First edition, 1993

Library of Congress Cataloging-in-Publication Data

Westall, Robert.
Demons and shadows : the ghostly best stories of Robert
Westall.—1st ed.
p.   cm.
1. Ghost stories, English.   2. Horror tales, English.
[Ghosts—Fiction.   2. Horror tales.   3. Short stories.] I. Title.
PZ7.W51953Db   1993   [Fic]—dc20   93-7949   CIP   AC

For Wes Adams
a good companion on a labyrinthine journey

CONTENTS

Demons and Shadows

RACHEL
AND THE ANGEL

RACHEL SAT on her bike in the vicarage gateway, twisting the handlebars and watching the front wheel screw up dust. The tire was going flat, but she couldn't be bothered to pump it up. It was half past nine in the morning and already too hot. Still cool in the shadow of the vicarage oaks, but beyond, the village street burned, little stalks of yellow straw chasing their tails in the swirls of heat. A car passed, going into the village too fast, blatting Rachel sideways with a gust of scorching air. She regained her balance just in time and kept on sitting.

Which way should she go? Back to the empty vicarage, the cold tap dripping on greasy plates in Mum's disorganized kitchen? She could wash up, but Mum would take it as criticism. Besides, the kitchen frightened her a bit when Mum wasn't there. Mum took her zany sense of humor with her, and left only the chaos.

No point going back. Or turning left, either. Beyond the vicarage trees the cornfields started, a heartless sea of gold, rising and falling, without hedges or shade, without cottages or gardens, people or animals, or even birds. The road crept through it, fenceless, like an unwanted dog, all four miles to Stensfield. On that road she'd see nothing but the distant lines of combine harvesters, eating up the wheat in square blocks like cornflake packets, spewing out their endless vomit of grain. You couldn't even see the men inside. On bad days she had the feeling the machines were doing it by themselves.

No point turning right, either. Beyond the rim of council houses, the cornfields bit into the village again. The village was drowning in a sea of gold, like a pretty head without a body anymore. It didn't use to be like this. When she was little, Daddy had taken her for walks. There'd been woods, birds, and hedgehogs.

All gone—swept away by the corn.

Only in front was there any life—the village street leading up to the church. If she rode slowly, there might be time for Dr. Diggory to pass, toot, pull up, and ask how she was, this fine morning? Then she'd lean her arm on the hot roof of his car, and they'd discuss something he'd just read in the *Telegraph*. Dr. Diggory was old, at least fifty, with a stiff, lined face that had watched too much pain. But talking to him made her feel grownup for half the day afterwards.

But most mornings he didn't pass. Of course, she could turn at the church and ride slowly back, giving him a second chance. But if she did that too often, the village women gossiping at their gates would notice and start gossiping about *her*.

Or she could go to the antique shop. Mrs. Venn let her help with dusting and talked to her about the deeper mysteries of porcelain. Sometimes, if Mrs. Venn had been to a sale, there'd be new treasures to unpack and admire. Mrs. Venn was a widow and nearly as old as Dr. Diggory.

No chicken, Mum said. Yet she was as pretty and cheerful as a married woman half her age, with her short blond hair and marvelous blue eyes. She had no children; she had nobody. Yet she had this happiness she shared with Rachel, as easily as she might share a seat on a bus.

But Rachel had spent all yesterday at the antique shop . . . Don't spoil a good thing, a little warning voice said.

Go and see Ziggy, who lived below the church with his huge garden and tiny cottage, one room up, one down? Good job Ziggy was so tiny or he'd never fit in. Ziggy and Molly were both small enough, because Molly was a fat black-and-white cat. Though when Rachel had first heard him talk about her, she was sure Molly was his wife. Ziggy talked to Molly constantly, quarreled with her bitterly at times. Rachel remembered coming up to the garden gate, hearing Ziggy's high-pitched shouts of "Mowderer, mowderer!" And there was poor Molly, cowering beneath the giant cabbages with a dead blackbird tied around her neck as if she was the Ancient Mariner . . . Or Molly huge with kitten, while Ziggy raged at her about the Catholic virtue of chastity. "She is no better than a streetwalker, Miss Rachel!"

But between them, they always found homes for the kittens.

Ziggy was Polish, a flotsam of war who'd appeared in the village in 1946, miles from any other Pole. Sometimes he talked of going home, to his sister who was a professor in Poland. Then he'd shake his head and say, "Poland is Poland no more, Miss Rachel. If I went back there, I wouldn't know it." So instead, each summer, his garden would blaze with the colors of the Polish flag.

"So this is Poland now, Miss Rachel!"

Or there'd be other flower beds, in the colors of the

Pope or the Virgin. "See, I am faithful to the Church, Miss Rachel. Even if they are not faithful to me because I drink too much!"

He made a living as a gardener, and every year won the prize for the biggest pumpkin. But she couldn't take Ziggy this morning. It was nearly time for the village show and he would talk of nothing but pumpkins. "Jack Sprigg's pumpkins, they are not well, I hear. Always they start well, but they fail. Perhaps they see Ziggy's pumpkins and lose heart!"

No, no pumpkins this morning.

Suddenly she realized there was nowhere in the world she wanted to go. It made her feel quite desperate. The blinding August sunlight closed in like a black cloud. Daddy and Mummy, gone to lunch with the Bishop, wouldn't be home till four. Time stretched ahead like a black sunlit tunnel.

In that instant, there was a shattering double bang overhead. Before she could flinch, she saw the two planes vanishing across the rooftops at the end of the village, curving up across the swelling corn. Phantoms, from the U.S. air base, eating up the blue sky as the combines ate up the fields, leaving behind their foul transparent tails of black smoke and the disgusting smell of a badly trimmed kerosene heater. Evil, with all the black pointed darts under their wings—devils from Armageddon. Breaking the rules, flying too low as usual. She had a sudden impulse of black hate, to ring up the base and complain, get them into trouble. But there would just be the usual calm and maddeningly reasonable American voice at the far end, assuring her the matter would be looked into, ma'am. Making her feel a silly little fusspot.

She knew she must do something quick or she'd get

into one of her black moods. Once she was in a black, she'd be a week getting out of it, and they *hurt*.

The church—she'd go to the church, always her final refuge. Halfway down the village street, on the corner by the post office, she passed a group of kids her own age, from the local high school. The girls looked at her, then flounced their pathetic blue and green hair and turned their backs, as if to say "Stuck-up bitch." One boy, the tall dishy one who delivered the milk in the holidays, gave her a smile. When she was past, another boy—she was *sure* it was another boy—gave a rather rude wolf whistle. But they'd never do anything about it. Farmhand's son and vicar's daughter . . . in this part of Lincolnshire? She might as well have been a green-eared Martian.

Nonetheless, her face burned all the way to the church. The sound of the gas-driven mower told her old Moley, the sexton, was cutting the grass between the gravestones. Thank God he was out of sight, around the back of the chancel.

SHE SWUNG the oak door shut behind her. The heavy clink of the iron latch was a comfort. She breathed in the air of her private kingdom: mildew and candles, incense and dusty kneelers. Dim and cool; but not as cool as she'd hoped. Daddy said the church stayed cool for a week in a heat wave; then the thick stone walls gave back their heat like storage heaters.

The tower base was friendly. The striped sallies of the bell ropes threw their looped-up shadows across the bell ringers' notices; a stone tablet, recording the ringing of Triple Bob Major to celebrate the Old Queen's Jubilee; yellowing cartoons of bell-ringing monks, fastened to the paneling with rusty pins.

Once when she was eight, greatly daring, she'd un-looped the sally of the smallest bell, the service bell, and rung it three times before it snatched itself from her hand. She'd caught it and rung it nine times more before a crowd of villagers rushed in, frantic to know which child of nine had died?

But today the sallies held no excitement; they looked dirty, like the tails of dead lambs. She could not shake off her blackness.

She walked on, stood beneath the great royal coat of arms that hung on the gallery. The village had paid a lot of money to have it carved in 1661, to prove their loyalty to the new-returned King—even though five village lads had died for Cromwell. She moved her head this way and that, letting the light from the windows bloom blue in strange patterns across the dark polished oak.

But it didn't help.

She went and stroked the coolness of her alabaster knight, where he lay with crossed legs and great mailed arm ever reaching across to draw his sword. Centuries ago, the village men had carved their initials in his soft stone, knocked off his nose to grind up as a cure for sheep colic.

But this morning he had nothing to say to her.

She didn't feel like playing her usual games, didn't feel like sitting in the choir stalls and singing the *Nunc Dimittis*, listening to her small voice echoing around the angel roof, as if all the great carved angels were singing, too. She didn't feel like finding and reading out loud the lesson for the day at the great brass eagle of a lectern. Didn't feel like playing the organ, or even mounting the shockingly high pulpit and preaching one of Daddy's favorite sermons, complete with every wickedly mimicked "Um" and "Ah."

Silly, empty, childish games. The church's deep sloping windowsills were thick with the bodies of small black flies, as usual. Why were they born in here, only to die trying to hammer their way out to the light of day? She brushed them off from habit; under her hand they mixed with the dust that always came off the limestone sills. By the time they hit the floor, they were no more than gray dust themselves.

As a last hope, she climbed into the south gallery, to look at the roof angels. Carved in oak, bigger than a man, they had intricate wings that stretched out to touch each other across the rafters. Remote calm faces and flowing hair. But all exactly alike. How could the old carver have borne to carve each face exactly the same, year after year? And though their shapes were beautiful, the wood was a dull gray-brown, and thick dust lay in every crevice of their robes. And the rest of the gallery was stuffed with old burst kneelers, and tawdry hoopla stuff from the village fete, and bundled-up Union Jacks from the coronation of 1953.

Nobody came up here but her. Not enough congregation to fill half the floor of the nave.

Dullness. Five hundred years of dullness. She could've screamed. If only something wonderful or terrible would happen, just once. Instead of dusty wooden angels, a *real* angel, like in the Bible . . .

In that instant, though she'd heard no one come in, she knew she was no longer alone in the church. Her arms and legs began to shake in the most peculiar way. Trying to control them, she tiptoed down to the front of the gallery. Even so, the dry boards creaked and cracked under her feet.

She could see all the opposite gallery and aisle, and the floor of the nave. Nothing stirred, not even a fly.

The sun was streaming in through the south aisle windows, beneath her feet, making pools of sunlight on the slabbed floor. If anything moved beneath her, she'd see the shadow.

Nothing moved . . . The bell sallies hung quite motionless in the tower base, telling her no one had opened the church door.

That only left the chancel and the altar.

There was something to the left of the altar that hadn't been there on Sunday. That had never been there before. Beyond the altar rail that Mrs. Munslow polished weekly, as if her life depended on it. Beyond Lady Wilbrook's grand but dying flower arrangement. Beyond the massive gold candlestick with its spring-white candle was something new and tall and dark.

Of course there'd be a perfectly sensible explanation. Always was. Not at all sure she wanted a sensible explanation, with a dark delicious fear squeezing her belly, she clumped down the gallery stairs like an elephant in hobnailed boots, as Mummy would have said. At the bottom, the only thing in the whole church she hated caught her eye. The Ten Commandments, lettered on the wall in a huge black Gothic script that crawled like spiders.

THOU SHALT NOT COMMIT ADULTERY

Mummy said those who committed adultery were called adults. Stifling a wild giggle, and with her guts still deliciously shrinking, she walked echoing up the aisle toward the altar.

As she got nearer, her steps slowed. She craned her neck, trying to peer past the huge flower arrangement, expecting every minute that the thing would become quite ordinary. It didn't. Even when she was past the altar rail, it refused to turn into anything sensible. Now she was only three feet away and it was the oddest thing she had ever seen.

Taller than Daddy—almost seven feet high. Curvy, sharp-edged, and a shining brown, with a purply glint where the light from the windows caught it. Must be metal—bronze. It was precisely cut and detailed, like a new coin, and she thought it *extremely* ugly. It seemed to have . . . wings. Three sets of wings, not so much feathered . . . more like the scales on a snake. Each pair of wings was folded—the top pair across where a face would be, the second across the body, and the third across the feet.

She wasn't a vicarage child for nothing. She knew the Bible text: "With twain he covered his face, and with twain he covered his feet, and with twain he did fly."

It was supposed to be a statue of an angel—modern art! Soft old Daddy had let some crazy modern artist dump the monstrosity on him, because nobody else would have it. God knew what the church council would say . . . They'd nearly gone mad when he introduced the second set of altar candles. And when he used incense, once a year at Christmas, they all coughed as if they were dying of pneumonia and the Russians had launched a poison-gas attack. Oh, *Daddy*!

She walked around it, pouting in disgust. The stupid artist had plastered the back with what looked like eyes, in the most revolting sort of way. That was in the Bible, too, of course.

"Full of eyes before and behind." The eyes weren't bronze but huge and shiny and dark like camera lenses. And clustered as thick and ugly as the spots on Derek Wharmby's cheeks . . . yuk!

But she couldn't resist reaching out to touch.

Two inches away, heat hitting her fingertips made her pull back. It wasn't icy-cold like bronze but red-hot, like the church stove in winter.

Don't be *silly*! She reached out and touched it.

And blistered her finger. She leaped back a yard and sucked her fingertip and watched the thing. The waves of heat coming off it made her break out into a sweat. Where a couple of leaves of Lady Wilbrook's flower arrangement touched it, they had crumpled and died. No wonder the church felt so warm!

Some new sort of central heating system, going full blast in the middle of a heat wave. How crazy could you get? It must have cost a ton of money to make . . .

Suddenly it all got too much. It was Daddy's worry, not hers. She began to walk away down the church. She hadn't got as far as the chancel steps when there came a strange creaking rustling behind. She whirled in a panic.

The wings were slowly opening. They might touch the altar hangings and set them on fire! Exasperated, close to tears, she ran back. And saw the most horrible thing. As the wings opened, the body she had thought was shining bronze began to wrinkle like skin, and she knew with horrid certainty it was alive.

The opening wings disclosed more pimply shining eyes, all over the face and body. And they began to glow dimly. And then they glowed brighter and brighter, until they were like the little red holes in a workman's brazier. As if the whole creature was full of fire. Black stalks extending from the head, like snails' eyes.

Oh, it must be a bomb, a missile from the air base. She must fetch old Moley the sexton, the police, the fire brigade . . .

But as she ran down the church, it seemed to stretch

to an infinite length, as if the great stone arches were made of elastic and she might run forever and ever. And then the aisle seemed to twist to the left and downward, and she tripped over her own feet and fell.

If she had nursed the hope that it was all a bad dream, the pain in her knees, the trickle of blood down her white shin told her it was not. She twisted around where she lay, to look back toward the altar. The dark figure seemed to fill the chancel arch. The altar seemed to have shrunk to the size of a silk-covered stool. The very fabric of the church seemed to be bending, as if trying to get away from the figure.

She knew she could not.

"I AM ZAPHAEL." The name was inside her skull like a clap of thunder, though she was oddly certain it hadn't got there through her ears. She was on her knees before it, because her legs simply refused to stand up. She felt she was going to be sick. She felt outraged at what this thing was doing to her and to Daddy's church. A small furtive part of her mind still played with the idea of getting a big hammer and smashing it. But already it was filling her mind again.

"I BEHELD SATAN AS LIGHTNING FALL FROM HEAVEN." It held no trace of joy or regret, no emotion at all, like a speaking clock. Less emotion than a speaking clock, for that at least *tried* to sound friendly. This just filled her mind until she feared it would burst apart with the strain.

"THERE WAS WAR IN HEAVEN. MIKEL AND HIS ANGELS FOUGHT AGAINST THE DRAGON AND THE DRAGON FOUGHT AND HIS ANGELS AND PREVAILED NOT NEITHER WAS THEIR PLACE FOUND ANY MORE IN

HEAVEN AND THE GREAT DRAGON WAS CAST OUT INTO
EARTH AND HIS ANGELS WITH HIM."

From her place on the floor, she looked at the scaly
bronze skin as it rose and fell, wrinkled and twitched,
and she shuddered. She had forgotten that the devils
had been angels once. Once, before they fought, they
must all have looked very much alike . . . been very much
alike. Not human, not human at all. All those silly artists
carving them and painting them looking like women with
beautiful faces and long golden hair and graceful white
hands playing harps and trumpets . . . If only they'd
bothered to look in the Bible for the real descriptions . . .
The Burning Bush that Moses feared to look upon, that
was not consumed . . . *that* had been an angel . . .

She felt the heat of the thing on her face, even from
this distance. It was glowing like a black cage of fire, like
a volcano about to erupt and throw down the whole
village.

She didn't even know which side this one had been on,
Mikel's or Satan's. There was no way of telling. It must
have been a terrible fight between Mikel and Satan . . .
She had seen two tomcats fighting on the roof of the
garage, the tangled, twisted bodies screaming, rolling
over and over, the blood, the tufts of ginger fur streaming
from them like autumn leaves on the wind . . . How
much more awful Mikel and Satan . . . their wounds . . .

"THE DRAGON FOUGHT . . . THE DRAGON FOUGHT . . .
THE DRAGON FOUGHT . . ." Now the creature sounded
like a speaking clock that was breaking down, going
wrong. Its head was lopsided. Had *it* been wounded,
dreadfully wounded?

"BEHELD SATAN . . . BEHELD SATAN FALL . . . SATAN
FALL."

There was something dreadfully wrong with the creature. It was not just terribly powerful but terribly going wrong. Like an elephant running amok . . . It might . . .

"THIS CITY IS UNDER JUDGMENT. I WILL DESTROY THIS CITY. I WILL DESTROY THIS CITY UTTERLY."

"But *why?*" Her voice was a wail. "What have we done?" It never occurred to her to question the thing's power.

"THIS CITY IS AN ABOMINATION OF WICKEDNESS."

"You can't destroy us . . . It wouldn't be allowed."

"HAVE YOU FORGOTTEN SODOM?"

"You can't . . . We know too much now . . . The whole world would notice . . . These things don't happen anymore . . ."

There was a long, hot silence. And then in the hot silence there was a familiar double bang overhead. Tiny trickles of dust fell from the ceiling, through the beams of colored sunlight from the stained-glass windows. The Phantoms from the air base had come back. Still flying suicidally low. God knew what destruction they held in those evil dart shapes under their wings . . .

And if the pilots made one split-second mistake . . . the village . . . if this creature even made the pilots blink . . . of course there would be a court of inquiry afterwards . . . regrets expressed . . . new regulations made . . . compensation paid. But Mummy and Daddy, Dr. Diggory, Mrs. Venn, Ziggy, and the boy who delivered the milk in the holidays would be tiny shapes under tarpaulins, shrunk by the heat of the inferno, if they still existed at all. No bigger than charred dolls . . .

She did the bravest thing she'd ever done, then. She rose to her feet, patted her hair back in place, and said to the dark shape, "I don't believe in you. I have made you up. You are only in my mind. I've been . . . upset

lately . . . alone too much. I read the Bible too much. I
hear about God's wrath destroying the world nearly every
day. I am frightened of the American bombers because
they fly too low. I shall go and fetch people now. If you
are still here when I come back, they will photograph
you and put you in the papers and do experiments on
you. You won't like that. And if you aren't here when I
come back, I will know you never really existed."

She knew she was being unfair; she wanted to be unfair
to it.

It said nothing.

She turned and walked away.

She was afraid the church would start to stretch and
twist again, but it didn't. The slabbed aisle stayed firm
beneath her feet. Oddly enough, the outside door was
slightly open, letting in a bar of sunlight across the rough
coconut matting of the tower base. She thought she'd
shut it when she came in, but the latch must not have
fallen properly and the wind had blown the door open
again. For some reason, she slid through the gap without
touching the door . . .

It was the silence that struck her first. Not a country
silence touched with a rustling of leaves, a passing car,
or the distant lowing of a cow.

Total, utter silence—the silence of a tomb.

And then the utter stillness struck her. The leaves of
the silver birch by the lych-gate had been blown back by
the wind, showing their pale undersides. But the wind
had gone, and still they stayed blown back, frozen. Frozen
like the chimney smoke of Miss Mulbridge's cottage,
where she kept a fire burning winter and summer to heat
the kettle for a cup of tea. Frozen like the clouds, which
looked painted on the blue sky.

Nothing in the whole world moved; yet still she ran for the safety of old Moley, the sexton. She noticed as she ran that the gravel of the path didn't scrunch under her feet. It felt fixed, immovable, as it did in a hard frost. The bumps in it hurt her feet through her sandals, like frozen ruts. She turned the corner of the chancel and saw old Moley. He was just curving the motor mower around the edge of the Granville tomb, head on one side in neat calculation, tongue half out with concentration, the beads of sweat standing out on his brow under the faded Panama hat. He had one foot off the ground, taking a step; the cut blades of grass flew from the front of his mower. But all, foot and sweat and blades of grass in mid-air, was frozen into stillness. She tiptoed closer: his chest wasn't moving; he wasn't breathing. Unless he breathed soon, he would die . . . She touched him. He didn't even rock on his feet; he was as immovable as a marble statue. She even tried to push one of the blades of grass that were suspended in mid-air. It not only stayed in position, unmoving; it cut her finger like a razor blade.

Zaphael had frozen the whole world.

But that meant everything was dead already.

Or else . . . Zaphael had taken *her* out of time itself. She was caught with Zaphael alone, forever in one moment of time. She could run as far as she liked through this frozen world; she would find no help, no food, no water.

The only thing to do was to go back into church and face him.

ZAPHAEL WAS STANDING where she had left him. His wings were still open, unfolded, but the light in his eyes was very dim. He might have been asleep.

But her mind was racing—the mind of a church child who had heard the Bible read, Old and New Testaments, since she could first remember anything. And suddenly she saw a trick that might work. She shouted, "Do *you* remember Sodom?"

The creature heard her; slowly its eyes lit up again, as she stood shouting at it, trembling with fright and eagerness.

She knew it remembered the destruction of Sodom.

"Do you remember Father Abraham? Do you remember his bargain with God?"

It remembered; its eyes glowed brighter and brighter until they were almost white with heat, until she feared she would melt with sweat, and the whole church burst into flame.

"Do you remember God's promise? *Do* you? That if Father Abraham could find ten good and just men in Sodom, God would not destroy it?"

Zaphael was silent; but she knew he remembered.

"There are good people *here . . .*" Sensing victory within her grasp, she felt so tense she was about to burst.

Zaphael was silent; she might almost have thought that Zaphael was waiting for something. Waiting for her . . . to . . .

Name the first name. She named it, feeling as if she was playing the first card in her hand at the parish Christmas Whist Drive.

"Ziggy," she said, not wanting to play her trump card too soon.

SUDDENLY SHE WAS in a different place. A small familiar room, only made unfamiliar by the light of an oil lamp and a fire in the grate. Ziggy's kitchen, and the curtains

drawn, and Molly sprawled contentedly in the wooden
rocker, her head hanging out on one side and her feet
and tail hanging out the other. Ziggy sat in the other
wooden rocker, on the other side of the fire, battering at
some liquid in a rusty old saucepan, with a big wooden
spoon.

Both Ziggy and Molly looked at her in such a natural
way that she said, "Hallo, Ziggy! Hallo, Molly!"

Ziggy looked straight through her, and went back to
battering the contents of the pan, warming it occasionally
over the red coals of the small summer fire. Only Molly
really saw her, the big green eyes following every move
she made, the black-and-white ears flying in all directions,
semaphoring alarm.

I'm a ghost, thought Rachel. Zaphael has made me into
a ghost. Only cats can see ghosts . . . It was all so absurd
she felt like giggling.

But now Ziggy was on his feet, spoon put down on one
side of the brick fireplace.

"Now we shall see! Now we shall show them!" he said
triumphantly. Rachel started with alarm, then realized
he was only talking to Molly, as usual. She watched while
Ziggy fetched a large black plastic bucket full of water
and squeezed the contents of the pan into it, through a
yellow colander. "Ah, good, good," he murmured to
himself, stirring vigorously. "And a good night of raining
to do it."

Only then did Rachel notice the whispering, drumming
of rain on the thatched roof of the cottage. But by that
time Ziggy was pulling on black wellies, a black rubber
mackintosh like the vets wore, and even a black sou'wester.
He looked comical, like a miniature black version of a
lifeboat cox'n off a box of matches. He looked even

funnier when he lifted from the corner of the kitchen an old wartime stirrup pump, the kind they used to put out incendiary bomb fires . . .

Then he went out into the dark and the rain, closing the door and locking it carefully. Rachel, who had by this time got back some of her sense of humor, decided to see if she really was a ghost who could pass through doors . . .

She passed through quite easily, and followed Ziggy into the night. She bet to herself that Molly's ears must be semaphoring like mad . . .

Outside, Ziggy stumped along through the rain, bucket in one hand and pump in the other. Rachel realized it was very late; all the lights in the cottage windows were out; the village was fast asleep. Ziggy stumped till he came to a high, well-trimmed hawthorn hedge. Rachel recognized the sagging white gate.

Jack Sprigg's house. For the first time, the whole thing stopped being comical. Rachel felt a slight twinge of unease, as if Zaphael had reached out a cruel black iron hand and gripped at her stomach.

Ziggy bent to his bucket and pump. He put the end of the pump into the bucket of black liquid and began to pump the handle. A thin jet of black water shot upward, fighting against the heavy falling rain. It went high over Jack Sprigg's hedge and curved down into Jack Sprigg's garden. Rachel heard it pattering down on big flat leaves, heavier than the rain, but disguised by the rain . . . as Ziggy was disguised in the darkness by his black raincoat and sou'wester. What was happening was invisible, inaudible to Jack Sprigg in his cottage, whether he was in bed snoring or awake, alert for intruders.

There was a thrumming, drumming, as if the black

water was falling on some big hollow drum-like object . . .

Like a prize pumpkin.

Somehow Rachel knew that this year again Jack Sprigg's pumpkins were going to lose heart.

In her mind, Rachel started to argue with Zaphael. C'mon, what's a few pumpkins? You can't destroy a village for a few pumpkins . . .

But she had to go on following Ziggy around. From garden to garden—from those of the greatest pumpkin growers to those of the very weakest, poorest pumpkin growers, who had no *chance* of winning. And everywhere, like a demon worm that flies in the night, the black rain fell with the clean rain, on the pumpkins. Until not one was left untouched. Though the clean rain would wash off every trace of black from the leaves, the black would be in the soil. And Ziggy worked so thoroughly, with such crouched intentness, like a murderer over his victim, like a weasel at the throat of a rabbit . . . His very intentness grew hateful.

And then she was back in the sunlit church. Zaphael, at the far end, was still, unmoving. He might have been asleep. But she was standing opposite where the Ten Commandments were written in black spidery letters on the wall.

THOU SHALT NOT COVET THY . . .

Thou shalt not covet thy neighbor's pumpkin, thought Rachel sadly.

"ALL RIGHT," she said, taking a deep breath. "Mrs. Venn." She would save Dr. Diggory for the next. Dr.

Diggory was an even stronger card. Dr. Diggory got up in the middle of the night to see to old ladies who were no more than lonely and frightened. Dr. Diggory saved babies' lives. People said Dr. Diggory was a saint.

Suddenly she was in Mrs. Venn's shop. This time it only gave her a slight jump, though again the two people in the shop looked first at her, then through her. She was getting used to it.

This isn't today, thought Rachel, because it's raining and gray outside, a miserable afternoon. Mrs. Venn had the lights on. And Rachel knew it was at least last week, because the grandfather clock was still there that Mrs. Venn had sold last Friday.

The other woman in the shop was called McNab. She was eighty or more and the nastiest, cattiest old woman in the village. Everybody loathed her. Even Mum said that some old people made their own loneliness.

Both women were staring at a black, gold, and orange plate that had for untold years hung on Mrs. McNab's wall, just inside her front door. Which was usually open to the village street so Mrs. McNab didn't miss anybody who went past, so she could grab them to do her an errand. Mrs. McNab had been known to have five neighbors doing her shopping for her at once. Each shopping for one item, they kept bumping into each other. Anyway, Mrs. Venn and Mrs. McNab were staring at the gold, orange, and black plate, as if it was a beloved pet about to expire.

"It's a real antique," said Mrs. McNab. "It was bought for me grandmother by me grandfather the week after they got married. My granny used to give me my cakes off it, when I wasn't five years old."

"When was your granny married?" asked Mrs. Venn, with a sort of weary compassion.

"It were . . ." Mrs. McNab did mumbling calculations, her lips trembling, the little black whiskers on them shaking. "It were 1887. . . . No, I tell a lie . . . 1888 . . ."

"That's not very old for an antique," said Mrs. Venn gently. "They're supposed to be a hundred years old. And it's part of a set . . . You haven't got the rest?"

"When me granny died, all her daughters got a bit of the set . . . It were split up between 'em . . . and me mam broke t'cup and saucer when me dad got . . . ill."

Mrs. Venn made a wry face behind the old lady's back. Everyone knew the old man had got his illness out of a bottle. "And I'm afraid it's rather chipped," she said gently.

"Just round the edge," said Mrs. McNab defensively. "And I got our Billy to touch it up wi' a lick o' paint . . . It hardly shows . . ."

"How much were you expecting to get for it?" asked Mrs. Venn, still gently.

"Twenty pounds," said the old lady, her eyes as sharp as black needles. "There was one of them on the Arthur Negus television show . . ."

Rachel gasped. The plate wasn't worth two; even *she* knew that. But Mrs. Venn said, "Are you needing the money for something special . . . ?"

"None of your business," said Mrs. McNab, though her lips trembled more. She looked as if she was going to break down and cry in the shop.

"I could give you five pounds," said Mrs. Venn. "If that would help?"

"And you sell it for twenty? After it's been on Arthur Negus? You're sharks, you dealers. You're all the same

. . . sharks." And she said it with real hate; yet her lips were still trembling, on the verge of tears. She grabbed her plate and fled. Suddenly Rachel thought Mrs. Venn looked every year of her age; and weary with it.

And then she looked up and smiled, and twenty years dropped away. And Rachel became aware she wasn't the only looker-on in the shop. Dr. Diggory was standing there, his raincoat open and splashed with dark rain, and his wet felt hat in his hand. And he was smiling, too—looking quite boyish and shy, in spite of his thinning hair and droopy little mustache.

"Trouble?" asked Dr. Diggory.

"Trouble!" said Mrs. Venn. They smiled again, together, and Rachel suddenly realized they were very good friends indeed. She'd hardly realized they knew each other . . . but she thought it was nice that two people she was so fond of should also be fond of each other. And how cozy to be with them, to overhear what they had to say. They might even speak about *her*, Rachel. Say how grownup she was getting, how intelligent, how fast she was learning about antiques.

But they didn't say anything to each other at first; just stood there staring silently, looking happier and happier, and younger and younger, till Rachel felt she would burst with happiness at such a miracle.

Then Dr. Diggory said, "I've only got an hour . . . I have a surgery at six."

And Mrs. Venn said, "Let's not waste it, then. Go on through. I'll make sure it's all clear and shut the shop . . ."

Waste? thought Rachel. Waste what? And why shut the shop?

But Mrs. Venn, suddenly businesslike and humming to herself with happiness, took her cashbox out of her

desk and locked it, turned the card that hung in the door
from OPEN to CLOSED, and with brisk flicks of the wrist
shot the bolts in the door, put out the shop lights, and
vanished after Dr. Diggory. Perhaps they're going to have
tea, thought Rachel. If he's got surgery at six, he'll need
his tea. She'd often had tea with Mrs. Venn herself.
Toasted tea cakes, homemade plum jam, and Earl Grey
tea, eaten in the deep chintz sitting-room chairs. So she
still followed . . .

But they didn't go into the sitting room. They were
climbing the stairs, hand in hand, happy and chattering
like a pair of schoolboys let out of school.

And the penny still didn't drop with Rachel. Dr.
Diggory was happily married; he had two grownup sons
at the university . . . Perhaps Mrs. Venn had bought
some new treasure that she was working on upstairs in
the storage room and couldn't move . . . ?

But they didn't go into the storage room. They paused
by the open door of Mrs. Venn's bedroom, and looked
at each other with faces as radiant as angels'.

Then they went in and closed the door.

And Rachel knew where Mrs. Venn's happiness came
from that she shared as willingly as a seat on a bus . . .

And then Rachel was back in the church, in front of
the black spidery lettering that read:

THOU SHALT NOT COMMIT ADULTERY

She grew afraid then. She had played three cards, and
Zaphael had trumped them all.

All she had left was Daddy. She was so sure of Daddy
—always kind, always patient, always with time to listen
to her. But they had all been kind: Ziggy, Mrs. Venn,
Dr. Diggory. They had all loved her and helped her.

And had feet of clay. She was still reeling under the
shock of Ziggy; but Mrs. Venn had overtaken Ziggy, like
a big wave on the beach overtaking a smaller wave. And
with Dr. Diggory it was like two waves together. She felt
like when you stand on the beach and the remains of
those waves run back out to sea under your feet and you
feel the whole beach is sliding away and you're afraid of
falling . . .

But Zaphael was cunning; she felt that. Broken and
lost, but cunning. Maybe he had pulled the trick in the
antique shop to stop her trying Daddy at all . . . She tried
to imagine what Daddy's feet of clay might be—secret
drinking like old Major Herbison, who tottered precar-
iously about the village smelling of the mints he swallowed
to hide the smell of alcohol?

Stupid. Daddy never tottered, or slurred his voice, and
never smelled of anything but his old pipe. And smoking certainly wasn't in the Ten Commandments even if
doctors did make a fuss about it . . . Daddy couldn't even
be bothered to finish up the wine they had for dinner
occasionally. Mummy always finished up his glass when
she cleared the table.

Sex? She giggled. The women of the village watched
Daddy like hawks, jealous if one old lady got ten minutes
more visiting than another. It was a joke in the family.
Certain old ladies always knew where Daddy was. If he
was late home to lunch you only had to ring up one of
them and ask her. No, Daddy was the most public person
in the village . . .

She suddenly felt like a traitor, sizing up Daddy's
chances as if he was a racehorse she was going to be
on . . .

So she walked straight up to the silent darkened
Zaphael and said "Daddy" with much more confidence

than she really felt. She felt she was putting everything she owned on Daddy.

SHE WAS in the car, sitting where she always sat, on the back seat, peering out through the windscreen between Mummy's and Daddy's heads. Through the windscreen, late-afternoon sunlight was slanting across the trees and fields. Mummy was wearing her best suit, and that absurd hat she only wore for church occasions. Rachel knew it was today, and they were coming home from lunch with the Bishop.

And they were coming home in silence. From the distance they sat apart, from the stiff way they held their heads on their necks, the silence had been growing for some time. And that was bad.

She sat and sat, while the pretty black-and-white cottages of Frondsby passed by and the rose gardens of Millborough, and the tarted-up water mill at Treesby. And still the silence continued. She watched Daddy's hand on the wheel and gearshift. The worse things got, the gentler his movements. Today his movements were very gentle indeed . . . The smell of the old car seat leather made her feel sick.

Finally, on the long straight stretch that led into Munton, Mummy stirred, straightened in her seat, and said, "You're not going to *take* it, are you?" Her voice was full of contempt and that horrid near certainty she used when she was trying to get things all her own way.

Daddy was silent still; if anything, his hands were a little gentler as he shifted down for a crossroads.

Emboldened, Mummy went on, "Being rural dean's an *old man's* job. It's a booby prize for also-rans . . . You wouldn't *want* it? You don't *want* it, surely?"

That was the point at which Rachel always gave in and

said to her, "Oh, all right, Mummy. I don't *really* want it," and Mummy said approvingly, "Of course not—you've got far too much sense to want a thing like that." And Rachel would feel a great cloud of gloom descend, knowing that she'd wanted the thing very much indeed, and that now her chance of having it was gone forever . . . So many things . . . The pilgrimage to Walsingham with the Youth Fellowship; the chance of riding lessons (so *bourgeois!*).

But Daddy still said nothing.

"Oh, so you *are* thinking of taking it? And then we shall see less of you than ever, I suppose? While you run about all over the county wiping the noses and backsides of silly young clergymen and middle-aged ones who should know better . . . Well, don't ask me to lay on tea on the lawn for them all. I'm not running a café—I'll not be their bloody waitress."

"I have never asked you to do anything to help with my church work," said Daddy. It was, if anything, said in a lower, softer voice than usual. But there was something in it that made Rachel shudder. A sound Mummy appeared not to hear.

"I should jolly well think not," she said.

"No," said Daddy. "I have left you free for much more important things, like criticizing the Mothers' Union and laughing at the Women's Institute and telling my church-wardens that they don't pay their farm laborers enough . . . and going on demonstrations about cruise missiles and appearing in court and getting your name in the local papers sailing paper boats down the river to commemorate Hiroshima."

"And so . . . ?" said Mummy defiantly.

"And slopping around in jeans you no longer have the

figure for, and a jacket a farm laborer's wife wouldn't be seen dead in, and moping around and playing the piano badly for days on end, when you can't even seem to see the wash piling up . . ."

Mummy had heard the note in Daddy's voice too late. Now she gave a gasp of pain and seemed to slump as if wounded in her seat.

"And," said Daddy, "the level in the sherry bottle goes down and down, until suddenly there's a brand-new sherry bottle from the supermarket, and nothing for tea except beans on toast. And, at that, the toast will be burned and the beans boiled out of their skins. And the house so smelly that the parishioners recommend cheap air sprays to me." His voice was still small and precise, like a surgeon's knife, cutting. Mummy was starting to sob, her great tearing ugly childish sobs. But still the small voice went on and on, cutting, while the hands were still gentle on the steering wheel . . .

Take me out of here, thought Rachel. Please.

Zaphael must have heard . . .

SHE STOOD BEFORE him, her head down, looking at the odd, unearthly shapes of his brazen feet. Her mind searched endlessly for anyone else in the village she could think of as good. She had tried a quick flick at the nice boy who delivered the milk, and had received in return from Zaphael a quick flick of that boy laughing over a bloody, struggling rabbit in a snare . . . She almost felt that Zaphael was sorry for her . . . In her mind, she gave up, consented. Silently she asked, "When will you destroy the village?"

"AFTER THE CORN HARVEST."

She looked up at him swiftly, in surprise. The end of

the corn harvest was three weeks off. Why should he wait so long?

It seemed to her that he wavered under her look—lost some of his massive bronze certainty.

"Why will you wait so long, Zaphael?"

Again that queer little wavering. She pressed in, and seemed to feel something yield.

"Why will you wait so long, Zaphael? You must tell me the truth, in the name of the Living God!"

"YOU WILL BE FAR AWAY THEN."

"You mean . . . while I am here you will not destroy it?"

The creature was still and silent. Something about its feel had changed. It felt different toward her . . . Was it sorry for her? But she took one look at the multi-eyed face, like the bronze face of a fly with leprosy, and knew that pity did not exist behind those many-faceted eyes. There had been no pity for Sodom and Gomorrah . . . No, it wasn't feeling pity; something else. Probing for weakness, she said, "I shall not go away, Zaphael, ever. Then when will you destroy the village?"

"YOU MUST GO AWAY, IN OBEDIENCE TO YOUR FA-
THER."

She saw the trap in time. She was being tempted to break a commandment. Honor your father and your mother . . .

"Oh, I shall honor him, Zaphael. But I shall tell him honorably that I want to live at home and get a job. That I don't want to go back to school. I am old enough to leave school now." She added, "I shall never leave this village while you are here, waiting to destroy it. I shall be trapped here, and you will be trapped here, till I die. Unless you choose to tell me you are going somewhere else."

She knew she had a grip on the creature now. It was like an immensely huge, immensely powerful dog that she had outfaced. "What am *I*, Zaphael?" She knew she could never bring herself to say it, or even believe it. But she had to make *him* say it, for all their sakes.

"YOU ARE A RIGHTEOUS PERSON." She wanted to giggle at the idea of *her* being righteous. But it was all to save the village.

"Where will you go, Zaphael?" She felt a touch of pity for him now. "Cannot you go and find your friends?"

"I BELONG NOWHERE. ON THE DAY OF BATTLE, I WOULD NOT CHOOSE. I WOULD NOT CHOOSE MIKEL. I WOULD NOT CHOOSE SATAN. SO I MUST WANDER . . ."

And then the church was suddenly quite empty. And the patch of sunlight on the floor of the chancel that had been as steady as a searchlight all the time they had talked developed the moving image of a cloud that passed across it and was gone. Then another cloud. She heard the wind sighing in the silver birch, and then it whistled around the buttresses of the tower. A strong draft blew in the open church door, carrying a pair of newly yellow autumn leaves.

Outside, the world was unfrozen and moving again.

There was a double bang, from the pair of Phantoms from the U.S. air base. But it was softer; they were now flying very much higher.

She knew it was all over.

She walked out into her new lovely sinful kingdom.

GRAVEYARD SHIFT

CEM ROBSON, WIDOWER, cemetery superintendent, finished filling in the last of the day's records, yawned,
stretched, and looked out of his sitting-room window.
The sun was westering, flooding golden light through
the weeping willows onto the life-size lichened angels and
the green-streaked splendor of the Irvine family tomb.
Glade after glade led out of sight, replete with cypresses,
clipped yews, and the weathered tombstones of well-
settled Victorian aldermen. He thought the Victorian
part, around his gate lodge, romantic. The Victorians
got things right. Here he concentrated his two gardeners
and the job-corps gangs.

The modern part of the cemetery, farther off, was as
boring as a filing cabinet full of dead daffodils.

He went and got his supper out of the oven with eyes
half blinded by the sunset. A busy day: seven burials.
Afterwards he settled in a kitchen rocker and read the
classifieds in the local paper. He found the offers of
scarcely used gas stoves and best Northumbrian lawn turf
soothing—a break between a busy day and what promised

to be a busy night. He sat a little slumped, a shy, slightly gangling man with wide shoulders and long legs, looking younger than his fifty years, with his tanned face, oddly innocent, faded blue eyes, and white, widely spaced teeth like well-kept tombstones. Women found him attractive, in spite of his profession. Perhaps they found the task of warming a mind filled with thoughts of cold clay a challenge.

He got on well with the undertakers, too; was always invited to their Christmas do. He didn't mind their odd sense of humor, their compulsive habit of measuring you for a coffin with their eyes. He found young Thompson a bit much, having his pet dog stuffed when it died and keeping it sitting in the corner of his office at the chapel of rest—but, considering their trade, not a bad lot.

WHEN THE EMPTY ROCKER opposite him creaked, he did not at first look up. But the smell of fresh-dug earth told him the first of today's newly buried was sitting there. Only in spirit, of course. But the newly dead were obsessed with the smell of the earth, as with a new perfume or after-shave.

Odd, too, how they always sat in his dead wife's chair. When she had first come back to him, she must have blazed a trail, shown them the way . . .

The rocker opposite creaked again, diffidently.

Then a small female voice said, "Please don't look at me. I look awful."

That would be plot 754, the funeral just after lunch. Sixteen-year-old Melanie Bowers, killed in a car crash.

He said gently, not looking up from his paper, "I don't mind, love. I'm used to it."

There was a stifled sob. "It's bad enough knowing your

body's marked like that. I didn't know it would mark your . . . spirit as well."

He could tell she was on the verge of real tears.

He said slowly, emphatically, "The spirit heals itself, love. Given time. It's all in your mind, see? When your mind turns to other things, it will heal. How's your mam taking it?"

"She cried terrible at the funeral. Me dad had to hold her up at the graveside . . ."

"Want to pop home for a few minutes, to see how they're getting on?"

"Can I? But suppose they see me? Like this?"

"They won't, love. People hardly ever do. They don't want to. Dogs and cats do. If you got a dog, he'll be pleased to see you, scar an' all. Dogs don't mind. An' you can leave your mam and dad a nice smell, if you like. Your favorite perfume, or your favorite flowers. That always helps cheer them up. So they know there's still a bit of you left . . . Off you go. Don't be too long, though. They're tired, and so are you."

"Where . . . do I go . . . after that?" He heard the panic surge in her voice.

"Come back here. That's what most of them do, to start with. Have a good sleep. Then . . . this cemetery's nice, this time o' year. There's the birds . . . still bees and butterflies . . . place is full o' life. And there's other people here, mebbe somebody you know. I've got a nice crowd in at the moment . . ."

"Thanks," said the small voice, a little brighter.

"Now—do you mind if I have a look at you?"

"If you want to—if you really don't mind."

He looked at her. Her green eyes tried to look back at him, bravely. The wound from the car windscreen, which covered the whole side of her face, was pretty dreadful. But it was starting to fade; the pretty, chubby face was starting to rebuild itself. They always started to heal, once they let themselves be looked at.

"Three days, hinny, and ye'll be as pretty as a picture again."

She tried a tentative smile; as if by magic, the wound healed a little more. "I didn't know we were allowed home, once we were buried . . ."

"Liberty Hall, this, hinny. Liberty Hall."

The rocker opposite was suddenly empty. He sighed, because she was so young. No bairns for her, no young husband, no love's young dream. Life was hard. He went back to his paper.

AFTER A WHILE, the rocker creaked again. Not the smell of earth this time. A strong whiff of lily of the valley. Winnie Bolam, late belle of the Golden Years Club . . .

No hurry. She was one of his regulars.

The rocker creaked again, indignant for his attention, and her voice said, "Eeh, Aah don't know what to do wi' him. He was back again this afternoon. Three hours, sitting on next door's grave. That's not respectful, sitting on somebody else's grave. Every day he comes and talks to me. It's not as if I was even married to him—we were just good friends at the club. He's dafter than one o' the young uns, and he's well over seventy. I don't know what our Harry would say, if he was here. Probably start a fight. Very possessive of me, Harry was . . ."

He looked up. It was funny how some of them were so ghostly you could see the pattern of the cushion through their bodies, and others were dead solid. Especially Winnie, with her stocky little figure, plump as a pigeon, wide blue eyes, and well-permed hair as golden as the Golden Years Club itself.

"Have you ever thought of . . . Going On . . . Winnie? You've been with me a long time. How long is it, now?"

She settled herself in the chair more comfortably, just as she had always done in life. "Eighteen month, come November. There's no hurry, is there? I've got all the time there is, now."

"You'll drive that poor feller that comes and sits by your grave mad. He knows you're still there, you know. That's why he keeps on coming back . . ."

"Aah always drove the fellers mad, from being a lass." She smiled complacently.

"But what about your Harry?"

"Let him wait. He might appreciate me a bit more when Aah do come."

"But this other feller . . . He might have things he ought to be doing . . ."

"He never had owt he ought to be doin', that one. He did nowt but run after me backside when Aah was alive . . ."

She faded. He wasn't worried about her. She came most nights. She wasn't complaining; she was boasting.

THE NEXT ONE was bad. A smell of sweaty leather and oil. The young biker from plot 751. His face young, fresh, and unmarked, apart from oil stains. The damage must be under his leathers, thank God.

"It's not fair."

"Life's not fair, son," said Cem as calmly as he could, reaching for his pipe with trembling fingers. The biker's rage, his rage to be back in the world, filled the room, crushing Cem down deep into his chair. The young were always the worst; they felt robbed. The old—sometimes they were just so glad to be out of their bodies, away from the pain at last.

"It was that bastard's fault," shouted the boy. "He was doin' eighty. On the wrong side of the road. He didn't even know the rules of the road . . ."

"He was inside a car, son. So he's alive, and you're dead."

The biker writhed in his chair, as if he was struggling against invisible bonds. His blackened, oily hands groped at the chair's arms, trying to grasp them, trying to make them feel real. Cem waited quietly, waited for him to find out it was no use. Finally, the boy gave up, exhausted. But he didn't give up pleading his case, trying to find some authority, judge or headmaster, who would excuse him from being dead.

"Me mum an' dad—I'm all they've got!"

"You should've thought of that afore you bought that big bike, son. Too late now."

"And I haven't paid off the bike . . ."

"Reckon your insurance will take care of that."

The boy was silent for a long time. He was a nice-looking kid, under the oil stains. The kind of tough, eager, cheerful kid you could be proud of. Cem had never had a son—just three married daughters who now looked after him like the treasures they were.

Finally, the boy shrugged and said, "Did you see me funeral—all them bikers? A hundred and five bikes. There was a pile of helmets six feet high at the chapel door . . ."

Cem thought he saw his chance. "There was a lad last month," he said slowly, "who had a hundred and seventeen bikes at his funeral . . ."

"Terry Sloane? I knew him—I was there. Is he still here?"

"Gone, son. Went on Ahead. There was no one here he could talk bikes with. He reckoned half his mates had Gone Ahead. Aah reckon there's more dead bikers than live ones."

The boy looked thoughtful. Cem pushed his luck. "Terry reckoned the lads must still get together up there. Still talk bikes. Mebbe still have races—through the clouds, around the Milky Way, mebbe. That's what Terry reckoned . . . Aah don't know."

The kid's face lit up. "Do you think so? I thought it would be all twangin' harps and sitting on clouds—boring."

"Only for them as likes twangin' harps, I reckon. Mind you, I can't be certain. Nobody comes back to tell me . . ."

The kid got up suddenly, slapping his leather gauntlets against his thigh. They were all sudden, bikers. Couldn't sit still five minutes; but at least they made up their minds quickly.

"I'll be off, then. Thanks a lot!"

"Don't forget to go and say goodbye to your mam and dad . . ." Cem settled back in his chair with a sigh of relief. He always felt he'd got it right, when they said thanks a lot.

HE HADN'T GOT his head down in his paper long when the rocker creaked again. A smell of peppermints and sweaty feet. So he knew it was Jack Timmins, even before the self-pitying sigh. Cem himself groaned inwardly. Your own friends, the ones you'd known in life, were the hardest to help; they didn't take what you said seriously.

And Jack Timmins would not have taken death well. Always a moaner, even at kindergarten.

So Cem sighed and said, "Hallo, Jack. How's it going, then?" He knew it was a foolish question to ask, but you had to say something.

"Why me?" asked Jack peevishly. "Why me? Aah didn't smoke, Aah never drank, Aah didn't go wi' women, like some Aah know. Why me? Two months into early retirement, wi' enough saved to keep Doris and me comfy for the rest of our lives. A nice new bungalow down Whitley Bay—Aah haven't even finished doing the crazy paving . . . Why me, Cem? What did Aah do wrong?"

"I'm not St. Peter," said Cem. "I just keep the cemetery tidy. If you're that keen to know, you'd better nip Up There and ask them . . ."

A cunning look came across Jack's face. "Oh, aye. And once they've got you up there, there's no gettin' back down here again, is there? You're stuck. You have to do what they tell you. Just like being back at work. 'Yes, boss' this, and 'yes, boss' that, and three bags full. Catch me . . . An' you can't even argue and ask for your cards. That's not democracy. That's dictatorship. That's what we fought against in the last war . . ."

"You were scarcely born in the last war," said Cem, a bit sharp. Jack had always brought out the worst in him.

"That's beside the point. Aah've worked for everything Aah've got, unlike some. It's mine."

"You better get back to it, then!"

"Aah've been back. Our Doris is as pissed as a newt, and laughing wi' that Fred Storey an' talkin' about old times. An' all her brothers are there, drinking my bloody whisky like there's no tomorrow. An' our Stan an' our Daniel are fighting over who's to have me Black and

Decker . . . Like vultures they are, bloody vultures. An' before Aah know where Aah am, that Fred Storey'll have his feet under my kitchen table, an' God knows where else. He's always fancied her, an' she's still a young woman—five years younger than me. An' she's weak, Cem, weak! She can't cope wi'out a man five minutes. They'll be using the leftover funeral sandwiches for the wedding breakfast. Aah know our Doris—she'll shove them in the freezer to keep. Six months Aah give her, just to stop folks talkin' . . ."

"I wouldn't spend much time at home, if I were you," said Cem cautiously. "Hang around here a bit. It's very nice in summer, though it's not much fun in winter. Some folks go off for a little holiday then, together. Show each other their favorite places, like the Channel Islands, or Torremolinos. I had a nice party set off to see the Taj Mahal, though they never came back to tell me about it. Mebbe there's too many ghosts in India—folk seem to die a lot out there—an' they just went straight Up instead."

"Riffraff," said Jack rudely. "You don't think Aah spent me life slavin' an' savin' up for a nice bungalow in Whitley Bay just to come back an' live wi' North Shields folk again . . . Aah'll just nip back home to make sure they've not stolen all the tomatoes out of me greenhouse . . ."

Suddenly the chair was empty. Cem sighed again. Jack was going to be a rare trial, if he stayed long. He'd upset the others . . . Then they'd start coming in twos and quarreling in the kitchen, and wanting him to judge who was right, as if he was King Solomon.

There must be easier ways of making a living. He wondered if other cemetery keepers had this kind of bother. He'd never dared to ask them, in case they thought he was mad. And Jack wasn't the worst. There was the nest of old ladies who inhabited the cemetery chapel, waiting for God to come and fetch them, as if the chapel was a bus stop, and God a number 11 bus. And there was the young mother of five who just sat in his rocker and wept, nearly every other night for a year now. And you couldn't even hold her hand or put your arm around her . . .

Weary, he dozed in his chair, the paper open across his chest like a too-short blanket.

HE NEVER KNEW if the rest of that night wasn't a dream, or whether he wakened and it really happened. All he could say was that he didn't usually have that kind of nightmare, and he sincerely hoped he'd never have another like it.

It seemed to be the cold that wakened him—an icy draft blowing up his body under the newspaper. He opened his eyes and saw Dr. Millwrick. Dr. Millwrick's funeral had been the last that day. Just the hearse and the pallbearers. No mourners. That was not surprising. He had no wife, no family. Nobody had liked Dr. Millwrick. He had been a very short, fat man, and he'd had a short, fat coffin. Which had given the pallbearers a lot of trouble. Maybe it was just that the gravediggers hadn't allowed for a man so fat, and dug the grave too narrow. But the coffin just hadn't seemed to want to go into the ground. It had stuck halfway down . . . The gravediggers had had to go down after it, ease the earthen sides with their shovels; jump on the coffin to get it in place. Afterwards . . . he had never seen the gravediggers shovel the earth back so hard and so willingly. The undertaker had mopped a pale sweating brow and said he was glad to have that one underground. Cem had had to give the man a big glass of whisky in his office. He had been curious; but the man drank his drink down in two gulps and left without saying another word.

There had long been stories about Dr. Millwrick—ever since he'd come to the town. Everyone knew he was a foreigner; everyone knew his real name had once been Milric. But people hadn't held that against him—just as they had nothing against Dr. Mukerjee, the Indian, who was highly thought of. Patients went to Dr. Millwrick; but they hadn't stayed long. People said it was the way he eyed them, once they'd taken their clothes off . . . especially the women.

Soon nobody went to ring at his bell. Even his receptionist packed in the job eventually, though he offered her extra money and there was a lot of unemployment about. Nobody else had applied for the job.

It didn't seem to bother Dr. Millwrick. He still drove around the town in his shiny black car. He still lived in his big house at Preston, though every year that passed, the trees in the front garden grew bigger and closer to the walls. He was pleasant to people in shops—smiled and made little jokes. The shop assistants broke out in a cold sweat when he left.

There was nothing to connect him with the children who began to disappear, about once a year. The police had made exhaustive inquiries . . .

And here was Dr. Millwrick in front of him, like all the other newly dead. Except . . . not quite like the others. As he shifted his fat little thighs in the rocker, under their pin-striped trousers, the chair not only creaked but actually *rocked*, backwards and forwards. When he brushed a few crumbs of damp soil off the trousers with a pale pudgy hand, Cem actually heard the crumbs of soil fall to the hearth rug. And they stayed there, slowly drying out.

Cem looked at his little red face, with the little black

mustache, and grew afraid, as he had never been afraid of the dead. The doctor was neither sad nor angry; indeed, he was smiling.

"It is all a matter of the *will*," said the doctor. Cem thought for a moment he meant his last will and testament, which was slightly reassuring. Lots of the dead were worried about that. Cem had had many a helpful word with a family lawyer; old people left their wills hidden in such funny places . . .

"Not *that* kind of will," said Dr. Millwrick. "I refer to the human will—or rather, the inhuman will, the superhuman will. With knowledge and experiment, and the superhuman will, one does not have to die. Ever."

"Get away," said Cem. He was so scared he couldn't think what else to say.

"You do not believe that I am not dead?" said the good doctor. He reached over and lifted Cem's drinking mug from where he had left it on the table. Then he put it down again, very gently. "You have talked to many dead, Mr. Robson, I think. You are not afraid of the dead, like most. You know the *dead* cannot harm you. They have no more power than dead leaves . . . I . . . am . . . not . . . dead. Oh, one of my colleagues from the hospital came and certified me dead. They are not difficult to fool . . . I repeat . . . I am not dead. I have the power to harm, still. I have the power to harm *you*, Mr. Robson."

"What do you *want*?" Cem's voice came out in a croak. His mouth was as dry as yesterday's dust.

"I wish you to dig me up, Mr. Robson. Tonight. Or rather to dig my coffin up. You will have little difficulty —you will find it quite empty—it will be quite light. Then you will replace the earth of my grave, respectfully and tastefully. Then you will take my coffin to my house— there is a spare key for the front door, hidden in the left-hand urn by the door. Put the coffin in the hall—I will see to it myself, later. Lock the front door again—put the key back in the urn—that is all. I will pay you well, for that favor."

"What good will that do you?" croaked Cem.

"Tomorrow, with my mustache shaved off and a pair of these new absurd large spectacles, I shall reappear as my own nephew, to whom I have left all I possess, in my *ordinary* will. Then, thanks to my *extraordinary* will, I will live as young Dr. Millwrick, grieving over the death of my kind uncle, old Dr. Millwrick."

It was a typical example of Dr. Millwrick's little jokes which made shop assistants break out in a cold sweat.

"And if I refuse?" said Cem, with what little remaining courage he possessed.

"If you refuse, Mr. Robson, I will do a small something to you, and you will become like me. You will never die, Mr. Robson. You will never lie, oh, so peacefully, in your own well-kept cemetery. You will never Go Ahead. You will live on to trouble the world; to be hated in shops; to have people shudder as you pass . . ."

Cem believed every word.

"Come," said Dr. Millwrick, beckoning. "You have work to do, Mr. Robson."

CEM NEVER KNEW what he might have done next, for the next moment there was another little chill draft, and when he looked up, the dead biker was standing there again. The biker nodded to him, casually. But all his attention was focused on Dr. Millwrick.

"Sod me, it's the Black Pig," he said, in a very offensive voice. "D'you remember me, Black Pig? I used to come at night an' break your windows . . . D'you remember our song?

"Black Pig, Fat Pig,
  Shove him in the sack, Pig!"

Dr. Millwrick remembered, if the look of black-eyed hate on his face was anything to go by. He snatched at the boy with a horrible insect swiftness, like one of those spiders that snatch butterflies—a movement that paralyzed Cem afresh with horror.

The boy didn't move. Dr. Millwrick's predator hands went straight through him, closing on nothing.

"I'm dead," said the boy. "You can't touch me now. The dead can do no harm, Black Pig. But they can't be harmed, either." He sang the song again.

Then he said, "We weren't scared of *you*. You were so fat you could only catch the little kids. We knew what you were. We used to use you for *dares*. You could never catch any of us. We used to stuff wild garlic through your keyholes, so you had to climb out of the windows. Do you remember when we stuffed your car wi' garlic? You couldn't use it for a week . . ."

Cem listened, dazed, as the boy kept up a flood of reminiscences, insults, and laughter. Dr. Millwrick seemed to be beside himself, striking out at the boy again and again, with a venom that was only equaled by its total ineffectiveness and yet was terrible to watch in its hate.

"Oh, they'll find you out in the end, Dr. Millwrick," said the boy. "And you know what'll happen in the end, don't you?"

Foam gathered grayly at the corners of Dr. Millwrick's plump little red mouth, around his little sharp green teeth. And then he seemed to calm himself, with an enormous effort.

"You are irrelevant," he said to the boy. "You can do nothing. Come, Mr. Robson. It is time for you to do my work . . ." He got to his feet decisively. The boy seemed to fade a bit.

And then suddenly the rocker right across the room creaked. And Winnie Bolam was there, plump as a pigeon, settling herself calmly, with a little smile of pure contempt on her face. Aimed at Dr. Millwrick.

"You were never a *proper* man," she said. "Never a proper man like other men. You could never go with a woman in your life. All you could do was muck around wi' little bairns . . ."

And again Dr. Millwrick was reduced to a clawing fury that achieved nothing but was awful to watch.

And again, in the end, he calmed himself.

Only to be faced by Melanie Bowers. And then by the young mother of five, whose weeping Cem had never been able to stem. The room filled up with all the dead from the cemetery. Even the nest of old ladies from the chapel. They all stared at Dr. Millwrick with a dreadful, undying scorn.

"Get out, get out, get out of our town . . ." It began as two or three chanting together, and grew and grew.

Again they reduced Dr. Millwrick to a frantic, hissing fury.

And again he eventually grew calm, and ignored them, and turned to Cem. Cem despaired. They could no more harm Dr. Millwrick than he could harm them. In the end, they, too, were irrelevant . . .

Except that, as Dr. Millwrick stepped forward, he suddenly flinched back. As if he had touched a red-hot poker . . .

Cem looked.

From a small crack between his thick curtains the light of day was peeping in . . .

With a small cry, as if he had stepped on a pin in his stocking feet, Dr. Millwrick vanished.

Cem looked around. All the dead had vanished, except the boy biker.

The boy looked at him, solemnly, wearily, but affectionately. "You know what you have to do . . . ?" he said. Then added: "All those daft old movies on the telly got *that* right, you know. But *any* kind of wood will do, for the stake."

Cem nodded, equally weary. At least the earth of Dr. Millwrick's grave would be soft and easy to dig.

"When I'm gone," said the boy, "don't kid yourself it couldn't happen just because it's North Shields. It happened. And he won't give you a second chance. We can't save you again."

"Aah'll do it," said Cem. "Aah promise."

"Thanks a lot," said the boy.

And was gone.

Cem shook himself and drew back the curtains. As the early-morning light flooded in, so did disbelief. There was an early blackbird hopping among the graves, looking for worms. The whir of the early-morning milk wagon was succeeded by the clink of bottles. The first bus passed, changing gears down Preston Road. The sky was a pure clear blue; it was going to be a smashing day. It couldn't possibly have happened. It was just a nasty dream.

He turned from the window.

The crumbs of earth from Dr. Millwrick's trousers still lay drying on his rug . . .

He looked at his watch. He had only two hours before the cemetery staff came in for the day.

He headed for the woodshed.

A WALK ON
THE WILD SIDE

TO LIVE WITH a cat is to live with fear.

You can keep dogs safe till they die of obesity: collar-and-leash and walks-in-the-park. But not cats; cats like a walk on the wild side.

You *can* deny cat nature. Like the childless couple down our lane, whose white Persians never leave the house except in spotless white cages for their monthly trip to the vet. Those cats sit endlessly in their upstairs bedroom window, staring out at the moving world, sometimes raising a futile paw to the glass. But mostly they're still; for a while, I thought they were stuffed toys.

Everything should be allowed to live and die, according to its nature. But cats have two natures. Take my tortoiseshell, Melly. Indoors, she's a fawner, onto my knee the moment I sit down, purring, drooling, craving my approving hand. A harmless suppliant . . .

My neighbors call her the bird catcher. She hunts their garden, filling their empty, pensioned lives with displays of predatory cunning better than TV safaris into Africa.

She's a diplomat; never brings a bird home.

I've seen her myself, late at night, crossing the back yards of our lane like an Olympic hurdler, under sparse orange streetlamps. I've called, but she ignores me, passing overhead without a break in her stride. On the wild side.

Two natures. A purring bundle in your arms; a contemplative Buddha by the fire. But those pointed ears are moving even in sleep, listening to the windy dark outside. Suddenly, though you've heard nothing, they're on their feet, away with a thunderous rattle through the cat flap. Sometimes they're back in your lap within five minutes; sometimes they're returned next morning (by a neighbor who can't look you in the face), a stiff-legged, sodden corpse in a plastic bag. You never get a chance to say goodbye. But everything according to its nature . . .

I used to enjoy a walk on the wild side. Even into my forties, the fire only had to burn blue on a winter's night and I was out walking under the frosty stars. But now my legs ache after a day at school; the blue-burning coals just make me fetch a whisky and snuggle deeper into my book. My cats walk the wild side for me, coming home with a hint of rain on their fur, or spears of cold, or the smell of benzine from the old chemical works. When I bury my face in their coats, I know what the world's doing outside.

Like the Three Kings, they bear gifts. Live worms, which I return instantly to the nearest patch of earth. Tattered moths, beyond saving, transformed from fun to food in one scrunch. Once my old tom, Ginger, taunted because he couldn't hunt like the girls, returned with that mournful yowl of success and a packet of fresh bacon in his mouth. I fried it for supper, gave him his tithe.

But the oddest thing Ginger brought home, on a Halloween of intense frost, was a tiny live kitten, exactly the same color as himself. That was the only reason we didn't think it was a rat, for its ears were still flat to its skull, its eyes unopened, and it was soaking in his mouth.

We shouted ridiculous things at him, demanding to know where he got it, insisting he take it back to its mother. He blinked his ridicule and left the house, implying he'd done his bit and it was now up to us.

My wife was a loving soul. She didn't love cats much —just all living things, and cats for my sake. Our hearth rug became an instant hospital of tumbled blankets and screwed-up towels, warm milk, and eyedroppers. She took over the fiddly business of six feeds a day.

Typically, the young female (for she was female, though ginger) repaid her efforts by becoming entirely devoted to me. From the beginning, she slept contented on my shoulder while I read. By four weeks, she would slowly and agonizingly climb my legs to get there.

I called her Rama, for no particular reason. My wife said it sounded like a brand of furniture polish. For all her poor beginning, Rama grew amazingly fast. At Christmas, in a fit of childish glee, we gave each of our cats a lump of chicken. There was a sudden spat, and when we looked again, Rama had one piece under each paw and one in her mouth. As young as she was, none of the others tried a challenge. That night, Ginger left home for good and took up residence at the village launderette.

Then came the battle for my lap, which any male owner of she-cats knows. The others would lie side by side, apparently peaceful, but occasionally stretching and trying to push each other off. Or they'd deliberately lie on top of each other, making me part of a cat sandwich.

They'd even come to blows between my legs, which is worrying if not downright agonizing.

Rama had no truck with that sort of thing. The moment she entered the room, she'd give one *look*, and the occupant of my knee would instantly depart.

She had the same effortless dominance at mealtimes. Four cats jostling at one saucer, and Rama eating lazily from the other. And they'd never dare *sniff* her leavings, even after she'd left the room.

And still she grew. Bigger even than old Melly, who was big for a cat. Every morning, as I brushed my hair before school, I would watch a little comedy. Rama would sit by our front gate, willing to receive all the world. And most passersby would come across to stroke her, for she was very beautiful, with her long, swirling red fur and plumed tail. But as they drew near and saw her great size and felt her confidence, they would grow . . . unsure. They would hover, hands half out, and then they would go away again, leaving her unstroked.

When she lay on me, she began to be oppressive. Her weight was just tolerable on my aching legs, but when, consumed by some catty passion, she insisted on lying on my chest with her paws around my neck, I had to strain to breathe. And she had this habit of staring into my face at a distance of five centimeters. No other cat ever did that, because, for cats, eye-to-eye is a challenge. But it was I that turned my eyes away; Rama had a heavy soul, as she had a heavy body.

But her delicacy made her bearable. The others have left my thighs, my shoulders, and my back a mass of tiny red scratches, with their ill-timed leaps, frantic landings, and convulsive, sleepy stretchings. I scarcely dare go swimming—people pass remarks that embarrass my wife.

But Rama never put a claw into me, save once. She was a lovely cat to doze with. After a cold, hard day at school, I tend to fall asleep over the roaring fire and the six o'clock news. With Rama on my knee, I dreamed pleasant dreams I could never remember and woke without a stiff neck, set up for the evening.

Then she began to haunt our bedroom at bedtime. Here my wife drew the line. Rama was carried swiftly downstairs and put out. She never struggled, but there was a laying back of ears that left her opinion in no doubt. Then she discovered my wife's reluctance to get up again, once warmly tucked in. So she would conceal herself early, behind the closed bedroom curtains or almost unbreathing in the moonlit shadow of the rubber plant. Sometimes as I undressed I'd spot her hiding place, but that great, cool green eye would swear me to silence. Then at my wife's first snore Rama would ghost across the carpet and purr softly up into my arms.

Then she tried to go too far and lie between my wife and me in bed. That was enough to get my wife up again, and out Rama would go.

There, for some time, the battle line stayed drawn . . .

MY SON PETER, too, has always lived by his nature. A Ph.D. in zoology, then the post of warden at a famous but utterly remote Scottish bird preserve. A wife not only beautiful but also zoological, and inured to their kind of genteel poverty. Happy with a three-bedroom cottage, a chemical toilet, and the use of the firm's Land Rover.

Usually they manage things so that their babies are born in late July, when we can go up to Scotland and hold the fort. My wife copes with the children. I clumsily take Sheila's place, putting plastic rings on ducks, cleaning oiled cormorants, stopping elderly ornithologists from

falling over cliffs, and being bossed around by Peter. My
son is always at his most touching when about to become
a father. For a few days he stops being a totally competent
thirty-year-old and runs his fingers through his hair like
a baffled teenager, his thin wrists sticking miles out of
the sleeves of his well-darned cardigan.

But this year, for all their Ph.D.s, they'd mistimed
things. The baby was due in November. My wife drove
up herself. There were snow warnings out, and I was
quite frantic until I got her call from the preserve. Then
I felt sorry for myself. Our house is large, Victorian,
rather isolated on the crest of the hill above the old
chemical works. In fact, the old manager's house. I'd got
myself a mansion on the cheap, because the view of the
works halved the price, though there's a splendid view
of the Frodsham Hills beyond.

Our social life is usually too busy for my taste, on top
of parents' evenings and all that nonsense without which
the modern parent does not think her child is being
educated. But now I learned that it was purely my wife's
creation; you can't hold dinner parties without cooking.
And I dislike going to the cinema on my own. In fact, I
discovered that after thirty years of marriage I disliked
going *anywhere* on my own. I got pretty lonely, but I was
too tired with the end of term to do anything about it.

I noticed the wind for the first time—the way the
Virginia creeper tapped on the windows. My wife's pres-
ence had always blocked out such things. I wasn't *scared*.
More like a primitive man, exploring after dark a cave
that had always been a bit too big for him and is now
much too big. My eyes noticed new shadows in the hall;
my ears twitched too often as I ate my lukewarm baked
beans in the big, cold kitchen.

The cats were a solace. With Rama on my knees, and

the others perched on the back of a chair and on the mantelpiece, we were famously snug. Only Rama came to bed with me. When I wakened in the night (which I never normally do), it was good to feel her weight on the bed and to reach out and feel her large, soft, furry flank rising and falling.

So I was all the more annoyed, one windy night, to be awakened at three by her insistently scratching at the door, demanding to be let out. You didn't leave Rama scratching long, if you valued your paintwork.

"Go on, then, damn you." She vanished like a ghost along the hall, and I went back to a cold bed, feeling thoroughly deserted.

I had just dozed off when the screaming started.

Now, as a headmaster, I consider myself an expert on the female scream—hysterical, expectant, or distressed. I really can tell from a scream outside our house whether a young woman is merely drunk, or quarreling with another female, or being sexually assaulted, enjoyably or otherwise. In fact, by sallying forth, I have prevented at least two rapes, for the area of unkempt grass and trees around the old works seems to attract far more couples than our pleasant municipal park.

But this was a man screaming, in such terror as I'd not heard since my army days. Inside my house. Downstairs.

I leaped out of bed, shaking from head to foot; my pajamas had a distressing tendency to fall down. The screaming went on and on. A door slammed. Other voices shouting. Breaking crockery.

I dialed 999 on the bedside extension and was glad to hear the policeman's voice. When I hung up, I felt braver, especially as silence had fallen. I went to Peter's old bedroom and got his .22 rifle, remembering the good times we'd had with it, harming nothing more than empty bottles floating in the old chemical sump. I found his box of cartridges and loaded them with trembling fingers. Then, against the policeman's advice, I went downstairs, switching on every light as I passed.

The kitchen was appalling: chairs tossed over, a sea of broken crockery scrunching underfoot, the back door swinging. Splashes of red among the broken saucers. I thought someone had broken my bottle of tomato ketch-up, but when I tasted it, it was blood.

Oh, my poor cats . . . They live in the kitchen at night.

But when I looked around, there they were—Melly and Tiddy and Vicky and Dunnings—perched high on the Welsh dresser, crouching under the gas stove, saucer-eyed, paralyzed with terror, but otherwise unharmed. All except Rama, my poor Rama, who had tried to warn me only ten minutes before.

The policeman came in through the swinging back door, the radio clipped to his jacket prattling.

"You the householder, sir?"

"I phoned you, yes."

He looked around. "Burglary or domestic quarrel?"

I wondered how some people must live, then said shortly, "My wife's away in Scotland. I'm alone in the house."

"Better put that gun down, sir. Is it loaded?"

I put the safety catch on. "I have a license," I said, wondering how out of date it was.

Another policeman appeared, dangled his hand know-ingly through a circular hole in the glass of the back door. "Burglary—pro job. There's a three-ton van parked down the back lane. Liverpool registration—some bookie called Moore—they're sussing him out on the computer now."

"Some burglary—you seen *that*?" The first copper

indicated a splash of blood with his shiny toe. "You're not injured, sir?" They surveyed my sagging pajamas.

"No, no!"

Their eyes went as hard as marbles. "You shot someone, sir? In the course of preventing the burglary?"

"No, no. Smell the gun—it's not been fired." They smelled it and looked even more baffled.

"I'm afraid they may have killed one of my cats," I said. It was absurdly hard not to cry.

They noticed the cats for the first time; poked their rigid bodies.

"One missing, sir? Lot of blood for a cat . . ."

"They've left a nice set of prints." The second policeman pointed to the wall behind the open back door.

On it was a complete print of a human hand, made in what appeared to be blood.

I WEARILY PICKED UP the last piece of crockery and put it in the waste bin. Ran some water into a bucket and began to wash the floor. The forensic experts had taken till lunchtime and made the mess a hell of a sight worse. I wasn't going to make it to school that day. I'd just telephoned my secretary when the doorbell rang.

White raincoat, felt hat. Sergeant Watkinson, CID.

"You'll be pleased to hear we picked up one of the gang, sir. *And* we got the names of the rest. He told us everything we wanted to know—when he came out of the anesthetic."

"Anesthetic?"

"We picked him up at Liverpool City Hospital. They'd dumped him there—couldn't cope. He'd lost an eye."

"An eye?" I said stupidly.

He changed tack, keeping me guessing. "They're a known gang, specializing in antiques. Come around the houses asking if you've got any antiques to sell; then they break in and take them anyway, a week later. A nasty lot. I'm glad you didn't . . . encounter them, sir."

"But what *happened*?"

"I believe you keep cats, sir?" He had a . . . hunting look on his face.

I nodded toward my shaken brood, still huddled around the kitchen. He reached out and stroked them tentatively, one by one. "Not very big, are they, sir . . . as domestic cats go? I mean, they *look* harmless enough. This cat that was missing . . . It hasn't returned, has it? How big was that one?"

"Just a big domestic cat . . . What are you getting at, sergeant?"

"Well—that bloke we've caught—he reckoned he got mauled by something big in the dark. You don't keep exotic cats, do you, sir? A leopard or a cheetah? Very popular they're getting, with folk who can afford them."

"Nothing like that. Just a large domestic cat. Of course, we do get tomcats visiting through the cat flap. A wild tom, cornered in a strange house, can get very nasty."

"Yeah." He didn't sound convinced. "That bloody handprint we found on the wall, sir, doesn't correspond to any named member of the gang—a woman's print, they think—long fingernails." He looked at me expectantly.

"I'm afraid I can't help you, sergeant. My wife keeps her fingernails short."

"Where's your wife staying, sir, at the moment?"

I gave him my son's phone number. "Can I wash that handprint off the wall now?"

"You can try, sir. Try a bit of biological detergent. Blood's hard to shift."

"Anything else?"

"Give me a ring if that other cat shows up, sir. I'd like to see it." He paused, one hand on the open front door. "I don't see why that villain should lie, sir—he wasn't in any fit state to lie."

"CUP OF TEA, sergeant?"

"If you're making one, sir." It was the third time he'd come back in search of Rama. Without success. After a week, she was still missing. But something kept drawing him to our house. CID, too, must live by their own nature.

"Your case is all sewn up," he said, spooning in two sugars. "We picked up the last lad yesterday, and he admitted twenty-five other break-ins. Pushover. All the stuffing knocked out of him—like the rest. We've recovered a fair bit of stolen property . . ." He stirred his tea again, needlessly. "They were a hard lot. If you'd gone downstairs that night, they'd have put the boot in, left you for dead. So you ought to be grateful to whatever was in your kitchen . . ."

Again, he left the question hanging in the air.

"Look, sergeant, I've never kept a leopard or jaguar. How could I, without half the town knowing? I'm a public figure. Can't afford funny business."

"I know, sir. We've made inquiries. Very solid gentleman you are, Mr. Howard Snowdon. Member of Rotary . . . well liked, too. A bit overfond of pussies, but quite *ordinary* pussies."

"You be careful, sergeant, or I'll start making inquiries about *you*."

"About me, sir?"

"Your inspector is one of my old boys—so are three of your subordinates. Headmasters have their powers, too, you know."

He grinned; I grinned. He'd been good company the last week. Which had been lonelier than ever in Rama's absence.

He stood up, and shook hands. "Well, you've seen the last of me, sir. Case all sewn up. Except I don't know what I dare put in my official report . . . that would stand up in court. I don't like loose ends . . ."

I saw him to the gate in the dusk, waited while he started his car, waved as he drove off. Turned.

Rama was sitting on the doorstep, the light of the hall behind her. At least, a silhouetted cat sat there—a very big cat, indeed.

I didn't walk directly to the front door; followed the curve of the drive, because the lawn was wet and I was only in my carpet slippers.

If it wasn't Rama, it would run away as I approached.

If it didn't run away, it must be Rama.

The cat watched me silently, only turning its head slightly as I walked around the curve. Surely it was the light behind her that made her seem so big?

Three meters away, I faltered. Suppose it didn't run away and it wasn't Rama?

"Rama? Rama?"

No response. There was a gardening fork stuck in the earth of the rose bed where I'd been turning over after pruning. Slowly, I reached out my hand. I felt much better, holding the fork.

Still the cat neither moved nor spoke.

This would never do—outfaced by a bloody alley cat? I advanced, thrusting the tines of the fork before me.

Immediately the cat stood up, stretched fore and aft luxuriously. Its plumed tail shot up in greeting, tip tilted slightly left. *Prook* of greeting.

Rama—almost as if she was laughing at me. I picked her up bodily and carried her in. She felt bigger, several pounds heavier. Living wild, eating fresh bloody protein. Plenty of rats in the old works—even rabbits, now it's been shut for years and the grass is growing between the cobbles.

She kneaded her paws against my chest ecstatically, extruding and withdrawing her claws. I felt them, I can tell you, right through my thick pullover. I told her to lay off, but she wouldn't. I grabbed the worst-offending paw, felt the heavy bones expanding and contracting, quite beyond my power to keep them still. It was a relief to dump her on the kitchen table.

"Where've you been, you bad girl? You've had me worried sick."

Then I realized she hadn't really; all through her absence, the other cats hadn't dared touch her food in the second saucer or lie on my lap. They'd known she was coming back, and so, subconsciously, had I.

She extended one forepaw along the tabletop. Splayed out, a cat's paw looks like a knuckled human hand in a velvety glove, with claws where human fingernails should be. She licked between her fingers, cleaning. I looked for signs of blood, human blood.

Her paws were spotless; but then they always were.

I sat watching her eating. Recently, I'd taken to drawing the kitchen curtains shut at dusk, because my back garden is full of conifers as tall as a man, and when the wind got into them, they moved in a way that worried the corner of my eye. The wind was moving them tonight. There was even a white plastic bag caught in one that might have been an idiot face. But I knew it was only a bag, because Rama was sitting on my table eating. Her eye caught its movement for a moment, fascinated; then she dismissed it with a slight splaying of the ears and returned to her plate.

I thought of phoning Sergeant Watkinson; but what was there for him to see? I much preferred Rama's company to Sergeant Watkinson's. Having finished eating, she set to, dragging one damp paw over her ear. Even the prospect of rain seemed cozy. She would sleep in my bed tonight, while the rain battered my windows.

And if she asked to go downstairs urgently?

She was doing no more than a good watchdog. O.K., the burglar had lost an eye. A Doberman pinscher would have torn his throat out. If watchdogs, why not watchcats?

Rama stopped washing and looked at me. In the dim kitchen, her pupils were dilated, round, like a woman's when she makes love. When that barrier of inhuman eye slits is removed, you can share souls with a cat, as well as with any human.

Rama loved me.

Still, I would show her who owned whom. I got down Ginger's old collar from the nail over the sink unit. (That was the one thing the couple at the launderette hadn't stolen; they'd had great pleasure returning it to me.) I wondered how Rama would take to a collar, as I fastened it with difficulty around her muscular neck. Some cats like them; some don't.

Rama seemed almost *too* pleased—rubbing her cheekbones against the knuckles of my hand with great affection.

IT OCCURRED TO me the next evening that I must change the note inside her little collar capsule. After all, she was called Rama, not Ginger, and as a headmaster, I value accuracy. I reached over to her and took the paper out. To my surprise, it was not the official name tag supplied by the pet shop but a roughly torn scrap brown with age. On it was scrawled, in old-fashioned, indelible pencil: I LUV U.

That was a phrase of my wife's, a standing joke between us. Whenever she left me a note on the kitchen table, asking me to turn on the oven or bring in the washing, she ended it that way. A taunt to my headmasterly prissiness, I suppose.

But this was certainly not my wife's writing. An illiterate hand, yet forceful; the pencil had torn the paper in two places.

I turned the paper over. It carried the printed heading: BRITISH RAILWAYS. Not BRITISH RAIL, which is the modern version. It seemed to be part of a time sheet for men doing shift work. Dates and times had been filled in with the same indelible pencil, but in the neat printing of some railway employee, no doubt. There was nothing more; the torn piece was, of necessity, very small so as to fit inside the capsule. As a last thought, I smelled it. Damp and mold and the faint whiff of benzine. It had come from the chemical works, I had no doubt.

Who on earth could have written it?

I had a strong suspicion it might be one of my own pupils. For the most puerile joke played on a headmaster is better than the best joke played on anybody else. Some of my colleagues have their phones unlisted for that very reason. I didn't bother. I got on pretty well with my lot. Some even say hello to me in the street. When I first came, they called me the Abominable Snowdon, but over the years it's softened to Old Abby.

Good joke to catch my cat, put a new message in her

collar. But why not something spicier, like "Old Abby's a poofter"? None of them would dare write I LUV U in front of his mates. A lone child, a lonely child? How would he know how my wife spelled it? And the writing was . . . odd, very odd. Someone trying to disguise his hand?

I put the note carefully inside our bone-dry spare teapot. Pity Watkinson couldn't test it for prints. But we don't carry fingerprint records of pupils, yet. Anyway, the surest way of encouraging this kind of nonsense is to take notice of it.

I put a new name and address in Rama's collar, hoping that if they caught her again, they'd keep their tricks to the same semi-civilized level. There were a lot of water-filled shafts in that works they could have thrown her down . . .

But I refused to keep her in; she must live according to her nature.

Then I carried her up to bed. She clung to me with flattering urgency.

IT WAS NEARLY bedtime the following night before I gave way to my impulse to look inside the name capsule again.

Again, the name and address were gone. Another brown scrap in its place. I placed it edge to edge with the first; they fitted exactly, torn from the same sheet. Same indelible pencil; same jagged, savage writing.

KUM UP N C ME.

Another of my wife's phrases. Used when she has a mild dose of flu and has retired to bed before I return home. Those notes I *never* leave lying around. In our younger days, they led to some wild and joyous occasions, and I would still be embarrassed if Mrs. Raven, our cleaning woman, were to find one and ask what it was.

Who on earth could have got their hands on *that* phrase? It was uncanny, almost as if my wife were hiding somewhere in the house, playing games on me.

Except for the savagery of the writing.

Just then, as if to confirm her absence, my wife rang up to tell me I was a grandfather again. A bouncing boy (why do they always bounce?). Howard Anthony George. That pleased me; two of the names are mine. But I did warn Peter when he came on the phone that the initials spelled "hag" and did he want his son so lumbered? We settled for H.G.A. in the end, which has a dignified ·cadence.

When I put the phone down, I felt much better. I placed both the evil-smelling notes into the teapot and wrote out my name and address for the third time.

"What's it all about, Rama?"

She gave a short, deep purr and splayed her ears in a noncommittal way that made me laugh.

I carried her up to bed again.

I LUV U. KUM.

The third quarter of the time sheet—the part with the signature: S. BALLARD, CHIEF SIGNALMAN. So I knew where the sheet had come from. There had been railway sidings on the far side of the chemical works. There would be a signal hut, where the switches were worked from. I thought I knew where it stood. Rama had just come back from it, smelling of must and damp and benzine . . .

But why should I trail up there in the wind and dark? That'd make the little monkeys laugh. Be all over the school in no time, rocking the discipline boat. Still (I looked at my watch), it was past eleven. All the little darlings should be tucked up in bed by this time or at least stuck in front of the midnight movie.

Might as well stroll across and see what they'd been up to. Make sure it was nothing dangerous. I took my old navy jacket off the kitchen door, got the lantern with the flashing red dome from the garage, made sure I had my door key, and set off. I'd left Rama eating a plate of cold fat pork, to the intent envy of the others. I think I had some idea of keeping her home, out of harm's way. But before I'd gone twenty meters, I heard the cat flap bang behind me and felt her weight streak past me in the dark.

And I was glad of her company, walking through the works. God, it's an awful place. The old company had no money left to run it, and the local council had no money left to demolish it. The children haunt the works, walking along the narrow overhead pipes, climbing the rusted conveyors and high girders. The most dangerous parts have been screened off by chain-link fencing, but the children beat the chain-link flat and go on with their deadly games. Graffiti everywhere, mingled with the old industrial notices, under the wavering beam of my lantern.

NO. 5 HOIST MUFC RULE OK?
DANGER CAUSTIC SODA BAZZER AND JEFF AND BILLY

We keep getting up petitions about it, and writing to our Member of Parliament, but we're wasting our time. Even St. George couldn't slay the dragon called No Money.

A bit of a moon broke through the clouds. The wind banged loose bits of corrugated iron, high up among the girders. My boot soles scrunched on the poisonous cinders. Dry dead leaves from God knows where, trapped like people in a disaster, scurried from place to place. I thought, if I have an accident here, it'll be days before they find me.

But the moon and my lantern saw me through, with a couple of frights, and I came out on the open plain of the sidings. Picked my way across the moonlit empty rails to where I thought the signal hut was.

But it wasn't. It was only some little plate-layers' hut with a stumpy chimney. The roof had fallen in, and boys had lit a fire against the outside wall.

LFC RULES. JACK BERRY'S A SLIMER

Inside, a mass of black soot and glinting shards of glass. Nothing had happened there for a very long time.

I was retracing my steps, feeling flat and foolish, when I saw a pale cat that could only have been Rama hurtling across the rails ahead of me. Following her with my eye, I at once saw the real signal hut, standing in the black shadow of the limestone furnace. Rama streaked up the outside stair and vanished inside. I hurried across, worried.

The flat roof was intact, though most of the small-paned windows had been broken, making it hard to see inside the shadowy interior. I clumped up the outside stairs, unnecessarily loud, as if to warn someone I was coming, and pushed the door. It yielded enough to let a cat in, then resisted with a metallic clink. Shining my lantern, I saw a heavy chain and rusted padlock. Giving a grunt of exasperation, I was turning to descend when I thought I heard my name called from behind the door.

"Howard?"

It must be the wind, which was getting up. Good heavens, it was nearly midnight . . .

I'd descended two more stairs when the voice came again.

"Howard?" If you insist I describe that voice, I would say it was a woman's—low, hoarse, and . . . unpracticed. Like a rusty gate creaking. But I didn't want to believe it was a voice, in that awful place. *Surely*, a trick of the wind?

While I was standing there hovering like a ninny, it came a third time, unmistakable. "Howard, I love you."

I wanted to run, but that works was no place to run through at night. So I went back and pushed the door angrily, so that the chain rattled. Called in my headmaster's voice, which sounded so hollow in the windy silence. "Who's there? What's going on? Open the door!"

"Howard, I love you. Howard!"

"What are you doing with my cat? If this nonsense doesn't stop immediately, I shall fetch the police."

There might have been a sigh at my stupidity; or it might have been the wind.

"Howard, help me. Fetch me some clothes. I'm so *cold*."

"Let my cat go, or I will fetch the police."

"Howard . . ." A yearning voice, a voice of endearment.

I ran down the steps, half in rage and half in terror. From a safe distance I stared up at the broken, multi-paneled signal-hut window. Tricky, because blowing moonlit clouds were reflecting in the glass. But I could have sworn I saw a tall shape walking among the signal-hut levers.

"Let my cat go," I bawled, "or I'll fetch the police."

Silence. I ran back up the steps, almost sobbing, and

tried to kick the door in. There was a flash at my feet, then Rama was past me, streaking across the tracks for home.

Well, I had saved my friend, and that was all that mattered. I followed her at top speed, and was never so glad to be through my own front door and switching on every light in the house. I made myself a hot whisky and lemon and sat drinking it till my shivering stopped. I was still shivering and drinking when the cat flap banged (not doing my nerves any good) and Rama came in, quite cool, and sat on the table, washing inside her hind legs. She gave me a couple of hard stares, as if to say "What's all the fuss about?" Then indicated it was time for bed.

Even with her beside me, it was a long time before I slept.

NEXT AFTERNOON, straight after school, I drove to the signal hut, to inspect it by the last glimmerings of December daylight. Solid brick, with a concrete-slab roof. Many broken panes, but the wooden window frames intact. Nothing bigger than a cat could have wriggled through. The only way in was through the upstairs door. Laughing at my stupid fancies of the night before, I climbed the stairs and rattled the chain. The lock was rusted solid; it would take an hour's work with a hack-saw . . .

"Howard?"

It shocked me more in daylight. God, how it shocked me. Cars were passing on the distant main road across the sidings, their headlights casting pools of sanity. But also reminding me it was getting dark again.

"Howard, *please*. I need clothes. I'm so *cold* . . ."

"Who are you? How do you know my name?"

"Howard, bring clothes . . . I need clothes."

"How did you get in there? What do you want clothes *for*?"

"Because I am *naked*, Howard. See!"

I put my eye to the crack of the door. Saw rough floorboards, the rusting levers sticking up at all angles, the broken glass.

Then an eye swam out of the gloom, opposite mine. An eye I knew yet somehow could not place.

"If you don't bring clothes, I shall come to you naked, Howard."

I ran all the way back to my car.

I was tempted to sleep elsewhere that night. But when headmasters start staying in hotels in our town . . .

I locked the doors and latched the windows. Drew the curtains. Told myself to be sensible. But it's less easy to be sensible after dark, especially alone. The wind's an enemy of common sense, and the Virginia creeper tapping, and the idiot face in the back garden . . .

My wife rang up, full of good news about mother and baby. For once, I couldn't be bothered with her. Her cheerfulness irritated, like a bluebottle buzzing against a window. I got rid of her as quickly as possible, cooked an early supper, and quite failed to eat it. Finally I scraped it into the dish for the cats.

Only to discover there wasn't a cat in the kitchen. Odd! When you keep five cats there are always a couple loafing around, ear cocked for the sound of a dish being scraped.

I suddenly felt immensely lonely; damned them for their ingratitude. Then steeled myself to open the back door and call them.

The wind snatched away my voice; none of them

answered. The wild bushes tossed their heads at me. The dead leaves in the yard scurried around like a trapped crowd in a burning theater. The sound of dead leaves is the deadest sound in the world; they sound the same at night in Pompeii.

I stepped out angrily to snatch the bobbing idiot-head bag from its bough. Lost my nerve halfway, ran back inside, and bolted the door. For a moment it shut out the noise of wind and leaves, and I heard, through the slightly open laundry door, the sound of a cat coughing. The sickening way they cough when they crouch flat to the ground and stick their necks out, so long you think they're choking to death.

A sign of fear in a cat. I followed the noise. The laundry room seemed empty. The arrangement of washing machine and blue plastic bowl that I'd left myself the day before seemed to sneer at me. I was just putting the light out, thinking I'd been imagining things, when the low, desperate coughing started again.

There was a deep, dark, narrow gap between the cupboard and the wall. I thrust my hand in and felt, at the back, a wire-tense bundle of fur, which I dragged out by the scruff. She fought all the way, digging in her claws and ripping the linoleum. Melly. For a second she lay still in my arms, eyes screwed tight-shut, ears back. Then she exploded back into the narrow gap like a furry missile, knocking over a chair that stood in her way. Leaving me with a torn shirt and bleeding arms.

I left her; I know terror when I see it. Perhaps she'd had a near miss with a car . . . By morning, she'd be herself again.

I was getting a whisky when it occurred to me there might be other cats hiding in the house. A careful search revealed the three little ones in the back of my tool cupboard, a huddle of mindless terror, quite impervious to the sharp edges on the saws and chisels they were crouching on.

They couldn't all have had near misses. Something was terrifying them. It made the bolted doors and curtained windows seem pretty thin. I wished Rama were here. Rama wouldn't frighten so easy. But of Rama there was no sign, even in the drafty attics.

I had an absurd desire to call Sergeant Watkinson. But what about? It was past eleven, and the world was away, asleep. It wouldn't want to know about my problems, at least till morning. Self-help, Howard, self-help! I went up to Peter's room to get the rifle. Again, the oily smell of cartridges reminded me of happier days. Would they still work, after ten years? Though God knew what I intended to shoot that night. Only *I* wasn't giving up my eyes without a struggle.

I made up a big fire in the lounge; pushed furniture against the windows, with some absurd idea of tripping up anything that tried to come through them. Settled in my armchair with another, very small whisky. Didn't want my wits fuddled. I tried playing some Bach on the record player, but the sound blocked out all other noises and I switched it off quickly. I finally settled with the gun across my knee, the lantern beside me in case the lights went out, and *The Lord of the Rings* balanced across the gun. But Frodo's journey—my favorite passage in all literature—was no comfort. I was listening, listening, checking each noise as it came. A hunted animal in its lair, but at least an animal with some teeth.

But we're not as good as animals at staying alert. Whether it was the whisky or the fire, I began to doze.

Twice, the book falling from my lap brought me leaping awake. Once, it was the collapse of coals in the fire. Once, the grandfather clock in the hall, chiming one, sounding as meaningless as it would to a cat.

And yet, in the end, my senses did not let me down. Suddenly I came out of sleep wide-awake, not knowing what had wakened me. But I somehow knew this was it. I remember putting my book and whisky glass carefully on one side, out of harm's way; picking up the gun and pointing it at the white door of my lounge, and not forgetting to slip off the safety catch.

At the back of the house, the cat flap banged. Which of the little cats was moving? Or had Rama come home? I wasn't tempted to go and look; just kept sitting in my chair, pointing the rifle with fairly steady hands.

I never heard any footsteps; just the floorboards in the hall, creaking. Something heavier than a cat.

The door handle rattled three times, as a cat will sometimes rattle it, wanting to be in. The third time, it began to turn, hesitantly, as if the creature wasn't used to opening doors. I had an awful temptation to shoot through the white door, just above the handle, to hear a heavy body fall and know that I was safe. To kill what stood there, without having to look at it. But I'm a man, not an animal.

The door opened only five centimeters; a five-centimeter gap of darkness, and something taking stock of me, out of that darkness. I nudged up the barrel of the gun, to warn whatever stood there not to try my patience too long.

"Howard?" It was the voice from the signal hut.

At that moment, I realized I was still wearing my reading spectacles, and everything more than a meter away was a blur. My outdoor spectacles were on the table beside me, but to reach them, I'd have to take one hand off the gun.

The door swung open, and I thought I was going crazy.

Mrs. Raven stood there in the shadows—Mrs. Raven, our cleaning woman, in her big-checked smock.

"Mrs. Raven," I said, dumbfounded. "What are *you* doing here?" I remember thinking, ridiculously, that this was Monday night—well, Tuesday morning—and Mrs. Raven came on Thursdays. Then the creature swam in from the shadows, and even wearing my reading spectacles, I realized I wasn't talking to Mrs. Raven but to something dressed in Mrs. Raven's smock. Which always hung on the back door, above the cat flap.

Where Mrs. Raven's scarf usually hid her curlers flamed a mane of burning red hair. Where Mrs. Raven's wrinkled gray stockings covered a pair of spindled legs . . . the smock, which enclosed Mrs. Raven like a voluminous sack, was no more than a minidress on this thing.

She flowed in like a wave of grace, filling the room. She'd have flowed right over me, but I raised the small, mean barrel of the gun.

That stopped her; whatever she was, she knew what a gun was for.

She curled herself smoothly down into my wife's chair, on the other side of the fireplace. Without human modesty; so I was glad I was wearing my reading spectacles. All her body hair seemed that same flaming red. She made my wife's chair look small; she made the room feel small; and it's not a small room. I wondered again about changing my spectacles, but she'd be across the hearth rug in a flash if I took my eyes off her.

"Howard?"

I peered. Got a blurred impression of large green eyes and, when she yawned, very white teeth. She was no more humanly modest with her yawn than with her body. Just yawned enjoyably to the fullest extent, without putting her hand over her mouth.

"You do know me, Howard." She tried to stretch again; but the smock was a constricting torment to her. She put up a hand and the cloth ripped open, as if it were paper. From the sound, I could imagine the size of her fingernails.

"You remind me . . . of my cat Rama," I said, forcing a laugh; not wanting to be totally outfaced. It seemed a good, brave thing to laugh at such a monster.

"I *am* your cat Rama."

Then I knew I was asleep and dreaming. The dreams of a lonely fifty-year-old whose wife has been away too long. But a man must act in his dreams as he would act in life. Or else he is a hypocrite. So I kept the dream gun pointing at her.

"If you are my cat Rama, you will behave like my cat Rama. At least while you are in *my* house. What you do outside is your own business."

I jumped awake to the rattle of the cat flap, to find I was in a cold and empty room. No wonder the room was so cold; the draft had swung the door open five centimeters . . .

I DIDN'T STIR from my chair for the rest of the night, though I stoked the fire several times and dozed till daylight. Some dreams can leave a heavier impression on you than reality. I wakened finally with bright early sunshine making streaks across the darkened hearth rug.

I pulled back the curtains, feeling a total fool, with a very stiff neck as a memento of my foolishness. The book, the gun, and the whisky glass were not a welcome sight.

I checked the house; every door and window was, of course, locked and secure. My five cats gave me their usual sleepy, stretching greeting when I entered the kitchen. I had to stroke their heads in turn; Rama first, of course. I tried staring her out and failed as usual. Otherwise, she seemed perfectly normal. I felt a certain reluctance to touch her at all but made myself. I am not the kind of person who blames a cat for my own silly dreams. Nevertheless, from that day there was a coldness, a distance between us.

Mrs. Raven's smock hung on the door as usual. Except that when I turned it around, all the buttons were missing and seemed to have been removed with unnecessary force. I found them in the pocket. That seemed a little odd, but then I'd never taken any interest in the garment before. Perhaps my wife or Mrs. Raven was busily engaged in taking it in, or letting it out, or some other mysterious thing that women seem always to be doing to garments. Certainly the smock wasn't seriously damaged. Nothing Mrs. Raven couldn't put right in ten minutes. I made a resolve to ask her about it but forgot and never did.

Life continued much as before, except that Rama seemed to get ever bigger and sleeker. And I felt an increasing reluctance to join my family in Scotland for Christmas and leave Mrs. Raven and Rama to each other's tender mercies.

But Christmas was still ten days off when it happened. I was buying my supper in the village off license when I heard about it. A young girl, on her way home alone from a Christmas dance the previous night, had been dragged into the old works and murdered.

"I saw the young copper who found her," said the woman behind the counter, her eyes wide upon the horror of some inward scene. "I had to give him a cup of tea, he was that shaken. He was sick all over the bathroom floor. He said it was like a wild beast had mauled her to death . . ."

I just stood there, with my cold Cornish pasties in my hand, afraid I was going to drop them. I remember that there was a young man standing across from me in the queue. A small young man in a black leather jacket, a workman of some kind, because he had a bag of tools in his hand, with the handle of a hammer and the point of a screwdriver sticking out. He kept staring at the woman and then staring at me, drinking in our faces, and I remember thinking he knows something, he knows about me and about Rama. I heard no more; I was only too eager to get out of the shop without disgracing myself.

When I got home, Rama was nowhere to be seen. Sergeant Watkinson rang the doorbell as I was sitting in the cold kitchen, staring blankly at the pages of an old color newspaper supplement.

I couldn't help glancing at Rama's usual chair as I showed him in.

"Something missing, sir?"

"No, no," I said, elaborately counting the four cats that remained. "Four—all accounted for."

"The other one never turned up, then?"

I shook my head. He'd never believe any of it, anyway. Besides, this was between me and Rama.

He asked if I'd heard anything the previous night. Living in the house nearest the old works . . . I shook my head with conviction. That much was true. I asked about the girl's injuries. He just shook his head. Nothing was being released.

When he'd gone, I went to Peter's room and took down the rifle.

The next week was hell. The gun was always ready, but there was no sign of her. The other cats began to eat her food, sleep in her chair. I don't know how I got through school. In the evenings, I drank. My wife sensed my mood over the phone; threatened to come home. I managed to put her off.

Then, the night before the end of term, I looked up at the uncurtained window (I no longer bothered to draw the curtains) and saw her great cat-mask peering at me. I wasn't frightened; only in despair that she would vanish like a ghost before I could fetch the gun.

But when I returned she was still there, staring in calmly, sadly—almost, I would have said, lovingly. I fumbled with the safety catch, raised the rifle to shoot her through the glass, and her head immediately vanished.

I ran outside into a clear moonlit night. She stood on the yard gate, silvered by the moon. I raised the rifle, and again she dropped out of sight.

I ran after her, like a mad thing, in my shirtsleeves. Saw her streaking down the grassy slopes to the old works, far ahead, too difficult a shot by moonlight. I ran without hope, then. She would lose me in the works, easily; be crouched on a girder, above my head, and I'd never notice.

But when I reached the works she was visible, a pale streak going along the main soda pipe. I began to suspect she was playing with me, as if I were a mouse. Leading me to what? Her death? My death? I no longer cared. My middle-aged breath scraped harshly in my throat, tasting foully of whisky and despair.

Half an hour later, on the slope of Brinkton Woods, I knew she was leading me on. Letting me draw nearer and nearer, yet always on the move; never giving me the chance of a straight shot.

Then, in the depth of the wood, she vanished. I sat on a fallen tree, sweating and gasping and wishing I were dead. Brinkton Woods is for lovers, not cats and crazy, middle-aged men. I felt too weak to walk the two miles home. Why had she *done* this to me? I didn't care if she killed me.

So why did I start up in fright at a crashing in the nearby bushes? It didn't sound like Rama anyway; much too noisy and disorganized.

Then a young girl screamed.

An ugly sound; a thud on flesh. Then the scream turned into a sobbing, a wild sobbing of sheer disbelief.

"Oh, no, oh, no, oh, no, please don't, please don't."

Another ugly noise, before it got into my thick skull that the girl might be being murdered. I'd never heard the sound of a killing before; it doesn't sound like you expect it to sound, from the telly.

I slipped off the safety catch and ran. Oh, Rama!

I burst through the bushes into a tiny clearing where the moonlight was full. A girl lay on her back, skirt up around her waist, pale, silken legs thrashing wildly while something dark crouched with horrible intentness over her head and neck.

As I raised my rifle, uncertain of getting in a shot, wondering whether to leap in and use it like a club, the girl gave one last, desperate, upward push with her bleeding arms. Just for a second, the dark shape hung above her, quite separate . . .

I fired at the center of the rib cage. No animal can do much harm once you've hit it in the rib cage, even if you don't find the heart.

I was too close to miss, even by moonlight. The beast fell sideways, pivoting on the girl's outstretched arms, and lay quite still.

"Goodbye, Rama," I mouthed bitterly, and walked across. The girl must not have been hurt too badly. She had jumped to her feet and began screaming again for all she was worth. Perhaps she thought I was the second murderer.

The beast had rolled into the shadow of a bush. I pushed it with my foot, still covering it with the rifle.

It was a man.

A small, dark man in a black leather jacket. A bag of tools lay beside him—hammer and screwdriver. He was quite dead, a small, damp, warm patch where his heart would be.

A feeling of being watched made me look up. Rising above the bush was a head, with two great, dark, sorrowful eyes and a mane of hair that managed to look red even in the moonlight.

Rama raised one hand.

"Goodbye, Howard." It had sadness and longing and contempt in it.

Then Rama was gone, forever.

THE MAKING
OF ME

YOU SEE THE STATE I'm in now, as I sit here.

Do not blame me. My grandfather made me what I am. With one blow. In one minute.

I had a happy childhood, except for one thing. I hated being "left with" people when my parents went off somewhere. You could never tell what people would *do* with you, once your parents had gone.

Like my holy aunt, for instance. No sooner had my parents waved goodbye than one of her holy friends would turn up, hold my head between her hands, look deep into my eyes, and ask if I said my prayers and hoped to go to heaven? I mean, what do you *say*?

Other times my aunt, who was Salvation Army, would take me off around the streets, marching with the band. I quite liked the band, though I hated the way people stared at us. Especially when we stopped on some wet and windy corner and the Major began shouting wildly about Jesus Christ and Salvation, to the two men and a dog who'd stopped to listen.

He lisped. He kept asking people if they were "thaved" or were still wallowing in their "thins." Some of my mates from school saw me standing next to him once, and I was regularly asked in the playground if I'd been "thaved" from my "thins." For a whole three years, till I went to secondary school.

My unholy aunt wasn't so bad. She might condemn God non-stop, for letting little children die of diphtheria or for sinking ships in storms, but at least she stayed home to do it, with nobody to hear but me. And she always had very good chocolate biscuits.

The person I really dreaded being left with, though, was my grandfather. He was not a *person*, like my mum and dad, or my little round laughing nana. He towered above me, six feet tall. I would sometimes glance up at him, as one might peer up in awe at a mountainous crag. The huge nose, the drooping mustache, the drooping mass of wrinkles. Then his eyes would peer down at me, too small, too close together, pale blue, wild and empty of everything but an everlasting, baffled rage. And my own eyes would scurry for cover, like a scared rabbit. He never spoke to me, and I never spoke to him, and thank God my parents never forced me to, as they would force me sometimes to kiss hairy-chinned old ladies.

There were old tales of his violence. How when his second child was born dead, he ripped the gas stove from the wall and threw it downstairs (and gas stoves were solid cast-iron then, and weighed a ton). How when he came home drunk on a Saturday night, Nana and my eleven-year-old father would hear his step and run to hide in the outside washhouse, till he fell into a drunken sleep before the fire. And then Nana would stealthily rifle his pockets for the remains of his week's wages, and go straight to buy the week's shopping before he woke. And when he woke, he would think he'd lost all his money in his drunken stupor.

But the Great War had done for him. Unlike anybody else I knew, he had a Chest, because he'd been gassed in the trenches. His Chest made a fascinating symphony of noises at the best of times. So I would listen to it, rather than the chat around the dinner table. But when he was upstairs in bed, bad with his Chest, the whole house was silent and doom-laden, and my parents tiptoed about and talked in whispers.

He was also shell-shocked. Nana always had to be careful with the big black kettle she kept simmering on the hob to make a cup of tea. If it was allowed to boil, the lid would begin to rattle, making exactly the same noise as a distant machine gun. And that would be enough to send him off into one of his "do's," when he would imagine he was back in the hell of the trenches and would shout despairing orders, and I would be sent out for a walk till one of his powders settled him.

They said he had killed an Austrian soldier in a bayonet fight and taken his cap badge. I was sometimes allowed to handle the strange square badge, to keep me quiet. It had a picture in brass of charging infantrymen, and strange, Eastern, Hungarian writing. When Granda was *really* bad, he thought the dead Austrian had come back for his badge.

And, above all, he still drank. Perhaps to drown the memories he never spoke of. Oh, the silent agony of waiting to eat Sunday lunch, because of him, at our house—my mother fretting and the painful smell of good roast beef being singed to a crisp in the oven. Every ear cocked for his wavering footsteps. The strange bits of French songs or German marches that he would hum while he pushed his food unwanted around his plate.

Afterwards he would fall asleep with his mouth open.

There was never any blackness for me like the blackness of the inside of his mouth.

While my parents were there, and the Nana I loved, he was just a fascinating monster, a fabulous beast. Safe to watch, like a tiger in a cage.

But being left alone with him . . .

A dreadful silence always fell. Perhaps he thought he had nothing in his mind fit for a child's ears. And my childish prattle, which so made the other grownups laugh, just got on his shell-shocked nerves.

Once, without warning, he clouted me across the ear. I think I wasn't so much hurt as *outraged*. Nobody had ever hit me, except my father twice, and that after plenty of warnings. The unfairness of it made the world reel about me. He told my father, afterwards, that I turned to him with tears in my eyes and said, "Why did you hit me, Grandfather?"

It sounds like something out of a Victorian novel. But it must have cut him to his shell-shocked heart. When my parents returned they found me barricaded safely inside the outhouse, and him rocking with his head in his hands, full of agonized remorse that he had hit that innocent bairn. And vowing never to do it again till the day he died, or might his hand wither and drop off.

The innocent bairn wasn't slow to make the most of such an opening. Next time I was left with him, I found him still silent, but strangely obedient. I soon grasped he would do anything I wanted, just to keep me happy.

To be honest, I don't think I meant to be cruel: I wasn't a cruel child. But I had suffered a kind of personal earthquake at his hands, and I was very keen to prove his present mood would last and the earthquake wouldn't happen again.

And I had a hopeless yearning to imitate my father, who was the engineer at the gasworks and, to me, a great wizard who dwelt among roaring furnaces and stamping cart horses, among great heaps of smoking slag and clouds of green gas, and who could start great steel dinosaurs of engines with one push of his small shoulder to an eight-foot flywheel.

I wanted to make a *machine*. A machine of brass and steel that swung rhythmically and jangled loudly, and flashed with steel and brass.

I asked Granda to get Nana's washline.

He did.

I asked that he string it around the room from the hook on the kitchen door where her apron hung, to the rail above the kitchen range where she dried her tea towels: from the handle of the cupboard to the hooks on the Welsh dresser. When it was firmly secured, we proceeded to hang from it every pot, pan, ladle, and spoon in her well-stocked kitchen.

I pulled on the line. Everything swung, danced, jangled with the most satisfying cacophony. It was like entering into a new world.

Two hours later they found me still happily pulling and clanging, with my grandfather cowering in the depths of his chair with his hands pressed over his shell-shocked ears.

He had kept his word; he had not laid a hand on the innocent bairn. I don't know why he didn't strangle me; it must have been a close call. Even I was scared at what I'd done—afterwards. When I saw the look on my father's face.

AND THEN my unholy aunt fell ill and was rushed to the hospital and was not expected to live. Suddenly the family

were going to see her every night, and my mother thought
that the hospital was no place to take a child. From now
on I was going to be left with my grandfather, not once
a month, but every night. A terrifying desert of silence
and strangeness stretched before me. If I'd had any pity
to spare from myself, I might have pitied Granda. But I
was just plain terrified. What were we going to *say*? What
were we going to *do* in that desert of time? I went, that
first evening, thinking the end of the world, so often
foretold by my holy aunt, was upon me.

I settled myself in the deepest chair, behind a mass of
old comics I'd read ten times already. But the *Wizard*
(and the famous Wilson, who had run the three-minute
mile at the Berlin Olympics when he was a hundred and
twenty years old, because he lived on rare herbs) had no
charms that night.

I furtively eyed my strange sighing Beast as his Chest
made its odd symphony of noises, and the terrifying
sweet smell of sick old man came through the air to my
cringing nostrils. I did not want to breathe the air he
breathed. As my mother might have said about something
I'd picked up in the street, I did not know where that
air might have been. It might still have had bits in it from
the trenches of the Great War, where dead men hung
rotting on the barbed wire. Particles of poison gas; or
the dying breath breathed out by the dead Austrian . . .

In the soft glow of the gaslight, his face was all wrinkled
and shadowed pits, mysterious as the craters of the moon.
He was fiddling with the tap of the gaslight, fixing a little
bit of wire around it. Perhaps it was his way of keeping
me at bay, as my comics were my way of keeping him at
bay.

He had dragged out of some cupboard a large old
stained tea chest. It was full of strange shapes, trapped

in tangled coils of wire. The strange shapes drew me irresistibly; perhaps I had some wild hope of building another jangle machine. I put a tentative hand inside. There was the most huge rusty hammer I'd ever seen . . . a long weird knife in a scabbard. I tugged at the knife; it resisted. I tugged harder . . . then harder. It leaped out of my hand, dragging behind it, in a web of tangled wire, a queerly shaped, huge brass tap, and a short brass cylinder. They all fell on the floor with a terrible bang. He swung around, ever jumpy . . .

I gabbled out, before he could hit me, "What's that funny tap, Granda?"

He picked up the tap, as if he hadn't seen it in a long time.

"By," he said dreamily, "that's a spare tap left over from the old *Mauretania*. Finest and fastest ship in the world, she was. Held the Blue Riband of the Atlantic for twenty years. The day she was launched—she had no funnels or nothing, mind—the shipyard workers got up steam in a little donkey boiler in the bows. The old Morrie was the only liner ever launched wi' steam up. And when she sailed on her maiden voyage, people lined the banks of the Tyne for eight miles to bid her Godspeed. As if the King was passin' . . . and when she came home from her last voyage, to be broken up to make razor blades, the people lined up again to say goodbye to her. Look, here's the pictures." And there, on the wall, were two photographs of the old Morrie sailing and the old Morrie coming home. And she looked the same in both.

"Why did they break her up? She looks as good as new."

"Aye, but she was tired *inside*," he said. "Things look the same, but they get tired inside." There was something in his voice I couldn't face. So I held up the short brass cylinder before the silence came back like the frozen Arctic.

"That's the lens of the film projector that showed the first movie ever shown in North Shields. The show was held in the Temperance Hall, and it cost a penny to get in. Fatty Arbuckle was the star—he got sent to prison in the end. We saw Charlie Chaplin through that. Rudolph Valentino. No talkies, of course—just a lady playing the piano for the exciting bits."

"How did you get it?"

"George Costigan gave it to me in Guthrie's Bar, the night the old King died . . ."

"And what's this?" I held up a worn long block of rubber.

"That's the brake block off me old bike—the one I used to ride around Holywell Dene, when I was courting your nana. I was taking that brake block off the night your dad was born . . ." A new kind of awe swept over me. My mother had often talked about the night *I* was born (and what a hard time I'd given her, and how she'd almost died of me), and that was mysterious enough. But the night my *dad* was born . . . That was as incredibly far off as the Pharaohs building the pyramids.

We were off in style now. Every object told a story. The dead rose up and walked again. Admiral Jellicoe and Earl Kitchener of Khartoum. Kaiser Bill and Marie Lloyd. Lloyd George and Jack the Ripper. They streamed out of my grandfather as they might have streamed out of the first cinema projector to show a film in North Shields.

Only once was he silent. About the long knife in the scabbard. He took it in his hand and was silent; then he put it back in the box. I knew it was the bayonet that had killed the Austrian, for his face went gray and his eyes were far away. I knew he hated it. I also knew he would never throw it away. Just like the cap badge.

"What did you do in the trenches—in between?" I asked.

"I'll tell yer." He pulled out a steel helmet, thick with rust. "See that little hole in the top?"

"Is it a bullet hole?"

He actually laughed. "No, no. It's a screw hole. We used to pull the screw out and stick a nail through the hole, and stick a candle on the nail. So we could see to play cards. Look—you can still see a bit o' candle wax. I was good at cards—three-card brag, a quick game—it didn't matter if you were interrupted, like. I won a lot o' money. Lot o' fellers still owe me money, but they're dead. So I took a little thing from their kit, instead. To remember them by. See . . ." He reached up and took down his shaving kit from above the sink.

"That's Gerry Henry's shaving brush, and Mannie Webber's bowl, and Tommy Malbon's mirror . . . Good chums, every one."

Now we were both silent, and it was all right. For I knew who was in the silence now. The good chums, every one.

It was Granda who broke the silence. "There was a joke as we used to have, us Shields lads out there:

> *"The boy stood on the burning deck,*
> *His feet were full o' blisters.*
> *His father stood in Guthrie's Bar*
> *Wi' the beer running down his whiskers.*

"We always said that, when we were down. It always got a laugh."

He laughed. I laughed. It seemed good to laugh with good chums.

WHEN MY PARENTS got back from the hospital, it was over for that night. I was reverently arranging objects in sections and patterns across the clippie rug, and Granda was peacefully snoring in his chair.

But he'd done enough. Taught me that every object tells a story, and every dent in every object tells a story. Within a week I was pressing my nose against the window of every junk shop in town. Regarding the scruffy little men who stood inside, rubbing their hands together against the cold, as the Lords of Time who knew all mysteries.

After that, museums. Like the museum I sit in now.

Then it was a dent in a tap made thirty years ago. Now it is a dent in a Pharaoh's head made four thousand years ago. All part of my journey back in time. The world goes forward to drugs and violence and slot-machine addiction. I go backwards, to where I am truly free.

My grandfather, long gone where old soldiers go, still accompanies me. His photograph is on my desk as I write; his photo before the gas got him, on the Somme. When my nana married him, she said he was the handsomest feller in Shields, with his bonnie blue eyes . . . He is much younger in his photo than I am now.

Each year I look more like him, as I remember him: the incredibly bushy eyebrows; the hairs that persist in growing on the end of my nose. When I laugh, I hear the echo of his laugh. Sometimes I hear myself wheezing in the mornings, though I was never gassed at the Battle of the Somme.

Time moves in all directions. My grandfather made me.

THE NIGHT OUT

ME AND CARPET were just finishing a game of pool, working out how to pinch another game before the kids who'd booked next, when Maniac comes across.

Maniac was playing at Hell's Angels again. Homemade swastikas all over his leathers and beer mats sewn all over his jeans. Maniac plays at everything, even biking. Don't know how we put up with him, but he hangs on. Bike Club's a tolerant lot.

"Geronimo says do you want to go camping tonight?" chirps Maniac.

"Pull the other one," says Carpet. 'Cos the last we seen of Geronimo, he was pinching forks and spoons out of the club canteen to stuff up Maniac's exhaust. So that when Maniac revved up, he'd think his big end had gone. Maniac always worries about his big end; always worries about everything. Some biker.

I'd better explain all these nicknames, before you think I'm potty. Geronimo's name is really Weston; which becomes Western; which becomes Indian chief; which becomes Geronimo. Carpet's real name is Matt; but he says when he was called Matt everybody trampled on him. Some chance. Carpet's a big hard kid; but he'd always help out a mate in trouble. Maniac's really called Casey equals crazy equals Maniac. Got it?

Anyway, Geronimo himself comes over laughing, having just fastened the club secretary to his chair by the back buckles of his leathers, and everyone's pissing themselves laughing, except the secretary, who hasn't noticed yet . . .

"You game?" asks Geronimo.

I was game. There was nowt else going on except ten kids doing an all-male tribal dance right in front of the main amplifier of the disco. The rest had reached the stage where the big joke was to pour somebody's pint into somebody else's crash helmet. Besides, it was a privilege to go anywhere with Geronimo; he could pull laughs out of the air.

"Half an hour; Sparwick chip shop," said Geronimo, and we all made tracks for home. I managed seventy up the main street, watching for fuzz having a crafty fag in shop doorways. But there was nobody about except middle-aged guys in dirty raincoats staring in the windows of telly shops. What's middle age a punishment for? Is there no cure?

At home, I went straight to my room and got my tent and sleeping bag. Don't know why I bothered. As far as Geronimo was concerned, a tent was just for letting down the guy ropes of, on wet nights. And a sleeping bag was for jumping on, once somebody got into it. I raided the larder and found the usual baked beans and hot dogs. My parents didn't eat, either. They bought them for me camping, on condition that I didn't nick tomorrow's lunch.

Stuck me head in the lounge. Dad had his head stuck in the telly, worrying about the plight of the Vietnamese boat refugees. Some treat, after a hard week's work!

"Going camping. Seeya in morning."

"Don't forget your key. I'm not getting up for you in the middle of the night if it starts raining."

Which really meant, I love you and take care not to break your silly neck 'cos I know what you're going to get up to. But he'd never say it, 'cos I've got him well trained. Me mum made a worried kind of grab at the air, so I slammed down the visor of me helmet and went, yelling "Seeya in morning" again to drown her protests before she made them.

Moon was up, all the way to Sparwick chippie. Making the trees all silver down one side. Felt great, 'cos we were *going* somewhere. Didn't know where, but *somewhere*. Astronaut to Saturn, with Carpet and Geronimo . . . and Maniac? Well, nobody expected life to be perfect . . .

Carpet was there already. "What you got?" he said, slapping my carrier box.

"Beans an' hot dogs. What you got?"

"Hot dog an' beans."

"Crap!"

"Even that would make a change."

"No, it wouldn't. We have that all week at the works canteen."

We sat side by side, revving up, watching the old grannies in their curlers and carpet slippers coming out of the chippie clutching their hot greasy packets to their boobs like they were babies, and yakking on about who's got cancer now.

"If I reach fifty, I'm goin' to commit suicide," said Carpet.

"Forty'll do me."

"Way you ride, you won't reach twenty."

Maniac rode up, sounding like a trade-in sewing machine. He immediately got off and started revving his bike, with his helmet shoved against his rear forks.

"What's up?"

"Funny noise."

"No funnier than usual," said Carpet. But he took his helmet off and got Maniac to rev her again, and immediately spotted it was the tins in Maniac's carrier box that were making the rattling. "Bad case of Heinz," he muttered to me, but he said to Maniac, "Sounds like piston slap. We'd better get the cylinder head off . . ."

Maniac turned as white as a sheet in the light from the chippie, but he started getting his tool kit out, 'cos he knew Carpet knew bikes.

Just as well Geronimo turned up then. Carpet's crazy; he'd sooner strip a bike than a bird . . .

"Where to, then?" said Geronimo.

Nobody had a clue. Everybody had the same old ideas and got howled down. It's like that sometimes. We get stuck for a place to go. Then Maniac and Carpet started arguing about Jap bikes versus British, and you can't sink lower than that. In a minute they'd start eating their beans straight from the tins, tipping them up like cans of lager. Once the grub was gone, there'd be no point to going anywhere, and I'd be home before midnight and Dad would say was it morning already how time flies and all that middle-aged smarty crap.

And Geronimo had lost interest in us and was watching the cars going past down the main road. If something interesting came past worth burning off, like a Lamborghini or even a Jag XJ12, we wouldn't see him again for the rest of the night.

So I said I knew where there was a haunted abbey. I

felt a bit of a rat, 'cos that abbey was a big thing with Dad. He was a mate of the guy who owned it and he'd taken me all over it and it was a fascinating place and God knew what Geronimo would do to it . . . But we got to go somewhere.

"What's it haunted by?" Geronimo put his helmet against mine, so his voice boomed. But he was interested.

"A nun. There was a kid riding past one night, and this tart all clad in white steps out right under his front wheel and he claps his anchors on but he goes straight into her and arse over tip. Ruins his enamel. But when he went back there was nothing there."

"Bollocks," said Geronimo. "But I'll go for the sex interest. What's a nun doing in an *abbey*?" He was no fool, Geronimo. He could tell a Carmelite from a camshaft when he had to.

"Ride along," he said, and took off with me on his shoulder, which is great, like fighter pilots in the war. And I watched the streetlights sliding curved across his black helmet, and the way he changed gear smart as a whip. He got his acceleration with a long hard burst in second.

I found them the abbey gate and opened it and left it for Maniac to close. "Quiet—there's people living here."

"Throttle down," said Geronimo.

But Maniac started going on about the abbey being private property and trespass—a real hero.

"Have a good trip home," said Geronimo. "Please drive carefully."

Maniac flinched like Geronimo'd hit him. Then mumbled, "O.K. Hang on a minute, then."

Everybody groaned. Maniac was a big drinker, you see. Shandy-bitter. Lemonade. He'd never breathalyze in a million years. But it made him burp all the time, like a

clapped-out Norton Commando. And he was always having to stop and go behind hedges. Only he was scared to
stop, in case we shot off without him. That time, we let him
get started and *went*. Laughing so we could hardly ride 'cos
he'd be pissing all over his bulled-up boots in a panic.

It was a hell of a ride, 'cos the guy who owned the
abbey kept his drive all rutted, to discourage people like
us. Geronimo went up on his foot rests like a jockey,
back straight as a ruler. Nobody could ride like Geronimo;
even my dad said he rode like an Apache.

It was like scrambling; just Geronimo's straight back
and the tunnel of trees ahead, white in the light of
Geronimo's quartz-halogen headlights, and the shining
red eyes of rabbits and foxes staring out at us, then
shooting off. And our three engines so quiet, and Maniac
far behind, revving up like mad, trying to catch up. I
wished it could go on forever, till a sheet of water shot
up inside my leathers, so cold I forgot if I was male or
female . . .

Geronimo had found a rut full of water and soaked
me beautifully. He was staring back at me, laughing
through his visor. And here was another rut coming up.
Oh, hell—it was lucky I always cleaned my bike on
Saturday mornings. Anyway, he soaked me five times,
but I soaked him once, and I got Carpet twice. And
Maniac caught up; and then fell off when Carpet got *him*.
And then we were at the abbey.

A great stretch of moonlit grass, sweeping down to the
river. And the part the monks used to live in, which was
now a stately home, away on the right all massive and
black, except where our lights shone on hundreds and
hundreds of windows. And the part that used to be the
abbey church was on the left. Henry VIII made them
pull that all down, so there was nothing left but low walls,

and the bases of columns sticking out of the grass about as high as park benches, like black rotten teeth. And at the far end of that was a tall stone cross.

"That's the Nun's Grave," I said. "But it's not really. Just some old bits and pieces of the abbey that they found in the eighteenth century and put together to make a good story . . ."

"Big'ead," said Geronimo. "Let's have a look." He climbed on the base of the first column and, waving his arms about, leaped for the base of the second column. Screaming like a banshee. "I AAAAAMM the Flying Nun." It was a fantastic leap, about twelve feet. He made it, though his boots scraped heavily on the sandstone blocks. I shuddered and looked toward the house. Luckily, there wasn't a light showing. Country people went to bed early. I hoped.

"I AAAAAAAAMMM the Flying Nun," wailed Geronimo, "and I'm in LOOOOOOVE with the Flying Abbot. But I'm cheating on him with the Flying Doctor."

He attempted another death-defying leap, missed his footing, and nearly ruined his married future.

"Amendment," said Carpet. "He *was* the Flying Nun."

"Never fear. The Flying Nun will fly again," croaked Geronimo from the grass. His helmet seemed to have turned back-to-front, and he was holding his crotch painfully.

"Amendment," said Carpet. "The Flying Soprano will fly again."

We were all so busy cracking up (even Maniac had stopped worrying about trespassing) that we didn't see the bloke at first. But there he was, standing in the shadow of his great house, screaming like a nut case.

"Hooligans! Vandals!" Sounded like he was having a real fit.

"Is that that mate of yours?" Carpet asked me.

"Mate of my dad's," I said.

"Your dad knows some funny people. Is he an outpatient, or has he climbed over the wall?" Carpet turned to the distant raging figure and amiably pointed the two fingers of scorn.

He shouldn't have done that. Next second, a huge four-legged shape came tearing toward us over the grass. Doing a ton with its jaws wide open and its rotten great fangs shining in the moonlight. It didn't make a sound; not like any ordinary dog. And the little figure by the house was shouting things like "Kill, kill, kill!" He didn't seem at all like the guy I met when my dad took me around the house . . .

Maniac turned and scarpered. Geronimo was still lying on the grass trying to get his helmet straight. And the rotten great dog was making straight at him. I couldn't move.

But Carpet did. He ran and straddled Geronimo. Braced himself, and he was a big lad; there were 180 pounds of him.

The dog leaped, like they do in the movies. Carpet thrust his gauntleted fist right up its throat. Carpet rocked, but he didn't fall. The dog was chewing on his glove like mad, studs and all.

"Naughty doggy," said Carpet reprovingly, and gave it a terrific clout over the ear with his other hand.

Two more clouts and the dog stopped chewing. Three, and it let go. Then Carpet kicked it in the ribs. Sounded like the big bass drum.

"Heel, Fido!" said Carpet.

The dog went for Geronimo, who was staggering to his feet; and got Carpet's boot again. It fell back, whimpering.

The next second, a tiny figure was flailing at Carpet. "Leave my dog *alone*. How *dare* you hit my dog. I'll have the SPCA on you—that's all you hooligans are good for, mistreating dogs." He was literally foaming at the mouth. "I don't know what this country's coming to . . ."

"It's going to the dogs," said Carpet. He pushed the man gently away with one great hand, and held him at arm's length. "Look, mate," he said sadly, wagging one finger of a well-chewed gauntlet, "take the Hound of the Baskervilles home. It's time for his Meaty Chunks . . ."

"I am going," spluttered the little guy, "to call the police."

"I would, mate," said Carpet. "There's a highly dangerous dog loose around here somewhere . . ."

The pair of them slunk off. Maniac returned from the nearest bushes to the sound of cheers. Geronimo slapped Carpet on the shoulder and said, "Thanks, mate," in a voice that had me green with envy. And we all buggered off. After we rode three times around the house for luck. Including the steps in the formal garden.

"There's another way out," I said, "at the far end."

The far drive seemed to go on forever. Or was it that we were riding slowly, because Carpet was having trouble changing gear with his right hand. I think the dog had hurt him right through the glove; but that was not something Carpet would ever admit.

Just before we went out through the great gates with stone eagles on their gateposts, we passed a white Hillman Imp, parked on the right well off the road, under the big horse chestnut trees of the avenue. It seemed empty as we passed, though, oddly enough, it had its sun visors down, which was a funny thing to happen at midnight.

Outside, Geronimo held up his right hand, U.S. Cavalry-fashion, and we all stopped.

"Back," said Geronimo. "Lights out. Throttle down. Quiet."

"What?"

But he was gone back inside. All we could do was follow. It was lucky the moon was out when he stopped. Or we'd all have driven over him and flattened him.

"What?" we all said again.

But he just said, "Push your bikes."

We all pushed our bikes, swearing at him.

"Quiet!"

The white Hillman glimmered up in the moonlight.

"Thought so," said Geronimo. A white arm appeared for a moment behind the steering wheel and vanished again.

Maniac sniggered.

"You can't *do* it," said Carpet. "Not in a Hillman Imp!"

"You have a wide experience of Hillman Imps?" asked Geronimo.

"Let's stay and watch," said Maniac.

Carpet and I looked at Geronimo uneasily.

"What do you think *I* am?" said Geronimo, crushing Maniac like he was a beetle. "Mount up, lads. Right. Lights, sound, music, enter the villain."

Four headlamps, three of them quartz-halogen, zeroed in on the Imp. I noticed it was L-reg., quite old. It shone like day, but for a long moment nothing else happened.

Then a head appeared—a bald head, with beady eyes and a rat-trap mouth. Followed by a naked chest, hairy as a chimpanzee's. The eyes glared; a large fist was raised and shaken.

"Switch off," said Geronimo. "And *quiet*."

We sat and listened. There was the mother and father of a row going on inside the Imp.

"Drive me *home!*"

"It was nothing. Just a car passing. They've gone now."

We waited; the voices got lower and lower. Silence.

"Start your engines," said Geronimo. *"Quietly."*

"What for?" asked Maniac plaintively.

"You'll see," said Geronimo, and laughed with pure delight.

He and Carpet and me had electric starter motors, which of course started us quietly, first press of the button. Good old Jap-crap. Maniac, buying British and best, had to kick his over and over again.

"I'm going to buy you a new flint for that thing," said Carpet.

Maniac's bike started at last.

"Lights," said Geronimo.

There was a wild scream, then an even wilder burst of swearing. The bald head reappeared. The car lights came on; its engine started and revved.

"Move!" shouted Geronimo, curving his bike away between the tree trunks.

"Why?" yelled Maniac.

"He'll never live to see twenty," said Carpet, as we turned together through the branches, neat as a pair of performing dolphins.

Then the Imp was after us, screeching and roaring in second gear fit to blow a gasket.

We went out of those gates like Agostini, down through the slumbering hamlet of Blackdore and up toward the moors. We were all riding four-hundreds, and we could have lost the Imp in ten seconds. But it was more fun to dawdle at seventy, watching the Imp trying to catch up. God, it was cornering like a lunatic, right over on the wrong side of the road. Another outpatient got over the wall. Even more than most motorists, that is.

And old Maniac was not keeping up. That bloody British bike of his, that clapped-out old Tiger was missing on one rotten cylinder.

He was lagging farther and farther behind. The Imp's lights seemed to be drawing alongside his. He was riding badly, cowering against the hedge, not leaving himself enough room to get a good line into his corners. I knew how he'd be feeling: mouth dry as brick dust; knees and hands shaking almost beyond control.

Then the Imp did draw alongside and made a tremendous sideswipe at him, trying to knock him into the hedge at seventy. The guy in the Imp was trying to kill Maniac. And there was nothing we could do. I pulled alongside Carpet and pointed behind. But Carpet had seen already and didn't know what to do, either.

Then Geronimo noticed. Throttled back, waved us through. In my rearview mirror I watched him drop farther and farther back, until he seemed to be just in front of the Imp's bumper. Up went his two fingers. Again and again. He put his thumb to his nose and waggled his fingers. I swear he did—I saw them in silhouette against the Imp's lights—though afterwards Carpet made out I couldn't have and that it was something I made up.

At last, the Imp took notice; forgot Maniac cowering and limping beside the hedge, and came after Geronimo.

"Out to the left," gestured Carpet, and we shot off down a side road, turned, and came back behind the lunatic's car.

So we saw it all in comfort. Oh, Geronimo could have walked away from him; Geronimo could do a hundred and ten if he liked. But just as he was going to, he saw this horse-riding school in a field on the left, on the outskirts of the next village, Chelbury. You know the kind of place—all white-painted oil drums and red-and-white-striped poles where little female toffs try to learn to show-jump.

In went Geronimo. Round and round went Geronimo. Round the barrels, under the poles. And round and round went the Imp. Into the barrels and smashing the poles to smithereens. He couldn't drive for crap—like a mad bull in a china shop, and Geronimo the bullfighter. *Boing, boing, boing* went the drums. Splinter, splinter, splinter in the moonlight went the poles.

Geronimo could have gone on forever. But lights were coming on in the houses, curtains being pulled back on the finest display of trick riding the villagers of Chelbury will ever see—not that they'd have the sense to appreciate it.

Just as Maniac turned up, minus a bit of paint, we heard the siren of the cop car. Some snot-nosed gent had been on the phone.

Of course the cop car, bumping across the grass through the shambles, made straight for Geronimo; the fuzz always blame the motorcyclist and the Imp had stopped its murder attempts by that time.

"You young lunatic," said the fuzz, getting out, "you've caused damage worth thousands . . ."

Geronimo gestured at his bike, which hadn't a scratch on it in the cop car's headlights. Then he nodded at the Imp, which had four feet of striped pole stuck inside its front bumper.

Then the fuzz noticed that the guy at the wheel was completely starkers. And that there was a long-haired blonde on the back seat trying to put her sweater on inside-out and back-to-front. The fuzz kept losing his grip on the situation every time the blonde wriggled. Well, they're human, too. All very enjoyable . . .

We got back to Carpet's place about seven, still laughing so much we were wobbling all over the road. We always end up at Carpet's place after a night out. It's a nice little detached bungalow on top of a hill. And we always weave around and around Carpet's dad's crazy paving, revving like mad. And Carpet's mum always throws open the one upstairs window and leans out in her blue dressing gown and asks what the hell we want. And Geronimo always asks, innocent-like, "This is the motorway café, isn't it?" And Carpet's mum always calls him a cheeky young tyke, and comes down and lets us in and gives us cans of lager and meat pies while she does a great big fry-up for breakfast. And we lie about till lunchtime with our boots on the furniture, giving her cheek, and she's loving it and laughing. I used to wonder why she put up with us, till I realized she was just that glad to have Carpet back alive.

And that was our night out.

ON MONDAY NIGHT, when I got home from work, Dad took me in the front room alone. I knew something was up. Had the guy from the abbey snitched on us? But Dad gave me a whisky, and I knew it was worse.

He told me Geronimo was dead—killed on his bike. I wouldn't believe it. No bastard motorist could ever get Geronimo.

Then he told me how it happened. On a bend, with six-foot stone walls on either side. Geronimo was coming home from work in the dark. He'd have been tired. He was only doing fifty; on his proper side, two feet out from the curb. The police could tell from the skid marks.

The car was only a lousy Morris Marina. Passing on a blind corner. The driver didn't stop; but the other driver got his number. When the police breathalyzed him, he was pissed to the eyeballs.

I believed it then; and I cried.

We gave him a real biker's funeral. A hundred and seventy bikes followed him through the town, at ten miles an hour, two by two. I've never seen such disciplined riding. Nobody fell off—though a few of the lads burned their clutches out. We really pinned this town's ears back. They know what bikers are now; bikers are *together*.

The Pope died about that time. The Pope only had twelve motorbike outriders; Geronimo had a hundred and seventy. If he met the Pope in some waiting room or other up above, Geronimo would have pointed that out. But laughing, mind. He was always laughing, Geronimo.

Afterwards, we all went back to the club and got the drinks in. Then there was a bloody horrible silence; the lads were really down, like I've never seen them. It was terrible.

Then Fred, the club secretary, gets to his feet and points at the pool table, where Geronimo used to sit, putting the players off their stroke by wriggling his backside.

"If he was standing there," said Fred, "if he could see you now, d'you know what he'd say? He'd say 'What you being so piss-faced for, you stupid jerks?' " And suddenly, though nobody saw or heard anything, he *was* there, and it was all right. And everybody was falling over themselves to tell Geronimo stories and laughing.

We all went to the court case too, all in our gear. The clerk of the court tried to have us thrown out; but one or two of us have got a few O levels, and enough sense to hire our own lawyer. Who told the clerk of the court where he got off. We were all British citizens, of voting age, as good as anybody else. Har-har.

And the police proved everything against the driver of the Marina. He lost his license, of course. Then the judge said six months' imprisonment.

Then he said sentence suspended for two years . . .

Why? 'Cos he belonged to the same golf club as the judge? 'Cos he was middle-aged and big and fat with an expensive overcoat and a posh lawyer?

The lads gave a kind of growl. The clerk was shaking so much he couldn't hold his papers. So was the Marina driver, who'd been whispering and grinning at his lawyer till then.

The clerk began shouting for silence; going on about contempt of court. Fred got up. He's 225 pounds of pure muscle, and he's about forty-five, with a grownup son in the club.

"Not contempt, Your Honor. More disgust, like."

I think the lads might have gone too far then. But Geronimo's mum (she looked very like him) put her hand on Fred's arm and asked him to take her home. And when Fred went we all followed; though a few fingers went up in the air behind backs.

Maniac and Carpet and me tried going on riding together. But it didn't work out. Whenever we rode together, there was a sort of terrible hole formed, where Geronimo should be. Maniac went off and joined the Merchant Navy, 'cos he couldn't stand this town anymore. He still sends Carpet and me postcards from Bahrain and Abu Dhabi (clean ones, too!). And we put them on the mantelpiece and forget them.

Carpet and I went on riding; even bought bigger bikes. I still see him sometimes, but we never stop for more than two minutes' chat.

But when I ride alone, that's different. You see, you can't hear very much inside your helmet when your engine's running. And the helmet cuts down your view to the side as well. So when we need to talk to each other on the move, we have to pull alongside and yell and yell. And when you first notice a guy doing that, it often comes over funny. Well, I keep thinking I hear him; that he's just lurking out of the corner of my eye. I just know he's somewhere about; you *can't* kill someone like Geronimo.

I got engaged last week. Jane's a good lass, but she made one condition. That I sell my bike and buy a car. She says she wants me to live to be a grandfather. And when my mum heard her say it, she suddenly looked ten years younger.

So I'm taking this last ride to the abbey in the moonlight, and I've just passed Sparwick chippie. And the moon is making one side of the trees silver, and I'm *going* somewhere. Only I'm not going with Geronimo; I'm getting further away from Geronimo all the time. Nearer to the old grannies with their hair in curlers coming out of the chippie clutching their hot greasy bundles. The middle-aged guys staring in the telly-shop windows.

And I'm not sure I like it.

THE WOOLWORTH
SPECTACLES

BEFORE THE WAR, you could buy spectacles at Woolworth's. Dealers gathered in lost spectacles, uncollected spectacles, dead men's spectacles, and they appeared in a black, spidery jumble on Woolworth's counter. There were stranger ways of making a living in the Depression . . .

You merely walked up to the counter, tried them on pair by pair, and if a pair suited, you pulled out your sixpence.

Mostly, pensioners bought them, having more troubled eyesight and less money than anybody else. Certainly my cousin Maude Cleveland had no reason, one warm June afternoon in 1938, to be patronizing that counter. Her father, as the town's leading solicitor, would have disapproved tremendously. He would have sent her to the optician immediately. Perhaps that's why she was standing there fiddling, turning her large blue beautiful and myopic eyes to the door at intervals, in case anyone she knew came in and saw her.

She was only *slightly* shortsighted, but blurring small

print, the need to hunch closer and closer, provoked her inordinately. Besides, if she went on squinting, it would make lines on her face in the end. She had been tremendously fit all her twenty-nine years—never been to the doctor since her mother died.

And once her father paid for spectacles, he would insist she wear them. All the time. In company. And men don't make passes at girls who wear glasses . . .

So she dabbled among the black, long-legged mass with her fine tapered fingers, holding her leather-bound New Testament in her left hand, open at the Book of Revelation, peering at it through each successive pair, in between peering at the door . . .

It was the feel of the strange spectacles that attracted her. The lively spring of metal, instead of the funereal smoothness of hornrims. She disentangled them with difficulty: they seemed reluctant to come. Then she realized they were on a chain, for hanging around the neck. This immediately disposed her in their favor. Lady Frome had such a pair, and fiddled and poked with them elegantly at meetings of the Parochial Church Council. And though Lady Frome was nearly fifty, her sprigged frocks and large hats were the quiet epitome of London elegance.

Maude examined the strange spectacles. Close to, her beautiful eyes had that near-microscopic accuracy that is the gift of short sight. The spectacles were very old-fashioned: half-moon lenses, with the palest green tint, and even a few tiny bubbles caught inside the glass. She could almost have sworn the frames were gold; and the chain, with its tiny links.

Her hand went to her purse swiftly. The shop could not know what it was selling . . . they were antiques . . .

Mr. Hazlitt, who ran the little shop in Church Walk, would be interested. She waved frantically for the assistant, who was gossiping, arms akimbo, farther down the counter.

"I'll take this pair!" She thrust the sixpence with force into the assistant's hand.

"Them's not ours, madam. We don't sell *that* sort." The slow country voice quickened with contempt. "Old-fashioned rubbish!"

"But they were here on the counter!"

"One of the old ladies must ha' left them when she bought a new pair. Give 'em here, madam, an' I'll throw 'em in the bin." The girl's plump hand rearranged the remaining spectacles protectively, as if they were sheep who'd had a wolf among them.

"But I *want* them!" Maude's voice rose to an indignant squeak.

"But they're not for sale, madam. Not ours. Lost property. I s'pose they should go along to the police station, by rights."

"Then I shall take them," announced Maude triumphantly. "After all, we don't want them ending up in the dustbin, do we?"

The girl hesitated, knowing she was lying. But Miss Cleveland was Miss Cleveland. And a complaint to the manager could cost her her job . . .

"Very well, madam. Shall I wrap them?"

"No, thank you." Maude clutched the spectacles even tighter, knowing she was being ridiculous. "Are you sure I can't pay you? I wouldn't want you getting into trouble."

"No, madam," said the girl, tight-lipped with stubbornness.

Outside, Maude stood appalled. She had behaved in a

most unchristian manner. Lying, avarice, theft, uncharity to someone less well off than herself. Sins that must go down in the back of her diary, toward her next confession at St. Michael's. More sins in five minutes than she'd been guilty of in the last month . . . She felt almost shockingly excited about it. Was getting excited about sinning a sin in itself?

In the heat, the High Street seemed deserted. Maude felt a foolish urge to try the spectacles on. She moved well clear of Woolworth's doorway so that the assistant couldn't observe her, slipped the chain over her long, smooth neck, felt her throat nervously, and popped them on.

They were pince-nez—clamped surprisingly firmly on the bridge of her elegant nose. Not painfully, like tweezers, but as if they knew where they belonged, and meant to stay.

What was more, they worked. Maude saw the world with a quite amazing clarity she'd forgotten existed. The black, half-shaven whiskers of that man coming toward her; the dirt-filled broken wrinkles descending cruelly from nose to mouth; the few greasy black strands fighting a losing battle across his balding pate. Worse, the way his beady black eyes roamed hungrily across her breasts and throat . . . It made her blush all over. Insufferable. She was a lady, but he was regarding her as if she were the lowest type of *woman*. A common workman . . . Would she ever feel safe again?

She whipped the spectacles off and relaxed back into her familiar peaceful blur. She was very good at reading that blur. That broad pink fuzz patch approaching, accompanied by a smaller gray fuzz patch, was undoubtedly what the county magazine referred to often as the genial Mrs. Forbes-Formby and her charming daughter, Patricia . . .

There was no time to remove the spectacles from around her neck; Mrs. Forbes-Formby would certainly notice such a furtive gesture. Instead, she tucked the spectacles down inside her discreet neckline. They lay flat, snugly, across the top of her breasts; a little chilly, but not unpleasant on such a hot day.

But some effect seemed to have lingered from wearing them. Certainly she had never seen Mrs. Forbes-Formby so clearly in her life. How heavy she had grown in the backside, how thick her ankles were, and how domineeringly she stood. Maude had always thought her a handsome woman, but now her nose, far from seeming noble, seemed merely too big and fleshy, and little beads of perspiration stood out unbecomingly all over it. The mouth, which had always seemed so decisive, drooped disagreeably.

Patricia looked worse; like a sweating sheep. Had her shoulders always drooped so much? Did she always keep her eyes down, so, when she was with her mother? She was two years younger than Maude, and she looked positively middle-aged. Gosh, thought Maude, you can't give up at *twenty-seven*! Do I look like that? She was seized with a sudden desire to peer into mirrors, to walk past reflecting shop windows. The conversation did not prosper. Mrs. Forbes-Formby looked positively affronted when Maude cut short her account of the cake judging at the Melton Women's Institute gala . . .

Let her look affronted, thought Maude, passing her first shop front. She treats her daughter like a child; and Patricia lets her.

Meanwhile, the shop window showed her shoulders

slightly rounded, though not half as badly as Patricia's. She pulled them back, as she'd been taught at school.

It made her breasts stick out with disturbing prominence . . . Another workman passed and admired them.

It occurred to Maude that she had reached a crossroads in her life . . .

She went on, her shoulders well back.

THE CLARITY OF SIGHT persisted. She noticed many things, few pleasant: broken upstairs windows above the shops' peeling paint, twitching faces. She had always thought Barlborough such a mellow town. There was a black-and-white cat sitting in the butcher's window, and several white cat hairs on the meat. She went into Flatt's the greengrocer's. Mr. Flatt gave her his usual genial greeting; she realized for the first time how shifty his eyes were . . . dipping down constantly to the apples he was weighing for her on his scales. It came to her quite suddenly that he was giving her short measure—something to do with resting his hand on the right side of the scales. She stared at the hand. His babbling increased; he broke out into a sweat and threw several more apples into the pan, bundled them all into a bag and couldn't get rid of her quick enough.

She had gained several apples and lost a friend. The thought so disturbed her that she decided to go and see Mr. Hazlitt. He always made her feel better, though he had to be used sparingly. For Mr. Hazlitt was persona non grata at home, and it would not do for gossip to reach Father. Ever since the night he'd come to Barlborough Archaeological Society and disputed with Father a little too long over the dating of the Barlborough Crosses. On which subject Father was a lifelong expert . . .

She surveyed the front of Mr. Hazlitt's shop with

pleasure: the wall clocks, the big brass Buddha she'd have loved to buy, the ginger cat . . . but the spectacles took over again, and showed her something less pleasant. The top corner of the shop window showed dampness; worse, green mildew was spreading everywhere. Worse still, the beam above was cracking into those little squares that could only mean dry rot . . . and a widening crack meandered through the brickwork above, right down from the level of the gutters.

She knew with dreadful certainty. She rushed into the shop, breathless.

"You've got dry rot. Your shop's going to fall down any minute . . ."

Mr. Hazlitt looked up from his ancient book with a smile. He was intriguingly ageless. White hair above a young face, and very bright blue eyes. Tall and slim, like an undergraduate. His mouth intrigued her: cruel or kind? She could never decide.

But one thing the spectacles showed clearly: his smile was one he would give a precocious child. He didn't take her seriously, not for a minute. If only Mr. Hazlitt would give her the kind of look those workmen . . . She brushed the thought aside, into the back of her diary.

"All right, Maude. Show me where you mean . . ." Amused, detached, kind, tolerant.

She showed him.

He suddenly ceased to be any of these things; he went berserk. He picked up the telephone directory and dropped it; trod on the cat; sent a hat stand crashing to the floor; paced up and down like a caged tiger. She had never had anything like this effect on Mr. Hazlitt before. It was she who finally got through to Theodore Brittan the builder, and calmly explained what was required.

By the time Theodore came and the beam was temporarily but safely shored up, Mr. Hazlitt had flopped into his best Sheraton armchair, totally exhausted.

"I'll make you some tea," said Maude, soothingly and greatly daring. As he did not reply, she went through the curtain into the back of the shop, where she'd never dared tread before. It was scrupulously neat and tidy, with a smell of clock oil, wood shavings, and tobacco smoke. Being so close to his life pleased her inordinately. She was satisfied he was what she would have called a proper man.

When she came out with the tray of tea (and some biscuits she'd found in a tin) he looked up at her in a new way. "Maude, what would I have done without you?"

"Rung up Theodore Brittan yourself," she said, with mock sharpness. But she blushed becomingly with pleasure, and thought she saw in his face not just a new respect but the merest flicker, gone in a second, of the look that had been on the workmen's faces. Though much more refined, of course . . .

It was then that she noticed the time and remembered it was Wednesday. Wednesday was the day Father came home early; Wednesday was the day Mr. and Mrs. Dewhurst always came to tea. At four. And already it was half past.

She hurried along, trying to work out why she was not reduced to a state of sheer terror. Not to be there to brew the tea and carry in the tray that the cook had left ready . . . not to be there to pour, while Father and Mr. Dewhurst delved deep into the business of the Archaeological Society, and Mrs. Dewhurst stared crossly around the room . . . It had never happened in all the years since her mother died. It was not to be thought of!

Father would be hungry, impatient, furious. Father

would tell her off in front of everybody. Mrs. Dewhurst would sniff disapprovingly; Mr. Dewhurst would be sorry for her, in his slow, stately way . . .

It was all the spectacles' fault. She put her hand to her neck to take them off; then paused.

The spectacles had not let her down so far. Wearing the spectacles, she had put to flight Mrs. Forbes-Formby, the greengrocer, and Mr. Hazlitt. Not a bad score . . .

She continued to wear them around her neck, under her frock, as she hurried up the drive, and saw Mr. Dewhurst's gray car parked next to Father's black one.

FATHER REARED UP from the sofa as she entered— rather, in his black suit, with his drooping white mustache and bald head, like a bull walrus defending his mating territory. She could not help smiling at the thought (quite unlike any thought she'd ever had before), saw he was disconcerted by the smile, and went directly into the attack.

"Haven't you started? You shouldn't have waited." She glanced at Mrs. Dewhurst, sitting like a full-bosomed judge about to pass the death sentence . . . implying that Mrs. Dewhurst could have poured boiling water into a pot, surely . . .

Her father opened his mouth three times to say something, then closed it again, and by that time she was past and into the kitchen, where she made firm, busy bangings with the kettle and the taps.

Then she was back with the tray like a whirlwind, pouring cups of tea and passing around sandwiches with disconcerting vigor.

"Another cucumber sandwich, Mrs. Dewhurst? Brown bread. Not at all *fattening*, I assure you."

Then she sat back and watched them coolly, elegant fingers poised over her own sandwich. And the magic of the spectacles continued . . . She saw that her father was wearing a suit that had been made for a bigger man; the waistcoat sagged over his once-broad chest and belly, like the skin of a fruit past ripeness . . . His double chin, once full and pink, was pale and hung like an empty flap of skin. He had adopted, unnoticed, the habit of taking off his gold-rimmed spectacles and rubbing his eyes. He was well over sixty . . . growing old. Not much left of the frightening bear who had icily, legally, bullied Mother.

The righteous bulk of Mrs. Dewhurst, as heavily corseletted as a knight in armor, appalled her. She could not be more than forty . . . What would she look like, undressed for bed, naked?

The thought shocked Maude. Another sin for the back of her diary? But Mr. Dewhurst, about the same age as his wife, looked so much younger . . . Another bear of a man, but kinder than her father—red-haired, red-mustached, in his ginger tweed suit and big brogues. A ripe man, a man still full of juice, not dead, like the other two.

Her mind was running away with her. She'd never *had* such thoughts! The spectacles . . . but there was no chance to take them off here, as the other three munched steadily, holding out their cups for a refill as they discussed the inexhaustible topic of Hitler.

Except . . . Mr. Dewhurst kept giving her more little glances than his requests for tea would seem to warrant. There was a look on Mr. Dewhurst's face: tiny, timid, glancing. But that same hungry look again.

The utterly respectable churchwarden and local historian desired her, just like a common workman. It aroused a little devil in her. There were so many ways a woman could lead a man on . . . *ladylike* ways. The pensive turn of a head on a long neck; fingers stroking the soft down of her own cheek. Mr. Dewhurst's glances grew bolder, till Mrs. Dewhurst noticed.

"We must be off, Henry," said Mrs. Dewhurst, pulling on her gloves and inspecting her revolting green hat in the tall dark mirror of the sideboard.

"But we're discussing the arrangements for the outing to the fort . . ." Mr. Dewhurst seemed disposed to argue; even Father looked affronted.

"Plenty of time for that later, Henry. Come, I must buy some Seville oranges for Cook to make marmalade. Flatt may sell out." She gave him a sharp look that got him on his feet, apologizing wretchedly to Father, looking a total, blushing, blundering fool. How could he stand her treating him like a lapdog in public? Then she remembered that his little bookshop hardly supported itself. He was no businessman; *she* had the money.

"I can't understand it," bleated Father, when they'd gone. "They never go this early. It's only five past five."

"Obviously marmalade is more important than Roman forts," said Maude.

"Woman's a fool . . ."

"Can *I* come to the fort? Mr. Dewhurst's always so interesting."

"I didn't know you were keen on the Romans."

"Yes," said Maude. "Oh, *yes.*"

She lay in bed that night, thinking what she'd wear. The blue skirt was a little short. If she walked ahead of Mr. Dewhurst, up the hill to the fort, looking back frequently over her shoulder to ask him questions, almost stumbling, so he would put out a hand to steady her . . . Delicious!

Then she remembered she hadn't said her prayers.

How had she forgotten to say her prayers? She never forgot to say her prayers. Father Whitstable . . .

At the thought of Father Whitstable, she realized the spectacles were still hanging around her neck, under her nightdress. How peculiar that she hadn't taken them off! Except that they gave her a pleasant sensation as they slid around in the valley between her breasts . . .

She shot upright. Maude Cleveland, you are a *sinful* woman! Get out of bed and say your prayers at once!

She still didn't want to. She wanted to go on lying in bed, thinking about the glint in Mr. Dewhurst's eye . . . and other things. The feel of the rough texture of his jacket, the roughness of his hands, his faint tobacco smell.

She shot out of bed with a great effort of will, and knelt on the cold linoleum as a penance. But still she couldn't pray . . . not wearing those sinful, sliding spectacles . . .

She took them off with an even greater effort of will, and put them on her bedside table.

Then she was able to pray. She was really very glad she'd taken the spectacles off.

She had never prayed so grayly, boredly, resentfully, in her life. The state of rebellion in her soul alarmed her. She would not wear those spectacles again.

She got back into bed and slept very badly, which was unusual for her. She dreamed about both Mr. Hazlitt and Mr. Dewhurst.

NEXT DAY, it rained. All day. The sky was the dull gray of a vicarage blanket. Maude attended weekday communion at St. Michael's, but her heart did not lift. Father Whitstable preached poorly, having a heavy cold. The sermon was all sniffs and handkerchief. He dropped his handkerchief three times and had to come down from the pulpit to search for it, and went on preaching as he searched . . . This did not do a great deal for the doctrine of the Transubstantiation, with reference to the Bishop of London's latest pseudo-scientific outburst. During the communion service, the knees of the woman in front creaked audibly; she was wearing a black hat with mauve flowers that smelled strongly of mothballs.

Going around the shops afterwards, Maude could find nothing she wanted. She left her umbrella in Elliot's, the stationer's, during a brief break in the rain, and having to walk back for it, she got thoroughly soaked. As she took off her hat and coat in the hall, her face looked pale and pinched, and (as she said to herself) wrinkled like an old boot. Her hair drooped lankly; she looked as unlikely an object for lust, let alone love, as she'd ever seen, and as a result, she had words with the cook.

As a further result, Cook produced a truly punitive dinner: tinned oxtail soup, fat mutton chops, limp white boiled potatoes, and watery green beans, followed by tinned peaches with over-solid rice pudding. And as an even further result of Cook's vengeance, and the fact that she had eaten too much of that vengeance in a hopeless attempt to cheer herself up, Maude went to bed with indigestion, and woke with it in the middle of the night.

She lay and thought of life slipping like sand through her fingers. Next year she would reach thirty, the fatal watershed. One of her back teeth was loose, and wobbled more than usual, wobbled so violently that it threatened to come unstuck altogether . . .

More unhappy than she'd ever been, she reached in the dark toward the bedside table for the glass of water and indigestion tablets.

Her hand touched the smooth glass of the spectacles.

And she thought that if the rewards of virtue were so wretched, could the rewards of vice be any worse?

In that moment, she was a lost woman.

She slipped the spectacles around her neck.

THE OUTING to the Roman fort was truly spiffing. The day dawned blue from horizon to horizon, so that Maude was able to wear her sleeveless blouse as well as the blue skirt that was a little too short. By the time the tour bus reached the foot of the suede-smooth green hill on which the fort lay, it was really warm, which left Maude pleasantly and becomingly glowing, and Mrs. Dewhurst sweating so badly that she got left behind over and over again as they climbed ramparts and descended counterscarps. Nobody was in the least interested in hauling Mrs. Dewhurst up; she finally had to retire, hurt, back to the bus with a desperate migraine, and spend her time applying her own wet handkerchief to her brow, in between casting malevolent glances uphill to where Maude was having the time of her life.

Maude was, it must be added, the principal cause of that migraine. For her effect on Mr. Dewhurst had been positively devastating. He seemed to have shed ten years as he made successful little jokes about ramparts and ditches, and handed Maude up as athletically as a schoolboy. Nor was he the only one. Mr. Hazlitt, similarly fascinated, was not to be outdone, either in handing up or in wit, and even Tony Smethurst, fresh down from Oxford and as boringly handsome as a Greek god, seemed to find Miss Cleveland irresistible, and was so bold as to inquire what Miss Cleveland was wearing on that little gold chain around her neck? If it should be a locket, was there room for a lock of his own golden hair?

"Never you mind," said Maude archly, "you *naughty* boy!"

Which reference to his youthfulness he seemed to take more as a challenge than as a discouragement, and grew bolder.

That was the moment Maude was to remember with pleasure for the rest of her days. The descending sun underlining every ridge and furrow of the earthworks, gilding even the individual stems of grass, and the wool of the few resident sheep. The warm early-evening breeze stroking the bare skin of her arms, and lifting her too-short skirt with gentle lasciviousness. Mr. Dewhurst's face, looking so bronzed and alive; and Mr. Hazlitt's and Tony Smethurst's, and those of the three humbler male hangers-on who stood slightly farther off, hopefully, rather like the resident sheep. And the angry distant glare of Lydia Dewhurst . . .

She felt a queen, with her little group of courtiers. What fun, playing one off against the other, encouraging them to compete, excel, yet not letting any get so discouraged that they despairingly went away. There was a skill in it, a knack in it, she would never have dreamed for a moment she had. She looked out at the distant sea peeping through the gaps in the coastal Dorset hills, and thought, "Can I do *anything*?"

Then innocent, harmless Tony Smethurst uttered the fatal words: "Who's your partner in the mixed doubles this year, Maude?"

Now, this was no trivial matter. Barlborough might have been despised as provincial in many things, but in tennis, never. The Tennis Club, even more than the Archaeological Society, was at the center of Barlborough life. They had been county club champions the previous year; seven members had at one time played for the county and two actually at Wimbledon, one getting as far as the second round. Membership was by invitation, recommendation, and reference. Once you were in, you were *in*; if you were out, you were nowhere. Maude, no mean player, had made a habit of losing gallantly in the quarter finals of the ladies' singles.

Now they all looked at her, expectantly. In the past, she had partnered Jack Simcock; but Jack had moved to Brighton. Now she looked around them all, her lips slightly parted, aware of a particularly furious glare coming up from the bus. Greatly daring, she asked, "Are you playing this year, Mr. Dewhurst?"

"Good God," said Mr. Dewhurst. "I'm thirty-eight, Maude. Nearly thirty-nine. I think I'll confine myself to umpiring again."

But he'd been one of those who'd played at Wimbledon; even after four years of umpiring, he was remembered. And suddenly his face glowed with recalled youthful glory.

"Go on, Henry," said Tony Smethurst. "Show us there's life in the old dog yet."

Mr. Dewhurst put him in his place with a look. But it was a look containing as much pleasure as rebuke.

"All right," he said, "I shall show you, young Smethurst. If my first service goes in, God help you. But I'd better get some match practice."

So it was done.

LIFE HAD NEVER BEEN so full for Maude. Her father felt the draft at home. Dinner became a solitary meal for him; and once he found a newly ironed shirt was missing two buttons. He spoke to Maude about it, but his icy diatribe had curiously little effect. She had this way of sitting back and looking at him these days, a little smile playing around her lips. His diatribe ran out of steam halfway, and he went back to his boring chop like a fugitive.

Maude *lived* at the Tennis Club, with its red gravel courts and low, pleasant green huts. Very often she practiced with Mr. Dewhurst. His first service terrified her deliciously, whether it whirled savagely up at her body or whanged like the crack of doom into the net. She liked to see him sweat, hear him grunt and groan, like a great red savage bear only separated from her by a three-foot barrier of netting. She saw and learned his every mood and movement.

And there was the leaning close, discussing tactics. He gave off heat like a red furnace; she felt it on her bare arms. And sitting talking afterwards, as the shadows of the high wooden fence that shut the world out crept across the court, and the swallows and swifts flew high and screaming in the dimming blue sky far above . . . there was no one left in the world but the two of them.

Of course, she never let him actually *touch* her. That was against the rules of the game . . . That would be playing into Lydia Dewhurst's hands.

She felt herself changing in many ways, as the gold spectacles bounced and joggled against the glowing pink skin of her breasts. Her own game, long based on good straight hitting, grew sneaky, in a way she would once have condemned. She tormented Mr. Dewhurst with evil little drop volleys; and her every stroke now carried a load of back spin, top spin, or side spin that could drift the ball back into the corner when everyone could have sworn it was going out. She admitted to herself that she was no longer a nice person to know. Sometimes she practiced with Mr. Dewhurst on Sunday mornings, instead of going to church. Her father grumbled that tennis was coming between her and her wits, and he would be glad when the tournament was over . . .

But she didn't neglect Mr. Hazlitt. Especially when she discovered, on his single shelf of antiquarian books, a couple of medieval herbals. The one by Gerard she liked so much that she drew out every penny she had in the bank to buy it. Mr. Hazlitt gave her a good discount, and they discussed the book frequently. When Maude read it at home, it seemed so often to fall open at certain pages.

"Foxglove, called by the ancients *digitalis*. A little taken strengthens the heart, but overmuch killeth."

Mr. Hazlitt was struck by her discrimination and eagerness to learn about antiques. He explained to her the significance of an object being parcel-gilt; how to tell a Sheraton commode from a design by Hepplewhite. She respected Mr. Hazlitt. His mind was good. She sensed that his thoughts were gathering toward a proposal; but she held him back gently. Certainly, not yet . . . Mr. and Mrs. Dewhurst were *much* more fun. For she found Lydia Dewhurst's seething, leaden hatred—totally denied expression even when she and her father went around to tea in the Dewhursts' great rambling house, full of strange uncouth African objects collected by Mrs. Dewhurst's missionary father—even more exciting than Mr. Dewhurst's great dammed-up bear-like passion.

But sometimes she mentioned the herbal to Mr. Dewhurst. What secrets were locked up in an innocent English hedgerow! How easy it would be to poison, without arousing suspicion! When, greatly daring, she gathered foxgloves to decorate the lounge and, when they were

past their best, did not throw them in the garbage but
boiled certain portions down, she showed the little bottle
to Mr. Dewhurst . . .

His fingers lingered on it, till she snatched it away; and
a look lingered on his face that was not lust but something
curiously, blackly like it. As before, she knew his moods.
He was happy with her, bitterly unhappy at home. He
often arrived for practice white and shaking; and when
the time came to part, a look of somberness would creep
across his face.

On the night before the tournament, they had booked
a final practice, late. The sun had dropped from the sky
before she arrived on her bicycle, and the last members,
snugly tired, with towels tucked around their necks, were
getting into their cars and waving goodbye. She sat on
the old wooden bench alone; she had time to think for
the first time in weeks.

Something surfaced in her mind, something of what
she might have called the old Maude—the Maude she
had been before she first put on the spectacles . . .
Recently, that little, weak, buried Maude had only approached her in dreams, leaving her to wake in the
mornings with a feeling that something indefinable was
terribly, terribly wrong. That she was running down a
hill—keeping her feet, just, but having to run faster and
faster, so that she couldn't stop now if she wanted to.
Then, as she got dressed, the little fearful Maude would
fade out of sight, banished by the busy excitements of
the day, the spite, the scheming, the power. Am I breaking
in two, she wondered. She shivered, as if someone had
walked across her grave . . .

Shadows were gathering; it was late; he had not come.
Something was terribly, terribly wrong. He had never

been late before, usually ridiculously early. The longer she sat, the more frantic she got. In the end she got back on her bicycle, shoving her tennis racket into the large basket on the handlebars, and cycled to his house. If she just cycled past, saw the lights on, she would be reassured.

She passed the gate; his car was in the drive; the house was in darkness. She turned the bike and cycled back. She was so worried now that she would even brave the cold, leaden dragon's wrath . . . All these weeks, little lost Maude had wanted her to feel sorry for the dragon, to understand. Little Maude had said that even the dragon had once been a baby . . .

But it had been no good; the dragon had never been a baby; had never been kind, or friendly, or even happy. She was a total blot on the light; the world would be better off without her . . . What use was she, for all her money—fat, ugly thing?

She cycled up the drive, rather wobbly, and rang the bell.

No answer.

But he never went anywhere except in his car! Had he had a heart attack? He was big; not young; he'd been pushing himself very hard . . .

She crept around the side of the house, holding her breath, peering through the windows at the darkness inside, shading the glass with her hand.

But when she reached the conservatory, he was plainly visible, among his beloved potted palms. Ready, wearing his tennis whites, but leaning forward in one of the cast-iron chairs, his head in his hands.

Was he ill? She tapped gently. He gave a start and reared upright, as if in terror of her. And his pale, staring-eyed face was spotted all over, with dark brown.

And so was the front of his tennis whites. The dragon had thrown gravy all over him, ruining his clothes. That's why he hadn't come. But he might have let her know.

She tapped again, more insistently. Slowly, like an old man, he rose, came across, and fiddled with the catch on the French windows.

What was the matter with him? A bit of gravy . . .

It wasn't gravy; it was red. It was blood. His tongue, like a little child's, came out and licked exploringly at a splash on his face.

"What? Where?"

He nodded limply, in the direction of the hall and staircase. She walked through.

He'd done it all right. The vast bulk of the dragon, in a vile purple afternoon frock, was sprawled at the foot of the staircase. Her skirt had ridden up, revealing pillar-like legs that had always been hideous and were more hideous now. The top of her head was crushed in like an egg, and an African knobkerrie, pulled from the wall, lay beside her, thick with matted blood and hair.

In that moment, she should have screamed. But, the spectacles cool and reassuring against her chest, she did not scream. Instead, her eyes noticed very clearly that the knob on the staircase newel post was nearly the same diameter as the knobkerrie he had used . . .

She felt *what* for him? No longer lust, certainly. Rage, at his unplanned spontaneous clumsiness, which had ruined everything. Disgust at his pathetic total collapse. A certain pity . . . and a rush of realization that if he came to trial, the cause of the quarrel between him and the dragon would certainly come out in court. Her whole future would be ruined. The papers . . . She would be painted a scarlet woman . . .

She walked slowly up the stairs, her eyes scheming, clear, conniving . . . She took hold of the banister directly above the knob on the newel post and began to pull at it. It was not very securely fastened to the wall. It began to sway from side to side, under her urgent hands . . .

"YES, THAT WILL DO for now, I think, madam." Inspector Groves, her father's friend and a keen member of the Archaeological Society, closed his official notebook with a snap. "Thank you for all you've done. A sad accident to a well-liked lady."

He led her out into the hall. The body of the dragon had been removed; and the matted hair and blood that Maude had so carefully removed from the knobkerrie and transferred to the knob of the newel post. And the broken banister, which had lain so convincingly under the dragon by the time the police arrived.

"That handrail was always loose," said Maude. "I must have warned her about it a dozen times."

"And she was a big woman," said Inspector Groves. "A heavy woman. It's a sad blow for him. I thought he took it very hard. I've seldom seen a man collapse like that . . . though it's a shocking accident, of course. Think he'll be all right? I was all for sending him to hospital . . ."

"Daddy'll have him at our house by this time. And that doctor gave him some pretty heavy sedation. He'll sleep the clock round. We'll look after him, Inspector, don't worry."

I shall, too, she thought. What a mess of a man! Clinging to her, crying like a baby, while she commanded his brute strength to do what was required. All men were weak, weak. But the worst was past. The fatal evidence was dispersing.

"Can I give you a lift, madam?"

"No—I've got my bicycle. If my light works."

"What's that you've got in your bike basket—oh, spare tennis things!"

"We were going to play. That's why I called."

"A rare shock for you, her falling like that, and you in the very next room . . ."

"We were just talking . . . I heard her call out as she fell."

Just at that moment, a dog came trotting along the pavement, out of the gloom, in the busy way dogs do. By the bicycle it stopped, sniffed eagerly up at the basket.

Maude stood frozen as the inspector moved forward. But he only kicked mildly at the dog. "Get away, you brute."

"It's the smell of . . . sweat he's after, I suppose," said Maude, delicately.

The dog howled in pain and departed. The inspector drove off past her with a wave, and Maude cycled home, only a little fatigued.

IT WAS AUTUMN. The wind had plastered wet yellow leaves along the bottom of Mr. Hazlitt's repaired window. Mr. Hazlitt and Maude were sitting drinking tea, as dusk fell. They were very close now. Mr. Hazlitt was a proper man. He would do as a husband.

"Any news of poor old Dewhurst?" asked Mr. Hazlitt.

"Had a card two days ago. He's landed in New Zealand. Went as soon as he got probate. Sold up the lot."

"Don't blame him," said Mr. Hazlitt. "Think I'd do the same. This town would always be full of memories—he would expect to see her on every corner. Lucky they had no children."

"Yes," said Maude.

Mr. Hazlitt switched on the shop light, and it winked on the gold chain around her neck which held the spectacles. "What *is* that thing you wear around your neck?" He reached across with the privilege of a fiancé and pulled up the spectacles . . . removed them.

And immediately went frantic, more frantic than he had been about his window.

"Why, Maude, where did you get these? They're old . . . really old . . . handmade . . . hand-ground lenses. Why, these are the kind of spectacles they wore in Hans Holbein's time . . . if they're genuine . . . fifteenth, early sixteenth century . . ." He pulled out a little round black jeweler's lens and screwed it in his eye. "There's a goldsmith's mark . . . and a little salamander . . . a salamander stamped into the gold."

"Oh!" said Maude weakly. The removal of the spectacles from around her neck was having a very strange effect on her. Suddenly she was her old self again—shy, diffident, half blind, helpless, terrified at the memory of the things she had done.

"A *salamander*, Maude. Symbol of the old royal family of France . . . why, Maude, Catherine de Médicis could have worn these spectacles."

"Who's she?" Maude managed to ask tentatively.

"*Who's she?* Only the Queen of France. The poisoner, you remember. Formidable woman. When I went to Blois, five years ago, they showed us the hidden wall cabinet where she kept her poisons. What tales these spectacles might tell! I must send them to the Science Museum . . . They'll know. You don't mind, do you? I expect they'll pay you a great deal of money for them. Where on earth did you get them? Family heirloom or something?"

"I bought them at Woolworth's," said Maude, and broke into frantic weeping at all she had done.

"There, there," said Mr. Hazlitt, hugging her as any good fiancé should. "You're a funny one—you're not the same woman two minutes running. I shall have to get used to coping. How many women *are* there inside you, Maude?"

Maude continued weeping.

How was she going to put all this to Father Whitstable?

A NOSE
AGAINST THE GLASS

THE TOWN SQUARE at Beaminster is pleasant in summer. Always space to park a car, on the cobblestones in front of the shops. In the middle, the warm stone of the market cross has, beneath its Victorian gothic arches, seats where long-legged teenagers endlessly lounge and flirt. On Saturdays in August the Morris dancers display their middle-class macho of ribbons, bells, and sweat.

But that particular Christmas Eve it was deserted save for a few women, huddled and shapeless as Eskimos, flitting from shop to shop for the last few things. Dusk was coming early, with the big wet snowflakes that fell and died in the shining blackness of the Bridport road. The lights of passing cars caught them in a last flurry of incandescent glory as they died.

And in one corner of the square, old Widdowson sat in his gilded cage. It was really a large antique shop, painted green with gilt lettering.

FINE ANTIQUES   T. F. WIDDOWSON   CLOCKS

But with its dim gold lighting from cunningly placed spotlights, with its flicker of brass on bezel and swinging pendulum, with the enduring patient stillness of the white-haired man sitting in one corner of the window, it did look, through the big falling flakes, like a gilded cage.

The passing women spared Widdowson a glance, a pang, a timid wave. They knew he'd be alone this Christmas, as he'd been for the last ten. They remembered all his past kindnesses. Never refused to open a village festival, old Widdowson; with a nice check to back it. Never failed to give a small but exquisite object for the first prize in the hospital's Christmas raffle. But there was nothing they dared do for him; he was too rich, too dignified, too old . . .

From his window, he missed none of this. Nothing wrong with his eyes and ears. They seemed to sharpen as he grew older. So did his mind, when he might have welcomed a little merciful blurring around the edges. Nothing wrong with him at all, for eighty-four. People called him wonderful; said *they* wouldn't mind living to eighty-four, if they could be like Widdowson.

But they never said it to his face . . .

The only thing wrong with Widdowson was the cold. Every summer, the sun seemed to lose a little more heart; every winter, the cold moved in a little closer. Oh, the shop had central heating; there was an extra fan heater at his feet. People who came into the shop in overcoats and mufflers soon felt the prick of sweat. But Widdowson had learned some time ago that this was not a cold that could be stopped by glass windows and thermostats. It seemed to him a cold within the earth itself which reached up into the bones of his feet through the soles of his shoes, which came through the window glass into his eyes, as the wet black road nudged toward freezing. Tonight in bed he would hear the cold, in the creaking of timbers and slates overhead; he would hear the crackle as ice crystals formed. At this time of year the earth herself seemed close to death, despaired of the sun's return, could not succor those who lived on her.

Killing weather, he said to himself. Killing weather. He noted that Thomas, his black neutered tomcat, had crept silently into the warmest place in the shop, under the corner radiator, clear of any drafts. He was glad Thomas was home for the night, out of the killing weather . . . but he mustn't limit Thomas's freedom! He wasn't two yet, sleek and well furred, with a lot of years before him. Widdowson had changed his will, last winter, to make sure Thomas would be properly cared for. He remembered still the cat's skull he'd found as a boy on Morecambe beach—white and beautiful and perfect, but so small and thinly made. He could no longer rejoice in Thomas's thick-muscled well-being, without that skull being stamped across it, like a postmark canceling out a bright postage stamp.

Morbid. An old fool getting morbid. An old fool sitting here on Christmas Eve, waiting for customers who wouldn't come. Nobody bought antiques on Christmas Eve. Tinsel was what they were scurrying around looking for; packets of dates and cocktail sticks. He could be sitting upstairs in comfort, with the curtains drawn closed and a new book, and the tray of tea Mrs. Talbot had left him, with the kettle ready boiled. Alone, of course. Alone for the next four days. With the sweet smell of old men. Ever since he'd been a child, cuddled by his grandfather, he'd hated the sweet smell of old men. Now it was always in his nostrils. Ten years ago he had first noticed it hanging about him. In a frenzy, he had bathed twice a day, changed his shirt three times, made a fool of himself with after-shave, till young girls looked at him and giggled. Now he despaired; the smell of old men would be with him now till the end.

Someone might still come into the shop; nosiness would be his last pleasure to go. Like that elderly couple yesterday, both collectors.

When the husband picked something up, on the point of buying, the wife said, "Not now, dear. We must hurry. Elsie's waiting." And he would put it down again.

Then the wife would pick up something else, and the husband would say, "No time now, dear . . . Elsie's waiting."

In the end they'd circled around for half an hour, jealous as cats, and gone away without buying, though they'd handled half the shop. Once, Widdowson would've been mad with chagrin, over a lost sale. Even ten years ago, he'd have felt sad for them, eternally denying each other's pleasure. Now he simply treasured them, as something as symmetrical and perfect as a Ming vase—popped them onto the shelves of his memory, to take down and dust and laugh over gently sometimes. While he could watch people he could drift through their lives painlessly, like an undemanding parasite . . .

He glanced out of the window again. In spite of the central heating, steam was condensing on the windows from the bottom sills like a subtle mist, cutting him off from the shop lights across the road, making them look like the lights of ships sailing away out to sea. It made him feel he was going blind. He rubbed at the nearest pane angrily, with his fist and sleeve. Which only produced a jagged blear in which car lights passed, distorted.

A jagged blear like a calligraphy of impotent anger; as if he had written his pain on the window as clearly as the greengrocer next door wrote up the price of Brussels sprouts. For all the world to stare at.

The world had always stared—ever since he grew so tall and thin as a boy. He had always been careful to give them something else to stare at. Let them stare at his rows of grandfather clocks, every one a beauty, restored within and without until anyone might have thought they were brand-new from the hand of Knibb . . . He gave a lifetime guarantee on every clock. That had been a bold gesture when he first started as a young man. Wasn't worth much now . . .

He looked at them, and they gave him no comfort; he thought they looked like big red highly polished tomb-stones. He grunted, either in disgust or in pain. Fifty years serving clocks, saving clocks, pulling them back from the brink of ruin in the forties and fifties when fools chopped them up for firewood . . . And then the joy went out of it, like the tide going out at Morecambe Bay in his boyhood. They said he bought and sold them more shrewdly than ever; asked him still to verify the clocks at the antiques fair at Olympia. But it was only habit now; simply refusing to lie down . . .

He turned again from the clocks to the window, like a driven thing. The mist of condensation had gathered again, mercifully erasing his angry calligraphy. All except one patch, little bigger than his hand.

And through that patch someone was staring in. A nose pressed against the glass, flat and white as a snail's belly. Two round blue eyes peering intently. Beyond the condensation's blur, a hint of pink lips and a fuzzy aureole that must be golden hair.

It made him jump. Then he had to laugh at himself for jumping. The face was so close to the sidewalk it could only be that of a child. A child staring in, wonder-struck. And he knew somehow there was no harm in the child; it was not the sort who threw bricks through antique-shop windows, and certainly not the older sort of child that mugged elderly antique dealers and some-times kicked them to death if enough money was not forthcoming. Which was as well for the child, for in the left-hand drawer of his desk was a Smith and Wesson of 1880 which might be antique but was loaded with live ammunition. It might mean prison, even at the age of eighty-four. But prison was better than the humiliation of being mugged.

He looked again at the window, fleetingly, shyly. The child was still staring in, staring at *him* now. With what expression? Wonder? Amazement? Love? How absurd! But he stiffly managed a wink at the child; a grin; and finally a wave. But the blue eyes went on staring at him, unfathomable. How absurd, thought Widdowson, to stare at a relic like me in wonder. It is indecent! And in a sudden rush of embarrassment he waved the child away, not in anger so much as in panic. He knew the incredible wrinkles of his face too well from the shaving mirror, and had never liked being stared at, even by the women he had loved.

The face vanished, leaving only darkness and the irregular metronome of car lights.

And Widdowson allowed himself a rare lapse into reverie—like his one cigar of the day . . .

That was how *he* had started, eighty years ago. Staring into the windows of junk shops when his nose could hardly reach the sill. Like Ali Baba's caves they seemed then, the tangles of old bicycles, Chinese wood carvings, fox furs, and engravings of the Old Queen, eyes hand-tinted blue and cold as the Arctic sky. His eye would explore farther and farther through the tangled jungle of wood and metal until it came to, at the back, silhouetted by the light of the rear premises, the tall figure of the owner standing, staring back at him. Magicians they had seemed to him then: sellers of mystery, sellers of history who knew the origins of all things. That was why he'd always wanted to be an antique dealer. Now that he was the best dealer in the southwest, he knew they had never been magicians, just dirty ignorant dishonest old men, desperately trying to scratch themselves a living sorting through the relics of the poor . . .

Suddenly he started up. What he needed was a stiff double whisky. Then he made himself sit down again. It was scarcely three o'clock in the afternoon. A double whisky now could be the start of the slippery slope. The one he'd slid down thirteen years ago, when Peggy died. The one he'd only just managed to climb out of . . .

With the help of a nose pressed against the window.

Margie Harrison. Thin as a stick in a pair of threadbare jeans and a washed-out Rolling Stones T-shirt that revealed her total lack of femininity at thirteen. He'd been frightened, at first, of the young female thing who simply would not leave him alone. Any time of the day or evening he might look up to see her, tongue peeping out of the corner of her mouth, peering at the antiques with desperate longing. In the end he had tried to solve it by inviting her in to look around. That had been a mistake. Once in, she was almost impossible to get out. Questions, questions, questions. And that naïve way of asking "Is it gold? *Real* gold?" He had explained it was merely ormolu, bronze with gilding. That had been the beginning of the teaching. She had tried to repay with sturdy offers to dust, to make him a cup of tea. He dared not let her dust; she could do damage worth hundreds in ten minutes of misplaced vigor. He dared not let her go upstairs to make a cup of tea; she might be a cunning street-smart thief. But he could not bear to send her away; she was the only flickering candle in the drink-sodden dark of Peggy's death. So in the end he taught her to dust, and let her go and make the tea. And then, even as a widower of seventy-two, he grew terrified of village gossip, of being thought a dirty old man . . . He went to see her mother in the end, and had been welcomed. In that poor house any chance of work or money had been welcomed. It was agreed she would come and dust for him, after school and on Saturdays, for three pounds a week. And be taught the antiques trade . . .

Three years it lasted. He taught her antiques, though she could never start to fathom the insides of a clock. He taught her how to speak properly, the meaning of the dealers' phrases, how to price an object. Until the incredible Saturday he had come back from delivering a long-case to find her so white and shaking he'd thought she'd been attacked. She could hardly speak . . . He'd had to shake it out of her. But no, it wasn't rape, it was a lady who had brought a pair of statues into the shop to sell. And she wouldn't wait . . . so Margie had bought them with forty pounds filched from the till . . . Widdowson had run through the shop to the back in a cold sweat. Forty pounds was forty pounds in those days.

But there in the back were a pair of Staffordshires, Victoria-and-Albert and Lord Nelson, genuine, filthy but unchipped, and worth at least a hundred pounds.

"Did I do right, Mr. Widdowson? Did I do right?" Her soul was in her eyes, her open mouth. He had hugged her; he had given her another ten pounds out of the till as her commission; he had told her she'd make a real dealer someday. And in his heart he had vowed to leave her the shop when he died. That would shake them at the sales, cocky beggars. The first real woman dealer—in these parts, anyway. He would start by taking her on full time, when she left school . . .

Then, quite suddenly, it had all gone wrong. A boy called for her at the shop one night, a young soldier with a cocky jerky manner and a handsome bony white face. Barry Manson, who had the gift of dirtying things just by looking at them. He walked around the shop lifting all the price tickets and whistling softly to himself.

As they left together, as the door was closing, he heard the soldier say, "You ought to ask for a raise; the old bugger's loaded."

He had been very patient, hoping it was a passing thing. She was used to handling things of quality now; surely she would see through Barry Manson . . .

But she hadn't. A month later, shamefaced, she asked him for the raise. He gave it to her; he'd been meaning to, anyway. But it made him bitter; he felt he was giving the money to Manson . . .

Of course, he'd always known she would get married; she was an attractive girl now, filling out. He'd hoped to give her away at her wedding, because her father had died by then. But he'd visualized something a lot better than Barry Manson. He'd hoped for a young auctioneer, or someone who came down regularly from Sotheby's. He'd looked forward to seeing her first child, perhaps being a godparent.

But not to Manson's child. A cloud grew between them; she still dusted well, and kept the shop with charm, but they didn't share their triumphs anymore. He would catch her watching him, in mirrors, hurt, baffled, wondering what she'd done. But he could never bring himself to tell her. And when she said she was leaving school, he hadn't offered her the job. She'd gone to work in the gift shop instead, where they liked her ladylike ways . . .

He sighed, and looked up at the window again, without thinking.

The eyes were back, peering in. So like her eyes. But not her eyes, for she was still around. A big strapping woman, pushing a pram with Manson's third snotty-nosed child in it, going to fat a little more with each baby. Yet the eyes did have the same hurt, locked-out look that hers had had, when she came to give notice before starting in the gift shop . . .

A sudden impulse made him get up and go to the shop door. He did not know what he meant to say to the person outside.

So perhaps it was just as well there was nobody there. Just Mrs. Peirson, locking up the greengrocer's next door. She turned and called, "Good night, Mr. Widdowson. Merry Christmas!"

Curiosity drove him across to her. "Mrs. Peirson? Have you just seen a child peering in my window?"

"No, Mr. Widdowson, I didn't see anybody. Mind you, I wasn't looking—a night like this. A child shouldn't be running about, a night like this . . ." She shivered, and he shivered in company. The snow was falling thicker, and sticking now, at least on the sidewalks. Quite thick —an inch deep below his shop windows.

And then he saw. There were only three sets of

footprints on the snowy sidewalk under his window. One set were his own; one set were large prints of a man in wellington boots; and the last were clearly a woman's.

Where the child should have stood, there were no prints at all.

Mrs. Peirson, following his glance, gave him an odd look and said, "Good night, Mr. Widdowson," and hurried away.

HE CLOSED THE DOOR and went back to his desk, shivering violently and not just with the cold. Was he going potty, as Walter Snowden had, and Violet Markham? He remembered the old people's home, Violet Markham's empty drooling face . . . Please God, not that. Heart attack, stroke, cancer, anything but *that*. His mind was his strong fortress, his house of defense . . . Even blindness he could have coped with, or deafness . . . But not to be himself, not to be in control of himself, to be a torn and whimpering rag of himself like Violet, or to go back to childhood like Walter . . . He would shoot himself first. He took the pistol from the drawer.

But it had an oddly soothing effect on him. It was not his destroyer, it was his child. *He* had bought it red with rust and broken. He had restored it till it gleamed subtly with the oil he had put on it. It clicked reassuringly in his hand. It worked perfectly, as he ejected the polished, gleaming shells.

Was his mind working equally perfectly? He reached for his desk diary, saw his appointments neatly inked in, all the way through to October next year. That wasn't a senile man's work . . .

One entry was merely penciled in. "Oatman—balloon clock? £175?"

He reached for the phone and dialed Harry Oatman's number. Remembered it without having even to think. Harry's voice came on the phone, a little rough. Harry had started celebrating Christmas a little early . . . A little cunning tiger wakened in Widdowson's mind. He might get the balloon clock for a little less than £175 if Harry was fool enough to drink during business hours. And Harry would be spent up, because he'd have given his feckless wife too much money to buy Christmas goodies. He'd *almost* promised to buy the balloon clock, but not quite. He'd said he'd think about it . . . But Harry, with his silly optimism, would by now be considering the clock sold, and would have been spending accordingly. Widdowson's voice took on a croon of sad regret. Not too much—just a tinge of unhappy discomfort . . .

"Harry, about the clock . . ."

He sensed Harry sensing the regret in his voice. And instantly panicking. *"What* about that clock?"

Harry tried to control his voice, but the panic showed through. Harry definitely had what he always euphemistically called a cash-flow problem. And if Widdowson didn't buy the clock, nobody else would, this side of New Year, when folk began spending their Christmas-present money. And the bills would be flooding in, for the end of the year . . .

"I don't think I can take that clock off you at the moment, Harry. I've just had one brought into the shop. A bit broken, but nothing I can't see to . . ."

A bit broken meant cheap.

"Look," said Harry, "I can see you right. A bit off . . ."

"How much off? I'm a little short of the ready myself."

"Will a hundred and sixty do you? Call it a Christmas present from me."

"You know I don't like stocking two balloon clocks at once, Harry. Makes people think they're ten-a-penny . . ."

"Look," said Harry desperately, "I'll be fair—after all, it is Christmas. Hundred and fifty to you, Widdowson. And that's a bargain. I won't take a penny less."

Which meant he would take more than a penny less.

"Hundred and forty," said Widdowson. The excitement of the chase filled his bloodstream like strong drink.

"Hundred and forty-five," said Harry weakly, seeing a glimmer of hope at the end of the long dark tunnel of Christmas.

"Done," said Widdowson. And with the chase over, he not only felt flat; he felt he had been intolerably mean. Harry Oatman was a fool, but he had three kids, and it was Christmas . . .

"Harry . . . ?"

"Yeah?" The pain and worry of thirty lost quid were in Oatman's voice.

"That old wreck of a Victorian long-case—the one you've had for years—the one that's supposed to play tunes and doesn't. How much d'you want for it?"

"What you want *that* thing for?" Oatman's voice was incredulous with hope. The long-case had been stuck in his shop so long, so broken, it was the joke of the county.

"I feel like a problem to work on over the holiday. I think I can do it—if I can get the bats' nests out of it."

"If anybody can do it, you can, Widdowson." Harry's voice was showing traces of maudlin admiration. "You can have it for a hundred."

"Ninety," said Widdowson sharply. He didn't want Oatman thinking he was going soft because it was Christmas.

"Ninety-five?"

"Ninety-five, then. When can you deliver?"

"Now if you like."

"Boxing Day will do. Boxing Day morning." He didn't want Oatman blundering through the snow with clocks in his present drunken state. Damn fool would probably get breathalyzed.

"God bless you, Widdowson," said Oatman, now thoroughly maudlin. "You're a good bloke. My missus—"

"Must go, Harry," said Widdowson crisply. "Merry Christmas." He hung up; he could never stand being thanked.

He felt better. He felt like a cat who has played with a mouse and mercifully let it go. And he knew he'd lost none of his old edge.

Senile? Rubbish!

He looked up.

The eyes were watching through the window again. Beseeching.

AGAIN HE RAN to the door. Again there was no one there, and no footprints in the snow. But the snow was falling very fast now. All the world was white for Christmas, and the lights of the shops across the square were hardly visible through the black falling flakes; as he watched, another shop window went dark. Only three left now—the gift shop where Margie had worked, the post office, and the Dumbledore Café. Not a soul was in sight; the scurrying housewives had all collected their Christmas stores.

Widdowson felt suddenly, bleakly alone.

He looked across the narrow street that led out of the village toward Crewkerne. Across the road, the restaurant still had its lights on, was still serving afternoon tea.

He hadn't been inside for years. But it looked just the

same, warmly red with its undrawn curtains, and a little lamp on each table, shining on silver plate and napkins.

He decided tea would be better than a whisky.

CLOSE TO, SHEILA WATKINS, who ran it, was just the same—a little plumper, a little more lined, a few more gray hairs, but the last ten years hadn't levied too sharp a price. She still bubbled with excitement, as she had when she was a plump schoolgirl, indulging herself in a treat at one of the same tables she now owned . . .

"Mr. Widdowson—how *nice*! I think we've got your usual table vacant for you!" Widdowson appreciated her gift of salesmanship. And indeed she had remembered his favorite table, back to the wall in the far corner, with a view over the square at his shoulder so he could keep an eye on everything, like a fading gunfighter in an old Western.

"Tea? Toasted tea cakes?" She had remembered his liking for tea cakes, too. She probably remembered he liked them well done, slightly black at the edges. A surge of warmth swept over him. She was a comfortable sort of woman, even in her widowhood. The sort any decent man could safely marry, if she'd have him. He'd toyed with the idea of asking her, after Peggy died . . . But women were vulnerable creatures, prone to cancer in middle age, and he couldn't have borne to be hurt again.

"Tea cakes," he said, to make up for not proposing to her twelve years ago. She went and gave his order, then came back, beaming. "Can you spare a moment, Mr. Widdowson—while they're toasting. I . . . I've bought a clock I'd like you to see. Of course, it's not like *your* clocks . . . but I think it's rather nice." She sighed comfortably. "When I saw it, I couldn't resist it."

She led him upstairs, across a landing that smelled pleasingly of polish. He felt a twinge of delightful guilt, imagining for a moment he was her lover . . . Then he was laughing at himself for being an old fool.

Her sitting room was as comfortable as she was, plump chintz and a smell of potpourri. He got a sense of her hidden life; there were two books on the table by the settee. *Hawksmoor* by Peter Ackroyd, and *Life in the English Country House* by Mark Girouard. The lady was no fool . . .

"Here's my clock." She paused and gestured, half proud, half self-indulgent.

The clock hung on the wall, neatly lit by a spotlight. It was a reproduction of a Dutch wall clock, with hanging brass weights and a crudely filed brass figure of Atlas holding up the world. It was perfectly *horrible*—expensive and vulgar, a travesty to anyone who'd ever seen a real Dutch clock. He had to stop himself gritting his teeth and closing his eyes in agony. He could have got her a genuine, honest mahogany schoolroom clock for the price she'd paid. If only she'd come to him . . .

But she was waiting for his opinion, eyes shining and mouth a little open, still looking like a schoolgirl, in spite of overwhite false teeth. Expectant eyes again . . . And she had made him welcome, and it was Christmas . . .

He said, still clinging desperately to his honor, "Yes— a Dutch clock. I've seen them in The Hague. The old ones are rather bigger . . ."

But she would not let him off the hook. "But do you like it, Mr. Widdowson? Do you *approve*?"

He forced the lies out, as if he was being sick. "I think it's very nice, Mrs. Watkins. Remarkable. Very sound craftsmanship."

"Well, that coming from you is a *real* compliment." Now she would be telling everybody in town what he'd said. People would be laughing at him behind his back. Thank you, Mrs. Watkins. You've just extracted my lifetime-earned good name as your Christmas present. Merry Christmas!

But he'd still like to have sat down on her chintz couch, have her fetch him a cup of tea and fuss over him; sit by the cozy log fire and warm his feet. He was weary; women gave warmth and food and love; all they demanded in exchange was your integrity . . .

"Yes, very nice," he said again, and trailed off.

"Your tea cakes will be ready by now," she said.

But he revived, downstairs. George McLoughlin came across to wish him a Merry Christmas, and show off his grandfather's golden hunter watch, which could truthfully be admired. Ken Smith, whom he hadn't seen for ten years since he moved to Bridport, clapped him on the shoulder patronizingly, and told him he didn't look a year older. He wryly consoled himself that Ken Smith looked a great deal older; he had halved his hair and doubled his waistline. A sort of little court gathered around him, hanging on his every word, as if he was minor royalty. And the tea cakes were unusually good and dripping with butter . . .

But it was the girl across the room who caught his eye. A tall, slim, elegant girl, carelessly but stylishly dressed. Not a local Dorset dumpling. She was with a plump young man, of a sort that Widdowson did not like, a type he seemed to see more and more. Young Tories he called them, as opposed to Old Tories. Always talking about how much money they were making. Always going a bit to fat, far too young. Too many expense-account lunches.

Spotty faces and sharp Italian suits and camel's-hair overcoats . . . vulgar. Always in accounting and City banks . . . No breeding. This one was holding forth on money now, and calling cabinet ministers by their Christian names. Norman and Leon and Nigel . . . Sickening.

Girl wasn't very impressed, either. Sexy bit—she had her legs crossed and was letting her shoe hang away from her heel. Widdowson had always taken that as a sign a woman was hunting for a man . . . Nice naked heel, in its silk stocking, nice elegant leg. But she wasn't much pleased with the man she'd caught this time . . . As he talked she was drawing little squares in the air with her dangling foot . . . sure sign of boredom.

And sensitive; she became aware he was watching her. Turned to look at Widdowson; he liked the long, elegant nose and the huge brown eyes. For a moment she looked at him as if he was a real person, not some old gaffer to be immediately discounted.

Delicately, wickedly, Widdowson glanced at her young man's averted head, and sketched a little pound sign in the air with his finger, and grinned conspiratorially.

She *was* sharp: she got it; she laughed out loud. Just for one glorious moment he was her brilliant and wicked grandfather. Then the young man turned and scowled at him, thunderously. A low-voiced row seemed to be breaking out between them. Then she was standing up and gathering her belongings . . .

As she swept past, he looked up a little timidly, a little appalled at what he'd done.

She gave him a wink, and a wide smile. For a blinding second, sixty years of age between them didn't matter. Then she was gone, leaving a hint of perfume that might have been Chanel No. 5, or didn't they make that anymore? Then the young man was blundering after her. If looks could kill . . . Widdowson met his eyes steadily, and the young man looked away first . . . But then, Widdowson told himself fairly, the young man had to look where he was going . . . As it was, he blundered into a table and knocked over a chair. Didn't stop to pick it up, either; threw money onto the counter to pay his bill and didn't wait for the change.

"Rudeness," said Sheila Watkins stoutly at his retreating back. "Well, he needn't bother coming here again. I can do without his kind of business."

And Widdowson was left with his Pyrrhic victory. If only he'd not interfered, he might have had another ten minutes to watch the girl. Still, he wished her luck with her life. She might know heartbreak—who didn't, sooner or later—but even as an old woman she'd have style.

The restaurant, without her glow, turned as bleak as a black-and-white movie. Widdowson sniffed in the air deep, like an old hound hunting for fox scent. But all trace of the Chanel No. 5 had vanished. She had sailed away like a glorious ship, laden with life and love and giggles and excitement and the sheer young health that surged in her from morning till night.

And he was left on the quayside, waving hopelessly. I would give the shop and the clocks and my bank balance and everything I own, he thought, to shed sixty years and run down the street after her, in rags. He had no doubts about his power to attract her, even in rags . . .

He poured himself another cup of tea, to cheer himself up; listened to a man trying to sell another man a car. The man was too quick and jumpy, too pushy . . . He failed to sell his car. Bad salesman, serve him right, thought Widdowson. He went and paid his bill in restored good humor, working out how *he* would have sold the car . . .

MRS. WATKINS TOLD the coroner later that Mr. Widdowson left her restaurant in apparently the best of health and spirits. She was the last person who really saw him alive . . .

THE COLD SEEMED to have got into the shop like a burglar while he was away. Thomas kept getting up and circling around as if trying to find a warmer arrangement under the radiator. Widdowson suddenly felt tired; he crawled behind his desk as if it was a refuge. It would have been wiser to go upstairs, where the windows were curtained against the frost; but he didn't feel up to the stairs yet.

The idea of starting all over again would not go away. He had exchanged his youth and strength for a lot of money. He was *still* making a lot of money. Now he no longer cared, everything he touched seemed to turn to gold; he could make a thousand pounds in a fit of abstraction—like the last auction he'd been to, at Sotheby's. Bidding for a huge funny-looking clock that nobody seemed to know much about that had mildly pricked his curiosity because it was covered with domes and minarets, though it had a French movement and a lot of seized-up works that must make a very funny noise indeed when they were freed of verdigris and actually functioning. He'd wanted it to fiddle with, really, in the long, dark evenings. Anyway, he had gone on bidding, languidly waving his hand and listening with half an ear to the rising price, to make sure he didn't pay more than it was worth, and all the time thinking about that last summer holiday he'd had in Normandy with Peggy.

He'd come to with a start, hearing the voice of the auctioneer giving the clock to him for five hundred and fifty. The next second he had been accosted by a tiny man in a business suit and a kaffiyeh. Obviously an Arab, though he spoke good English in spite of his panic, and spat saliva all over Widdowson's lapels. He had made so much fuss the auctioneer had three times called for silence before he began the next lot.

The little man was really very upset, indeed. Widdowson, amid stares, had led him out into the foyer, and managed to calm him down and get his story.

The clock was a French clock, made for the Mohammedan Middle East market in the middle of the nineteenth century. It had been sold to the Sultan's ancestor, but mislaid during some palace insurrection in about 1920. The present Sultan had just heard of the clock's existence while on a trip to London. He had sent his aide-de-camp to bid, but the aide-de-camp had had a hard time finding a taxi, got stuck in several traffic jams, had trouble establishing his master's credit with the auctioneer's clerk, and heard the clock sold as he entered the room . . . The aide-de-camp's face was working pitifully; his master's instructions had been to buy the clock at *any* price, and not return without it. The aide-de-camp dare not return without it; reduction to the rank of camel driver was the least of the punishments he feared . . .

Widdowson had felt sorry for the little man, with his beaky nose and large dark tear-filled eyes. He pitied any man who worked for the powerful. He had put his arm on the shoulder of the rather absurd brown pin-stripe

yearning. He knew those eyes, too, were looking for the pearl of great price, one each side of the nose pressed like a snail's belly against the window. He wondered, half numb with cold, if the eyes were those of his own infant self. He looked at the eyes sadly and shook his head.

"Go on, then, look. Go on looking. But I tell you, young man, it's a snare and a delusion. There is no pearl of great price. Why don't you go off and have fun, instead, while you can? Go and get warm! Grow up and find a good woman, and go to bed with her as often as you can . . ." Maudlin old bugger, he thought, a maudlin old bugger talking to himself.

But, to his great amazement, the eyes responded. They moved rapidly from side to side of the bare patch.

The child outside was shaking its head, very emphatically. The child outside was insisting there *was* a pearl of great price.

"All right," he said to the eyes, which were now still and watching him intently again. "Have it your way; it's your life."

Again, through the steamy glass, the child shook its head vigorously. For some reason, Widdowson became convinced the eyes would not run away this time; it was worth the effort of going to the shop door once more. He almost tiptoed across to it; he kept on looking across to the patch, to see if the eyes had vanished. But they hadn't.

He swung open the shop door, heard the shop bell clang above his head. Took a step outside, a big swift step; and felt the thickening snow slide treacherously under his feet. So he finally went out onto the street with a rush and slither. When he recovered his balance, he looked up.

The child was still standing there; it was smaller than

he thought. But—and he gasped in horror—it was only wearing some thin threadbare nightgown thing that didn't come down to its bare knees.

And the small thin feet were bare on the snow.

An icy gust of wind came around the corner, ruffling the child's nightgown; it was so cold it tore right through Widdowson's sheepskin coat and thick turtleneck sweater. He thought with anguish, closing his eyes against it, how cold the child must be. Then he opened his eyes, hoping the child was only a figment of his imagination, and would have vanished.

But it was still standing there, looking at him. He noticed how thin its legs were; the feet were almost transparent against the snow; he could see their blue veins and thin anklebones standing out. The arms below the short sleeves were like sticks. The face was huge-eyed, hollow-cheeked. The stomach was large, swollen with hunger. The face seemed to be bruised down one side. And yet still the child looked beautiful. He remembered the newsreels from Ethiopia; he remembered how the children there still had this way of looking beautiful, even when they were dying . . .

But this wasn't an Ethiopian child; it had fair long hair that whipped in the cruel wind; the huge eyes were blue, like his own.

A terrible sense of disorder filled Widdowson; it was impossible that any *English* child should be in this state, any *Beaminster* child. What were the teachers doing . . . the social workers from Bridport? He became incoherent with the outrage of it . . . but then there had been stories in the papers about English children. But not in Beaminster. Everybody knew everybody's business in Beaminster.

Then he snatched himself back to looking at the child.
To thinking straight. Perhaps the child was a Christmas
ghost from long ago. From the hungry forties, the
eighteen-forties. Children must have starved in Beaminster *then* . . . under the Corn Laws and the Speen-
hamland system. After all, the child had left no footprints
outside his window.

But now the child put one pale bony foot forward,
then took it back again. And Widdowson could see, quite
clearly, a five-toed footprint in the snow. It was a real
child. It was telling him it was a real child.

He moved toward it, his arms outstretched, mumbling
incoherently about coming into the warmth, having food.
He heard himself mumbling something about milk and
biscuits . . . Christmas cake.

The child began to back away from him.

Then it turned and ran. Vanished around the corner
. . . Two cars passed Widdowson in rapid succession,
their headlights showing snowflakes as big as goose
feathers, reminding him of that childhood nursery
rhyme.

He looked back into his shop. The door was swinging
wildly in the gusts of wind where he had left it open.
Flakes of snow were swirling into the shop and onto the
fitted carpet, melting to damp dark spots. The papers
were blowing off his desk, the smaller pictures fluttering
on the wall. He saw Thomas's tail, fleeing up the stairs.
He even thought he saw one of the taller, thinner clocks
sway . . . impending chaos. And another searing gust of
wind tore into him, making him gasp and nearly knocking
him off his feet. He felt, with all his eighty-four years,
how frail the human body is.

He must get back into the shop and get the door shut.

The temperature in there must be dropping like a stone, the humidity going up . . . Damp was bad for clock veneer. Cold blowing up the stairs, invading his living quarters . . . It would take the central heating all evening to get back to normal. Once back inside, he could ring the police about the child. Teddy Hollings, the local constable, was Beaminster born and bred. He'd know every nook and cranny. He'd know how to contact the Social Services.

He got back inside and forced the door shut, and sat at his desk. He made a feeble attempt to pick his papers off the floor, but the effort to bend made his head swim. Besides, he must dial the local police station. He was a long time doing it; his fingers felt like frozen sausages.

Finally, he got through. Mrs. Hollings. Teddy wasn't in; there'd been a serious pile-up near the tunnel on the Crewkerne Road—people hurt. The ambulance was being slow in getting through. It could take hours to clear. The nearest available patrol car was back in Bridport . . .

He hung up in despair. No help there tonight. He rang the Social Services number; the answering machine was already on, and gave a Dorchester number to ring for the duty officer. What the hell would Dorchester know about finding a child in the alleyways of Beaminster?

He looked out of his window, across the square; the last of the shop lights had gone out. He looked at his watch. Of course, it was nearly six o'clock. Normally his own lights would be off; only the dim security lights would be left on. Even the restaurant lights were off. Sheila Watkins wouldn't open again on Christmas Eve; everyone was home with their families, getting ready for Christmas; the poorest night in the year for dining out, she always said. He rang her upstairs flat anyway, but she didn't reply. She had probably gone to stay with friends. Hardly anybody else lived over the shops around the square. Nobody whom he'd care to tell about a child in a nightgown; they'd think he was drunk and babbling . . .

The thought of a drink was like manna in the wilderness. He went to the cabinet in the office at the back of the shop where he kept a few choice bottles for extra-special customers. Poured himself a large whisky, infuriated at the way his shaking hands spilled it on the leather top of the desk. He was so cold, cold . . .

Not as cold as the child. Not dying of cold, as the child must be. Why the hell didn't it have the sense to go home to the warmth? Then he remembered the bruise on its face. Perhaps it didn't go home because it was frightened of being beaten? Battered? Murdered?

He paced up and down the shop, whether to get warm or to work off his anxiety even he couldn't tell. He stopped every five paces to gulp more whisky, feeling it dribbling down his chin. The windows were all steamed up now; the hole the child had stared through was gone. It was, to his coward self, a source of relief. It kept the child . . . outside. He didn't have to see it anymore. After all, he'd offered to have it in, get it warm, feed it, find it help. If the silly little thing had run away from him, was it *his* fault? He'd done what he could . . . risked his life. He'd nearly fallen; and at his age, a fall often meant a broken hip, and a broken hip usually meant the end. There was no point in them *both* dying . . . You couldn't expect a man of eighty-four . . .

And then the weeping started. Right outside the window. A weeping that would have broken anybody's heart. As if all the world was weeping.

He forgot everything. He ran to the door and ran out

into the snow. He almost caught the child; one second his arms were closing around it, and the next his foot had slipped and it was gone out of his arms.

It ran across the square to the shelter of the Market Cross, where the teenagers lounged in summer. No shelter there tonight; the wind would be howling through the four gothic arches . . . but he could see it underneath those arches by the lamplight that filtered dimly, through the snowflakes, from the few streetlamps. It was only a dim flicker of white nightgown and golden hair blowing in the wind, but he knew somehow the shadowed blue eyes were still watching him. Perhaps it would talk to him on its own ground.

He gathered his strength and ran. There was a sudden flare of headlights, a blare of horn, the long screech of tires on packed snow, and something large and dark missed him by inches; he felt the size, the weight of it in the wind of its passing, and the eddies it caused in the snowflakes. The driver later told the coroner he'd seen this old white-haired gaffer running like the wind. But was sure he hadn't hit him—quite sure.

Widdowson had shot his bolt by the time he reached the Cross; he felt the snow which had dropped inside his shoes start to melt; he felt his old lungs creaking like bellows. He knew he was spending more strength than he had, and he'd never overspent his strength in his life. Fool, said a voice in his head, a voice whose sense he'd always trusted in the heat of the hottest auction. Fool, go back before it's too late.

But the child was gone from the Cross. Widdowson thought it had vanished altogether, till he saw a flicker of blowing gold in the gutter outside the gift shop. The child was lying in the gutter, motionless . . . unconscious?

Crippled by the fall? In any case, it'd be no bother now . . .

Widdowson ran on at half speed—well, a fast totter really, he thought with a grim flick of humor. He pulled up in a heartrending skid, just kept his feet, and reached down to pick up the child . . .

. . . who catapulted from between his outstretched hands like an untamed cat, and was running away down the road toward the church. Then slipped and fell again, as it reached the corner, and again lay still. Was it injured in some way, concussed? Or was it playing up? Funny thing, playing up, if it meant lying on the freezing snow in a nightgown. But if it was concussion, which would fit in with the bruise on the face, it might mean the child *couldn't* get up again—might lie in the snow and freeze to death like a newborn lamb. He *must* get to it. The slope down to the church was steep and treacherous; he hadn't even brought a stick, which he usually carried when the road was slippery. He made progress slowly now, clinging to whatever he could, drainpipes, windowsills. He crept past the windows of the other antique shop, and noticed she had a bronze Chinese vase with cloisonné enamel in her darkened window, which at £55 was definitely undervalued. Funny how bits of your mind worked on their own, in the most ridiculous circumstances . . .

Behind him, his shop door was blowing in the wind again, his papers scattering, his pictures fluttering, a clock, taller and thinner than the rest, rocking. No burglar alarms were set. Had certain gentlemen well known to Scotland Yard's Fine Art Squad passed that way with a furniture van that night, they could have helped themselves to stuff worth a quarter of a million . . . but it was

an hour before anybody noticed. Teddy Hollings, returning exhausted but thankful from the traffic accident
at the tunnel, was still alert enough to stare aghast and
nearly crash his own car. He searched the ground floor
and found nothing but weather damage, though the
fluttering sheets of paper blew around the shop like
birds, and whispered like ghosts. He went upstairs,
fearing to find the worst, and found nothing. He re-
ported the incident to headquarters, and thought about
a search . . . but search where?

WIDDOWSON MADE the journey to the bottom of the
hill with his head down all the way, placing every foot
with infinite care, fighting for his life as a younger man
might have fought on Everest. From the various houses
came little bursts and squeaks of Christmas noise. Children shouting and laughing; a record player playing
"Silent Night," which Widdowson had come to dislike
more than any TV jingle, through the sheer amount of
repetition. He could have called for help, but he was too
proud and stubborn, and he knew if he met anyone he
was too shaken to talk coherently. He had a terror of not
being coherent . . .

When he reached the bottom of the hill, the child was
gone. He might have thought himself deluded, but he
could see where the child's body had dented the snow,
and a trail of naked tiny footprints, leading uphill now
to where the church tower bulked black and huge above
the mounded snow. There was a haloed moon behind
the black flakes of falling snow, and by its light he thought
he could see something white flicker in the church porch.
Moaning to himself, clinging to the rough wall of the
churchyard, he climbed up hand over hand, past the

wrought-iron gates which stood open ready for Midnight Mass, and into the porch.

The porch was empty—only the notices fluttering like sleepy restless white hens on the notice board. But he was glad to reach it; it was quiet and warmer, out of the wind. And the door into the church was ajar . . . Aha, he thought. Got you! He pushed the creaking door open, went in, closed it with an effort behind him, and locked it with the key and put the key in his pocket. You won't get away from me now, my lad!

The church was dark, but very warm. They must be warming it up for Midnight Mass. It would be a help if he could put the lights on, but he hadn't been in the church for thirteen years, since he buried Peggy. And forty years before then, when he married Peggy. Would the switches be by the door, which was logical; or would they be somewhere up by the pulpit and organ? There was a little light coming in now, through the huge dark-blue windows. It bounced and flickered on the tops of the pews; and the east window showed the light of one streetlamp through its stained glass, enough to outline the rood screen and the cross fixed above it. Beautiful black pattern. And the glowing tiny red light above the altar . . . But of switches he could see no sign, as he groped from pew top to pew top, afraid of falling over something hidden by the darkness of the floor.

Very well. If there were no switches, if he couldn't see, he must listen. He sat down heavily in the front pew, and was grateful that the aches in his legs eased. He took out his handkerchief and wiped the damp that melting snow-flakes had left on his face; brushed the thick snow off his coat and trousers . . . Then he settled to listen. His hearing seemed extra-acute now. He turned his head this way and that, listening to every sound. And found the church full of sound—the creaking of rafters and pews as the church warmed up. Noises from outside, voices, the sound of a bicycle freewheel, oddly distorted and magnified.

After a while he became convinced the child was there; he could sense it waiting in the dark, listening with equal intentness.

"Boy?" he called with some authority, now he had got his breath back. "Boy? Come here, boy! I won't hurt you!" He tried to make his voice gentler and gentler, as you would with a timid or abused animal; he had always been good at making friends with animals. Then, as nothing happened, he would grow cross, try to command the boy. Then he would grow ashamed of his own self-defeating anger, and make his voice soft again.

And all the time he felt the child watching, drawing nearer . . .

But it was still a terrible shock when he saw the child standing at the foot of the chancel steps, only about six feet away, and quite still. And Widdowson knew with equal shock that the child was no longer afraid. The child seemed utterly at home here . . . so that it was Widdowson who grew a little afraid of the child's sureness and stillness. But he said, with a gruff bravery he did not feel, "Well, you have led me a dance! What're you doing out on a night like this? We're going to have to get you sorted out!"

Still the child neither spoke nor moved. And Widdowson hardly dared to speak to it again; he might have the church key in his pocket, but he knew he was the prisoner now. Not that he much cared; it was so warm in the church, and his legs had stopped hurting. He felt himself dropping into a cozy doze, and leaped back awake, thinking this would never do. People coming into church for Midnight Mass might find him snoring, with his mouth open, like some old tramp that had crept in out of the wind. He made a last effort. An attempted joke.

"Looking for the pearl of great price, were you? Well, you'll not find it in my shop."

But the child slowly shook its head. As if to say it would.

"I don't know where, then, boy. I've been looking for it myself, for eighty years, and *I've* not found it."

The child raised its hands in a gesture toward Widdowson, as if offering him something. As if offering Widdowson Widdowson himself.

Widdowson laughed—a frighteningly creaky laugh, as if his lungs were going off-duty. "What, an old wreck like me? You'd find better in Thompson's second-hand shop."

But the child shook its head again. With the utmost sureness. So that Widdowson cried out in panic, "Who are you, boy?"

The child raised its hands again, fully open now.

Widdowson could see dark dribbling marks, in the center of each wrist . . .

Widdowson remembered what night it was, and was flatly and unquestioningly satisfied. He began to fall asleep. But there was one thing he must do. Must write. He fumbled in his pockets and after a long while found a pen. There were carol sheets glimmering white all along the pew, laid out for Midnight Mass.

He just managed to finish writing.

IT WAS a great shock for the churchwardens when they arrived. The door locked unexpectedly, when they were sure they'd left it open, ready. They had to send to the verger for the spare key. And when they put the lights on, there was this man sitting in the front pew. A man who'd been inexplicably sitting in the dark. They called out to him; he did not reply . . .

"Looks like old Widdowson!"

"Never seen *him* in church before!"

But they were trembling as they walked up to him.

"Mr. Widdowson!"

"He's dropped off!"

They shook him gently. The awful coldness of his face told them he was dead.

He just sat staring, staring at the wooden angel that held up the lectern and the Bible—an angel with a white-painted robe and long, golden hair. It was about four feet tall, about the size of a child, with upraised hands to support the Bible above its head . . .

"Good God!"

"He's . . . smiling."

"Grimacing . . . Musta been his heart."

"Poor old bugger, he was a good age."

"About eighty-five."

"Not a bad innings . . ."

"I'm glad the women didn't walk in and find him. Go and ring the police. I'll keep the women out of the church. Enough to ruin their Christmas. Here . . . what's this? He's written something."

"Don't touch it. Leave it for the coroner."

"It's not a suicide note—it's a sort of will."

About my money—give it all to the children. Signed, T. F. Widdowson.

"Not much of a will—that won't stand up in court. Not witnessed, is it?"

"And I bet he's left a packet, too. Go on, go and ring the police. I'll stay with him."

TERENCE FAIRFAX WIDDOWSON was found by the coroner to have died from a massive infarction of the heart, probably brought on by undue exertion.

The will he left in the church was not granted probate, lacking any witnesses that he was "of sound testamentary disposition." His earlier will prevailed. Thomas the cat has been well looked after, but finds it difficult to find a draft-free spot to settle in in his new home.

The antiques business was sold as a going concern; it still has Widdowson's name over the door, but a new man sits in the gilded cage.

AUTHOR'S NOTE: *I apologize to the antique dealer of Beaminster, whose shop, complete in every detail, I have borrowed for this story. I know nothing of the real owner except that he or she sells very good clocks.*

GIFTS FROM
THE SEA

THE NEXT BOMB was the closest yet. Its slow, descending screech got louder and louder and louder.

Brian began to count under his breath. If you were still counting when you reached ten, you knew it hadn't blown you to pieces. He stared at the curving white wall of the shelter, the candle flickering in its saucer. The last things he might ever see on this earth . . .

Seven, eight, nine . . . the bunk he was lying on kicked like a horse. The candle fell over and rolled around the saucer, still burning, and starting to drip wax onto the little table. From the top bunk, his mother reached with a nearly steady hand and set it upright again. They listened to the sound of falling bricks as a house collapsed, the rain of wood and broken slates pattering down on the road and thudding onto the earth on top of their shelter.

"Some poor bugger's gotten it," said Mam.

After the all-clear had sounded, they climbed out wearily into the dawn and saw which poor bugger had gotten it. Number 10 was just a pile of bricks. Eight and

12 had lost their windows and half the slates off their roofs. The road was littered. A big black dog was running around in circles, barking at everything and everybody. An ambulance was just disappearing around the corner of the road, and a crowd of people were breaking up, where number 10 had been. Dad came across, filthy in his warden's uniform. Mam stared at his face silently, biting her lip.

"It's all right, hinny." He grinned, teeth very white in his black face. "They were in the shelter. We got them out. They're not hurt. But she cried when she saw what was left of her house."

"She kept it like a little palace," said Mam. "She was that proud of it."

Dad looked up at the sky, the way the German bombers had gone.

"Aye, well," he said, "the R.A.F. lads got one of the buggers."

They trailed around to the back door of their house. The kitchen seemed just as they'd left it; only a little jug with roses on it had fallen on the floor and broken into a hundred fragments.

"That was a wedding present," said Mam. "Your Auntie Florrie gave us that." She bent down wearily and began picking up the pieces.

But it was when they opened the front-room door that they gasped. The windows were still whole and the curtains intact. But everything else was just heaps of whiteness, as if there'd been a snowstorm.

"Ceiling's down," said Dad. Brian stared up at where the ceiling had been. Just an interesting pattern of inch-wide laths, nailed to the joists. Dad ran upstairs and shouted that the bedroom ceilings were down, too.

"Eeh, what a mess," said Mam. "How we ever going to get this straight?" Brian could tell she was on the verge of tears. "Me best room. Where can I put the vicar now, if he calls . . ."

"Just thank God you've still got a house to clean, hinny," said Dad gently. "But," he added, looking at Brian, "*you'd* better go and stay at your gran's, till we get this lot cleared up."

AN HOUR LATER, still unwashed, still without breakfast, Brian was on the little electric train down to the coast. He had Mam's real-leather attaché case on the seat beside him, with a change of underpants, pajamas, a hot-water bottle, and his five best Dinky toys. He felt empty and peculiar, but excited. An adventure; you couldn't say he was running away like those evacuee kids. Gran, at the coast, was nearer the Jerry bombers than home. It was more like a holiday; no school for a week. And even more like a holiday because he was setting out before most kids were up. The train was full of men going to work in the shipyards. Blackened overalls and the jackets of old pin-stripe suits; greasy caps pulled down over their eyes as they dozed. Everybody grabbed a nap when they could these days. But they all looked like his dad, so he felt quite safe with them.

He turned and looked out of the window, down at the river far below. Greasy old river, with brilliant swirls of oil on it. Packed with ships, docked three-deep on each bank. Big tankers; the rusty gray shapes of destroyers and corvettes. Already some welders were at work, sending down showers of brilliant electric-blue sparks, like fireworks in the dull gray morning.

Britain can make it, thought Brian. Britain can take it.

He often heard Mr. Churchill talking inside his head, especially when he felt tired or fed up. It helped.

The man beside him spoke to the man opposite. "Aah see Gateshead's playin' Manchester City on Saturday."

"Andy Dudgeon'll hold them."

"City's good . . ."

"Andy'll still hold them."

Brian was last to get out. At Tynemouth. He walked down empty Front Street, sniffing the smell of the sea that came to greet him. *Just* like being on holiday. A wagon was delivering milk. Brian felt so good and grownup he almost stopped and told the milkman all about being bombed. But only a kid would've done that, so he only said good morning.

GRAN GAVE HIM a good breakfast. She cut her toast much thicker than Mam, and always burned the edges in an interesting way because she toasted it with a fork on the open fire. It tasted strongly of soot, but there was a huge lump of butter in the dish that made up for it. He didn't ask where the butter had come from; he'd just be told that Granda knew a feller who worked down the docks.

After breakfast he helped Granda hoist the Union Jack on the radio mast in front of the row of Coast Guard cottages on the cliff. An act of defiance against Hitler. Granda ran it up the pole, broke out the tightly wrapped bundle with a vigorous tug on the rope. The flag fluttered bravely in the wind. Granda said "God save the King" and they both saluted the flag. Then Granda said "God help the workers," but that was just a joke. They always did it the same, when he stayed with Granda. Then Granda went to work, and Gran got out the washtub and the poss-stick, it being Monday morning, and started thumping the washing in the water as if Fatty Goering was somewhere down there in a midget submarine.

Washday was no time to be in the house. Wet wash hung in front of the fire, steam billowed, the windows misted up, and even your hands felt damp. Brian got out, followed by a yell that twelve o'clock was dinnertime.

Everything was terribly *early*. Brian felt hopelessly ahead of himself. Still, he had plenty of *plans*. First he called at the school, to stand grandly outside the railings and watch the local kids being marched in, and feel *free* himself. Then he went on to tour the defenses: the sandbagged antiaircraft pom-poms on the seafront. He spent a long time hovering from foot to foot, enjoying the guns' shining, oily evilness, till a grumpy sentry asked him why he wasn't in school.

Then he headed down the pier. The pier was like a road, running half a mile out into the gray of the sea. It was like walking on the water. It was like walking into the wide blue yonder, like the song of the U.S. Army Air Corps. It was like playing dare with the Nazis, across the sea in Norway. It was even better when waves were breaking over the granite wall, as they were today. You tiptoed along, listening for the sound of the next wave, and if you were lucky you just managed to duck down behind the wall before the wave broke, and stayed dry. Otherwise, you got soaked to the skin, all down your front.

He dodged successfully all the way, feeling more and more omnipotent. At the far end he stood in the shelter of the enormous lighthouse and watched an armed trawler put to sea. It came speeding up the smooth water of the estuary, and then pitched like a bucking bronco as it was hit by the first sea wave. The wind blew its sooty smell right up to him, with the smell of grilling kippers from the galley chimney. Soot, salt, wind, spray, and kippers blew around his head, so that he shouted out loud for joy, and waved to the men on the deck; and one of them waved back.

And then he suddenly felt lonely, out there so close to Hitler. Getting back to land was harder and scarier. The waves might creep up behind your back; so might a German bomber. They'd machine-gunned the lighthouse before now; they would machine-gun anything that moved, and most things that didn't. He took much longer getting back to shore, running sideways like a crab, looking back over his shoulder for waves and Germans.

At the end of the pier he met a dog, on the loose like himself. A big Alsatian, all wet and spiky-haired from swimming in the river, and thirsting for mischief. It shook itself all over him, then put its paws on his shoulders and licked his face with a long, smooth, pinky-purple tongue.

Then it stood by the steps down to the rocks and barked encouragingly. Brian stood doubtful. It was good fun going around the tumbled rocks at the base of the Castle Cliff, but risky. The cliff was brown and flaky and crumbling; there'd been rock slides. When his dad was a boy it had been called Queen Victoria's Head because, seen sideways, it had looked just like the profile of the Old Queen on a coin: nose, chin, bust, everything. Then the cliff had fallen and the Queen was gone, and now the cliff looked like nothing at all.

The boulders at the foot were huge and green with seaweed, with narrow cracks in between, where you could trap and break your ankle. And if you trapped your ankle or broke it, and you were alone except for a dog that didn't know you, you would just have to lie there till the tide came in and drowned you and swept your body out to sea. Nobody else walked around Castle Cliff rocks on a weekday . . .

The dog barked, insisting. Brian looked at the line of damp on the rocks, and decided the tide was still going out.

He followed the dog onto the rocks, waving his arms wildly as he leaped from boulder to boulder, and his hobnailed boots slithered on the green seaweed and only came to a crunching stop in the nick of time, as they met a patch of white barnacles.

But almost immediately he was glad he'd come. He began to find things brought in by the tide. First a glass fishing float, caught in a veil of black, tarry net. He scrabbled aside the net; underneath, the float was thick, dark green glass, half the size of a football. He dropped it inside his shirt, where it lay cool and damp against his belt, because he had to have both hands free for the rocks. Mam would like the glass float for her mantelpiece; it would help make up for the damage the Nazis had done to her house.

Then there was a funny dark piece of wood, about as big as an owl. At some time it had had a bolt driven through it, for there was a dark round hole, like an eye, at one end. It had been burned, too. It had ridged feathers of damp blue-black shiny charcoal. Brian looked out to sea, remembering ships bombed and burned and sunk by the Nazi bombers, within sight of the shore . . .

But the sea, and the grinding rocks, had worn the lump of wood into the shape of folded wings and a tail, so that when he held it upright in his hand, it *did* look like a bird, with a round dark eye each side of its head. The dog thought it looked like a bird, too. It ran up, barking frantically, and neatly snatched the bird from his hand with one slashing grab. Then it discovered it was only wet wood and let it drop. It barked at it some more, then looked at Brian, head on one side, baffled.

He picked it up and held it out at arm's length again, waggling it to make it look alive. And again the dog thought it was a bird, and leaped and grabbed. Then dropped it, shaking its head vigorously, to get the sharp taste of salt out of its mouth.

He threw it for the dog, as far toward the sea as he could. It hit a boulder and leaped in the air with a hollow clonk. On the rebound, the dog caught it and slithered wildly down a sloping rock, ending up with a splash in a deep rock pool. It brought the piece of wood back to him, and shook itself all over him, soaking him anew.

The fourth time he threw it, it clonked down a crack in the rocks and vanished out of sight. The dog tried to get down after it, but couldn't, and stood barking instead. Brian was suddenly sad; he would have liked to take it home and give it to his dad. His dad might have set it on a base and varnished it and put it on the mantelpiece. His dad liked things like that. As he stood, he heard the cautious voice of his dad inside his head telling him to be careful, or he'd be a long time dead. It made him check on the state of the tide, but he was sure it was still going out.

He explored more cautiously after that. Found evil-smelling cods' heads from the fish gutting, hollow-eyed like skulls, with teeth sharp and brown as a mummified alligator. He sniffed at the stink of rotting flesh, was nearly sick, and sniffed more gently a second time, till finally he could stand the smell without being sick. It was part of toughening yourself up for the War Effort . . .

And then he found the patch of limpets, clinging to a rock. He hovered again. Limpets were his great temptation. They clung to the rocks so hard you might have thought them stuck there forever with glue. But he'd found out long ago they weren't. Under the shallow cone of the ribbed shell was a sort of snail which clung to the rock with a great big sucker-foot. If the limpet heard or felt you coming, it put on maximum suction and you'd never get it off the rock. But if you crept up quietly, you could get the blade of your knife under it before it knew you were there, and you could flick it off upside down into the palm of your hand.

And there it was, all pale soft folds, gently writhing in its bed of liquid, all beautiful with its two eyes coming out on stalks, like snails' eyes . . . It somehow gave him a squishy feeling, like the photos of semi-nude girls at the Windmill Theatre in London, which he snitched out of *Picture Post* after his parents had read it, and which he hid in an old tobacco tin of his father's, under a pile of his own *War Illustrated*s.

He took his fill, till the feeling wore off, and then he carefully chose a smooth wet patch of rock and put the limpet back on it, right way up. He tested it; the limpet had resumed its grip on the rock, but only feebly. When the tide came back in, the waves might knock it off, and whirl it around and smash it . . . He felt somehow terribly, terribly guilty and wished he hadn't done it. But he could never resist, till afterwards.

The dog barked impatiently, summoning him on, not understanding why he was wasting the wonderful morning. He scrambled on after it, trying to stop worrying about the limpet.

THEY CAME AROUND Castle Cliff at last, safe into King Edward's Bay. Little, snug, a sun trap his dad had called it, when they came down for the day before the war. Chock-full of bathers then, deck chairs, ice-cream kiosks, and places where you could get a tray of tea for a shilling, and a shilling back on the crockery afterwards.

Not now. Totally empty.

And divided into two halves by the wire—huge rolls of barbed wire, stretching like serpents from cliff to cliff. Inland of the wire, the beach was dead mucky, full of footmarks, dropped cigarette butts, rusting, broken bits of buckets and spades. People still came here for a smell of the briny, even in wartime. Holidays-at-home . . . the government organized it . . . Fat girls in their pre-war frocks, dancing with each other in the open air on the promenade to the music of the local army band in khaki uniform—pretending they were having a hell of a good time, and hoping one of the band would pick them up afterwards . . .

Seawards of the wire, the beach was clean, smooth, pure, washed spotless by the outgoing tide. Sometimes the waves, at the highest tides, passed through the wire. Nothing else did. For there were notices with a skull and crossbones, warning of the minefields buried under the sand to kill the invading Jerries, or at least blow their legs off.

Unfortunately, the dog could not read. It went straight up to the wire and began to wriggle through, waggling its hips like a girl trying to catch a soldier's eye. Brian shouted at the dog, leaping up and down, frantic. Feeling responsible, feeling he'd brought it here. Forgetting *it* had brought *him*.

The dog took no notice. It finished its wriggling and leaped gaily onto the clean, wet, flat sand. It became sort of drunk with space and wetness and flatness, tearing around in ever-increasing circles, cornering so sharply its feet slid and it nearly fell on its side. Brian waited terrified for the small savage flash and explosion, braced to see large, furry, bloody bits of dog fly through the air, as if they were legs of pork in a butcher's shop before the war.

But nothing happened. The dog changed its tactics and began dive-bombing bits of wreckage that were strewn about, leaping high in the air and coming down hard with all four feet together. Throwing things up in the air and catching them.

Why didn't the mines go off? That dog was as heavy as a grown man . . . Then Brian looked at the sand under the wire. There were all sizes of dog tracks running through it. The dogs of the town had obviously found out something the humans didn't know.

There were no mines. The army couldn't afford them. All they could afford were notices warning of mines. Then the people who read them would think they could sleep safe in their beds at night, thinking the mines were protecting them from the Germans.

Fakes. Like the fake wooden antiaircraft guns that Tommy Smeaton had found up the coast toward Blyth, guarded by a single sentry against the English kids who might wreck them. Fakes, like the airfields full of plywood Spitfires that kids played in around the Firth of Forth . . .

Brian didn't know whether to laugh or cry.

Then he followed the dog through the wire. Ran around in circles with it, teasing it with a long lump of seaweed. Jumped up and down, expecting still, with a strange half thrill, that there would be a bang under his feet at any moment, and he would go sailing through the air . . .

No bangs. He sat down breathless, and all that happened was that the damp sand soaked through the seat of his shorts.

When he got his breath back, he began to explore along the tide line. Oh, glory, what a haul! A sodden sheepskin boot with a zipper down the front, obviously discarded by a pilot who'd had to ditch in the sea. And it was a size 7, and the 7 had a strange crossbar on it, which meant it was Continental. A German pilot's boot!

Then he found a dull brown tin that clearly said it contained ship's biscuits. Iron rations, floated from the lifeboat of some sunken ship! British, so not poisoned, like people said German things were. He'd take them home to Mam.

A cork life jacket, good as new. Oh, glory, what a place for war souvenirs, and not a kid in the whole town must know about it! A near-new shaving brush for Dad . . . German or British, it didn't matter. Dad's old one was pre-war, and nearly worn down to a stump.

His shirt front began to bulge like a lady who was having a baby. Seawater ran down under his belt, down the front of his shorts, but he didn't care. A brier pipe, an aluminum pan without a dent, a good broom head, a lovely silver-backed mirror. He had his pockets stuffed, his hands full, things tucked under both armpits, so he could hardly walk. In the end he had to make dumps of useful stuff every few yards above the tide line. He couldn't carry everything home all at once; he must hide some, bury some in the dry sand, and come back for it later.

The last find took his breath away. A violin in its case. The strings had gone slack; no sound came when he twanged them, but surely it must be worth a shilling or two? Dad would know.

He moved on into sudden shadow. He looked up and saw that he was nearly at the foot of the far cliff. Where the Mermaid's Cave was.

Nobody called it the Mermaid's Cave but him. He had found it in the last year of peace. There was nothing in it but a long floor of wet, glistening pebbles, full of the smell of the sea. But each pebble glowed wonderfully in the blue-lit gloom. It was a miraculous place—the kind of place where you might expect to find a mermaid . . . if anywhere on earth.

Not that, at thirteen, he believed in mermaids anymore. Only in soppy poems they taught you at junior school. "The Forsaken Merman." Hans Christian Andersen's "Little Mermaid." And his cousin George's R.A.F. joke, about what are a mermaid's vital statistics . . . 38–22–18 pennies a pound!

But he wished there *were* mermaids. He had a daydream about coming into the cave and surprising one combing her long blond hair down to half conceal her rosy breasts, as in fairy-tale books or the photos from the Windmill Theatre. It would be nice to . . . His mind always sheered away from what it would be nice to do with her.

Ah, well. No mermaids now. Just war souvenirs. You couldn't have everything, and already today had been better than Christmas. Still, he'd look inside, like he always had. Might be a lump of Jerry airplane or something . . .

There was *something*. Something long and pale, stretched out. Almost like a person lying there . . .

Barmy! Things always changed into something else when you walked right up to them boldly. But that could almost be a long leg, a long bare leg, as shapely as the girls' at the Windmill.

He shot upright so hard he banged his head painfully on the rock roof. But when he opened his eyes after the agony, she was still there. The Mermaid. Her hair was gracefully swirled across the pebbles, the way the sea had left her. Her wide gray eyes were looking straight at him, with an air of appeal. Her face was pale, but quite untouched. She'd been wearing a dress, but there wasn't that much left of it. Just enough to pass the censors at the Windmill.

Transfixed, he slowly reached out and touched her. Her face was cold. Not human cold, like when somebody comes in from a winter's day or has been bathing. No, she was as cold as a vase full of water. As cold as a thing that is not alive.

Dead. But death and the sea had been kind to her; and to him. Nothing had touched her except the thing that had killed her. If there had been blood, the sea had washed it away on her voyage ashore. She was dead, but she was entirely beautiful. She was beautiful, but entirely dead. On the beautiful pebbles of the cave, with her hair around her. No smell but the clean smell of the sea. She might have been a lovely ship's figurehead, washed ashore after a shipwreck.

He just stood and stared and stared. She must have come off some ship. What was she? Norwegian, Dutch, Danish? Sometimes their coasters carried the captain's wife and family.

He was there a long time. Somehow he knew that once

he moved, nothing would ever be the same again. She would change into something else, like the piece of wood that wasn't a bird; like the minefield that wasn't really a minefield.

He would have liked to take her home.

He would have liked to keep her here, and come to see her often.

But he was a realist in the end. He remembered the cods' heads on the rocks. Once he moved, they would put her in a hole in the ground. Once he moved, she would only exist on a written form. And she was so beautiful, here in her cave . . .

He might have stayed . . . how long? But he heard the roar of the waves, the roar of the returning tide. He ran out in a panic. Waves were starting to stream up the beach, and the dog was nowhere to be seen.

He began to run up the beach. There was a khaki-clad figure on the cliff, striding to and fro on sentry duty. Brian waved and shouted, and then began to cry as he ran.

He had no idea why he was crying. All the rest of his life, he could never quite work out why he had been crying.

THE CREATURES
IN THE HOUSE

DAWN BROKE OVER Southwold seafront.

The wind was blowing against the waves; white horses showed all the way to the horizon—smaller and smaller as if painted by some obsessional Dutch marine artist. On the horizon itself sat a steamship, square as a pan on a shelf, scarcely seeming to move.

Seafront deserted; beach huts huddled empty in the rain. The only movement was a flaking flap of house paint on the pier pavilion, tearing itself off in the wind.

Miss Forbes opened her eyes on her last day. Eyes gray and empty as the sea. She eased her body in the velvet reclining rocker in the bay window—luxurious once, now greased in black patches from the day and night shifting of her body. It was some years since she had been to bed. Beds meant sheets and sheets meant washing . . . She seldom left the bay window. She took her food off the front doorstep and straight onto the occasional table by her side. Once a week she took the remains to the dustbin. Otherwise, there were just the trips to the toilet, and the weekly journey to the dripping tap in the kitchen for a pink-rosed pitcherful of water. She opened her eyes and looked at the sea and wondered what month it was. Her mind was clearer this morning than for a long time. The creature in the house had not fed on her mind for a week. There wasn't much of Miss Forbes's mind left to feed on. A few shreds of memory from the forties; a vague guilt at things not done. The creature itself was weakening. The creature knew a time would come soon when it had nothing to feed on at all. Then it would have to hibernate, like a dormouse or hedgehog. But first the creature must provide for its future, while there was still time. There was something Miss Forbes had to do . . .

She rose shakily, after trying to straighten thick stockings of two different shades of gray. She went out into the hall, picked up the 1968 telephone directory, and, her eyes squinting two inches off the page, looked up the solicitor's number.

She had difficulty making the solicitor's girl understand who she was—an old-standing client and a wealthy one. She mentioned the name of partner after partner . . . Old Mr. Sandbach had been dead twenty years . . . Young Mr. Sandbach retired last spring. Yes, she supposed Mr. Mason would have to do . . . Eleven o'clock?

Then she slowly climbed the stairs, slippered feet carving footprints in dust thicker than the worn stair carpet. In what had once been her bedroom she opened the mirrored wardrobe door, not even glancing at her reflection as it swung out at her.

She began to wash and comb and dress. With spells of sitting down to rest, it took three hours. The creature had to lend her its own waning strength. Even then, Miss Forbes scarcely managed. The creature itself nearly despaired.

But between them they coped. At half past ten, Miss Forbes rang for a taxi, the ancient black stick phone trembling in her hand.

The taxi driver watched her awestruck in his rearview mirror. Two things clutched tightly in her gloved hand. A door key and a big lump of wallpaper with something scrawled on the back in a big childish hand. Like all his kind, he was good at reading things backwards in his mirror.

"I leave all my worldly possessions to my niece, Martha Vickers, providing she is unmarried and living alone at the time of my death. On condition that she agrees, and continues, to reside alone at 17 Marine Parade. Or if she is unable or unwilling to comply with my wishes, I leave all my possessions to my great-niece, Sarah Anne Walmsley . . ."

The taxi driver shuddered. *He'd* settle for a heart attack at seventy . . .

"SUPPOSE I SPEND all the money, sell the house, and run?" asked Sally Walmsley. "I mean, what's to stop me?"

"Me, I'm afraid," said Mr. Mason, wiping the thick fur of dust off the hall stand of 17 Marine Parade, and settling his plump pin-striped bottom. "We are the executors of your aunt's estate . . . We shall have to keep *some* kind of eye on you . . . It could prove unpleasant . . . I hope it won't come to that. Suppose you and I have dinner about once every six months and you tell me what you've been up to . . ." He smiled tentatively, sympathetically. He liked this tall thin girl with green eyes and long, black hair. "Of course, you could contest the will. It wouldn't stand up in court a moment. I couldn't *swear* your aunt was in her right mind the morning she made it. Not of sound testamentary capacity, as we say. But if you break the will, it would have to be shared with all your female aunts and cousins—married and unmarried. You'd get about three thousand each—not a lot."

"Stuff *them*," said Sally Walmsley. "I'll keep what I've got." She suddenly felt immensely weary. The last six months had happened so fast. Deciding to walk out of art school. Walking out of art school. Trailing around London looking for work. Getting a break as assistant art editor of *New Woman*. And then lovely Tony Harrison of production going back to his fat, frigid, suburban cow of a wife. And then this . . .

"I must be off," said Mr. Mason, getting off the hall stand and surveying his bottom for dust in the spotted, stained mirror. But he lingered in the door, interminably, as if guilty about leaving her. "It was a strange business . . . I've dealt with a lot of old ladies, but your aunt . . . She looked . . . faded. Not potty, just *faded*. I kept on having to shout at her to bring her back to herself.

"The milkman found her, you know. When the third bottle of milk piled up on her doorstep. He always had the rule to let three bottles pile up. Old ladies can be funny. She might have gone away. But there she was, sitting in the bay window, gray as dust.

"He seems to have been her only human contact— money and scribbled notes pushed into the milk bottles. She lived on what he brought—bread, butter, eggs, yogurt, cheese, orange juice. She seems to have never tried to cook—drank the eggs raw after cracking them into a cup.

"But she didn't die of malnutrition . . . The coroner said it was a viable diet, though not a desirable one. Didn't die of hypothermia, either. It was a cold week in March, but the gas fire was full on, and the room was like an oven . . ." He paused, as if an unpleasant memory had struck him. "In fact, the coroner couldn't find any cause of death at all. He said she just seemed to have faded away . . . Put down good old natural causes. Well, I must be off. If there's any way I can help . . ."

Sally nearly said, "Please don't go." But that would have been silly. So she smiled politely while he smiled, too, bobbed his head, and left.

Sally didn't like that at all. She listened to the silence in the house, and her skin crawled.

A primitive man, a bushman or aborigine, would have recognized that crawling of the skin. Would have left the spot immediately. Or if the place had been important to him, a cave or spring of water, he would have returned with other primitive men and performed certain rituals. And then the creature would have left.

But Sally simply told herself not to be a silly fool, and forced herself to explore.

The library was books from floor to ceiling. Avant-garde—fifty years ago. Marie Stopes, Havelock Ellis, the early Agatha Christie, Shaw, and Wells. Aunt Maude had been a great reader, a Girton girl, a bluestocking. So what had she read the last ten years? For the fur of dust lay over the books as it lay over everything else. And there wasn't a magazine or paper in the house. So what had she *done* with herself, never going out, doing all her business by mail, never putting stamps on her letters till the bank manager began sending her books of stamps of his own volition. Even the occasional plumber or meter reader had never seen her; only a phone message and the front door open, with scrawled instructions pinned to it . . .

Aunt Maude might as well have been a cloistered nun . . .

But the house with its wood-planked walls, its red-tiled roof, its white gothic pinnacles, balconies, and many bay windows was not in bad shape—nowhere near falling down. Nothing fresh paint wouldn't cure. And there was plenty of money. And the furniture was fabulously Victorian. Viennese wall clocks, fit only for the junk shop twenty years ago, would fetch hundreds now, once their glass cases were cleared of cobwebs and their brass pendulums of verdigris. And the dining-room furniture was Sheraton, genuine, eighteenth-century Sheraton. Oh, she could make it such a place . . . where people would bother to come, even from London. Everybody liked a weekend by the sea. Even Tony Harrison . . . She thrust the thought down savagely. But what a challenge, bringing the place back to life.

So why did she feel like crying? Was it just the dusk of a November afternoon, the rain-runneled dirt on the windows?

She reached the top of the house—a storeroom under the roof with sloping ceiling, and a yellow stained-glass window at one end that made it look as if the sun was always shining outside, and the massed brick of the chimney stacks at the other. A long, narrow, tall room— a wrong room that made her want to slam the door and run away. Instead, she made herself stand and *analyze* her feelings. Simple, really: the stained glass was alienating; the shape of the room was uncomfortable, making you strain upward and giving you a humiliating crick in the neck. Simple, really, when you had art-school training, an awareness of the psychology of shape and color.

She was still glad to shut the door, go downstairs to the kitchen with its still-dripping tap, and make herself a cup of tea. She left all the rings of the gas stove burning. *And* the oven. Soon the place was as warm as a greenhouse . . .

. . .

IN THE DARKEST corner of the narrow storeroom, far-thest from the stained-glass window where the sun always seemed to shine, up near the gray-grimed ceiling, the creature stirred in its sleep. It was not the fiercest or strongest of its kind—not quite purely spirit, or rather decayed from pure spirit. It could pass through the wood and glass of doors and windows easily, but it had difficulty with brick and stonework. That was why it had installed Miss Forbes in the bay window; so it could feed on her quickly when it returned hungry from its long journeys. It fed on humankind, but not all humankind. It found workmen in the house quite unbearable—like a herd of trampling, whistling, swearing elephants. Happy families were worse, especially when the children were noisy. It only liked women, yet would have found a brisk Women's Institute meeting an unbearable hell. It fed on women alone, women in despair. It crept subtly into their minds, when they slept or tossed and worried in the middle of the night, peeling back the protective shell of their minds that they didn't even know they had—rather as a squirrel cracks a nut, or a thrush a snail shell—patient, not hurrying, delicate, persistent . . .

Like all wise parasites it did not kill its hosts. Miss Forbes had lasted it forty years; Miss Forbes's great-aunt had lasted nearer sixty.

Now it was awake, and hungry.

SALLY HUGGED her third mug of tea between her hands and stared out of the kitchen window, at the long, dead grass and scattered dustbins of the November garden. The garden wall was fifty yards away, sooty brick. There was nothing else to see. She had the conviction that her new life had stopped, that her clockwork was running down. I could stand here forever, she thought in a panic. I must go upstairs and make up a bed; there was plenty of embroidered lavendered Edwardian linen in the drawers. But she hadn't the energy.

I could go out and spend the night in a hotel. But which hotels would be open in Southwold in November? She knew there was a phone, but the post office had cut it off.

Just then, something appeared suddenly on top of the sooty wall, making her jump. One moment it wasn't there; next moment it was.

A gray cat. A tomcat, from the huge size of its head and thickness of shoulder.

It glanced this way and that, then lowered its forefeet delicately down the vertical brick of the wall, leaped, and vanished into the long grass.

She waited; it reappeared, moving through the long grass with a stalking lope so like a lion's and so unlike a cat indoors. It went from dustbin to dustbin, sniffing inside each in turn, without hope and without success. She somehow knew it did the same thing every day, at the same time. It had worn tracks through the grass.

Hard luck, she thought, as the cat found nothing. Then, spitefully: Sucker! She hated the cat, because its search for food was so like her own search for happiness.

The cat sniffed inside the last bin unavailingly, and was about to depart, empty-handed.

Welcome to the club, thought Sally bitterly.

It was then that the hailstorm came—out of nowhere, huge hailstones, slashing, hurting. The tomcat turned, startled, head and paw upraised, snarling as if the hailstorm was an enemy of its own kind, as if to defend itself against this final harshness of life.

Sally felt a tiny surge of sympathy.

It was almost as if the cat sensed it. It certainly turned toward the kitchen window and saw her for the first time. And immediately ran toward her, and leaped onto the lid of a bin directly under the window, hailstones belting small craters in its fur, and its mouth open—red tongue and white teeth exposed in a silent miaow that was half defiance and half appeal.

You can't let this happen to me.

It made her feel like God, the God she had often screamed and wept and appealed to, and never had an answer.

I am *kinder* than God, she thought in sad triumph, and ran to open the kitchen door.

The cat streaked in, and, finding a dry shelter, suddenly remembered its dignity. It shook itself violently, then shook the wetness off each paw in turn, as a kind of symbol of disgust with the weather outside, then began vigorously to belabor its shoulder with a long, pink tongue.

But not for long. Its nose began to twitch, began to twitch quite monstrously. It turned its head, following the twitch, and leaped gently onto the kitchen table, where a packet lay wrapped in paper.

A pound of minced beef, bought in town earlier and forgotten. Sally sat down, amused, and watched. All right, she thought, if you can get it, you can have it.

The cat tapped and turned the parcel, as if it were a living mouse. Seemed to sit and think for a moment, then got its nose under the packet and with vigorous shoves propelled it to the edge of the table and sent it thumping onto the stone floor.

It was enough to burst the paper the butcher had put around it. The meat splattered across the stone floor with all the gory drama of a successful hunt. The cat leaped down and ate steadily, pausing only to give Sally the occasional dark suspicious stare, and growling under its breath.

O.K., thought Sally. You win. I'd never have got around to cooking it tonight, and there isn't a fridge . . .

The cat extracted and hunted down the last red crumb, and then began exploring the kitchen—pacing along the counters, prying open the darkness of the cupboards with an urgent paw.

There was an arrogance about him, a sense of taking possession, that could only make her think of one thing to call him.

When he finally sat down, to wash and survey her with blank dark eyes, she called softly, "Boss? Boss?"

He gave a short and savage purr and leaped straight onto her knee, trampling her about with agonizing sharp claws, before finally settling in her lap, facing outward, front claws clenched into her trousered knees. He was big but painfully thin. His haunches felt like bone knives under his matted fur. The fat days must be in the summer, she thought sleepily, with full dustbins behind every hotel. What do they do in November?

He should have been an agony; but strangely he was a comfort. The gas stove had made the room deliciously warm. His purring filled her ears.

They slept, twisted together like symbiotic plants, in a cocoon of contentment.

THE CREATURE SENSED her sleep. It drifted out of the storeroom and down the intricately carved staircase, like a darkening of the shadows—a dimming of the faint beams that crept through the filthy gauze curtains from a distant streetlamp.

Boss did not sense it, until it entered the kitchen. A she-cat would have sensed it earlier. But Boss saw it, as Sally would never see it. His claws tightened in Sally's knee; he rose up and arched his back and spat, ears laid back against his skull. Sally whimpered in her sleep, trying to soothe him with a drowsy hand. But she didn't waken . . .

Cat and creature faced each other. Boss felt no fear, as a human might. Only hate at an intruder, alien, enemy.

And the creature felt Boss's hate. Rather as a human might feel a small stone that has worked its way inside a shoe. Not quite painful; not enough to stop for, but a distraction.

The creature could not harm Boss; their beings had nothing in common. But it could press on his being, press abominably.

It pressed.

Boss leaped off Sally's knee. If a door had been open, or a window, Boss would have fled. But no door or window was open. He ran frantically here and there, trying to escape the black pressure, and finally ended up crouched in the corner under the sink, protected on three sides by brick, but silenced at last.

Now the creature turned its attention to Sally, probing at the first layer of her mind.

Boss, released, spat and swore terribly.

It was as if, for the creature, the stone in the shoe had turned over, exposing a new sharp edge.

The creature, exploding in rage, pressed too hard on the outer layer of Sally's mind.

Sally's dream turned to nightmare—a nightmare of a horrible female thing with wrinkled dugs and lice in her long gray hair. Sally woke, sweating.

The creature was no longer there.

Sally gazed woozy-eyed at Boss, who emerged from under the sink, shook himself, and immediately asked to be let out the kitchen door. Very insistently. Clawing at the woodwork.

Sally's hand was on the handle when a thought struck her. If she let the cat out, she would be *alone*.

The thought was unbearable.

She looked at Boss.

"Hard luck, mate," she said. "You asked to be let in. You've had your supper. Now bloody earn it!"

As if he sensed what she meant, Boss gave up his attempts on the door. Sally made some tea, and, con- science-stricken, gave Boss the cream off the milk. She looked at her watch. Midnight.

They settled down again.

Three more times that night, the creature tried. Three times with the same result. It grew ever more frantic, clumsy. Three times Sally had nightmares and woke sweating, and made tea.

Boss, on the other hand, was starting to get used to things. The last time, he did not even stir from Sally's knee. Just lay tensely and spat. The black weight of the creature seemed less when he was near the human.

After 3 a.m., cat and girl slept undisturbed. While the creature roamed the stairs and corridors, demented. Perhaps it was beginning to realize that one day, like Miss Forbes and Miss Forbes's great-aunt, it, too, might simply cease to exist; like the corpse of a hedgehog, by a country road, it might slowly blow away into particles of dust.

A WEAK MORNING sunlight cheered the dead grass of the garden. Sally opened a tin of corned beef and gave

Boss cat his breakfast. He wolfed the lot, and then asked again to be let out, with renewed insistence.

Freedom was freedom, thought Sally sadly. Besides, if he didn't go soon, there was liable to be a nasty accident. She watched him go through the grass and reach the top of the wall with a magnificent leap.

Then he vanished, leaving the world totally empty.

She spent four cups of coffee and five cigarettes gathering her wits, then opened her suitcase, washed at the kitchen sink, and set out to face the world.

It wasn't bad. The sky was pale blue, every wave was twinkling like diamonds as it broke on the beach, and her brave new orange Mini stood parked twenty yards down the road.

But it was Boss she watched for—in the tangled front garden; on the immaculate lawn of the house next door.

Then she looked back at number 17, nervously. It looked all right, from here . . .

"Good morning!" The voice made her jump.

The owner of number 16 was straightening up from behind his well-mended fence, a handful of dead brown foliage in one hand.

He was everything she disliked in a man. About thirty. Friendly smile, naïve blue eyes, checked shirt, folk-weave tie. He offered a loamy paw, having wiped it on the seat of his gardening trousers.

"Just moved in, then? My name's Mike Taverner. Dwell here with my mama . . ."

Half an hour later she broke away, her head spinning with a muddling survey of all the best shops in town and what they were best for. The fact that Mr. Taverner was an accountant and therefore worked gentleman's hours. That he was quite handy around the house and that anything he could do . . . But it was his subtly pitying look that was worst.

Stuff him! If *he* thought that *she* was going to ask *him* around for coffee . . .

She spent the day using Miss Forbes's money. A huge flashlight for some reason; a new transistor radio, satisfyingly loud; a checked tablecloth; three new dresses, the most with-it that Southwold could offer. She ordered a new gas stove and fridge, and got the promise that the post office would reconnect her phone tomorrow . . .

She still had to go home in the end.

She put her new possessions on the kitchen table, all in a jumble, and they seemed to shrink to the size of Dinky Toys. The silence of the house pressed on her skin like a cold moist blanket.

But she was firm. Went upstairs and made the bed in the front bedroom with the bay window. Then sat over her plate of bacon and eggs till it congealed solid, smoking cigarette after cigarette. The sounds that came out of the transistor radio seemed like alien code messages from Mars.

She went to bed at midnight, clutching the radio under one arm, and cigarettes, matches, flashlight, magazines with the other.

But before she went, she left the kitchen window open six inches. And a fresh plate of minced beef on the sill. It was like a hundred-to-one bet on the Grand National . . .

BOSS LEFT THE HOUSE determined never to return, and picked up the devious trail through alley and garden, back yard and beach house that marked the edge of his territory. Smelling his old trademarks and renewing them vigorously, he stalked and killed a hungry sparrow in one alley; found some cinder-embedded bacon in another; but that was all. He was soon hungry again.

By the time dusk was falling, and he rendezvoused at the derelict fishermen's hut with his females, he was very hungry indeed. The memory of the black terror had faded; the memory of the raw meat grew stronger.

He sniffed noses and backsides with one of his females in particular, a big scrawny tortoiseshell with hollow flanks and bulging belly. But he could not settle. The memory of the meat grew to a mountain in his mind, a lovely, blood-oozing, salty mountain.

Around midnight, he got up and stretched, and headed out again along his well-beaten track.

Ten yards behind, weak and limping, the tortoiseshell followed. She followed him farther than she had ever ventured before; but she was far more hungry than he was, her plight far more desperate. And she had smelled the rich raw meat on his breath . . .

The creature felt them enter the house; now there were two sharp stones in its shoe.

It had been doing well before they came. Sally had taken a sedative, and lay sleeping on her back, mouth open and snoring, a perfect prey. The creature was feeding gently on the first layer of her mind—lush memories of warmth and childhood, laughter and toys. First food in six months.

Uneasy, suddenly it fed harder, too hard. Sally moaned and swam up slowly from her drugged sleep; sat up and knew with terror that something precious had been stolen from her, was missing, gone forever.

The creature did not let go of her; hung on with all its strength; it was so near to having her completely.

Sally felt as cold as death under the heaped blankets; the sheets were like clammy winding-sheets, strangling, smothering. She fought her way out of them and reeled about the room, seeking blindly for the door in the dark. Warm, she must get warm or . . .

The kitchen . . . gas stove . . . warm. Desperately she searched the walls for the door, in the utter dark. Curtains, windows, pictures swinging and falling under her grasping hands. She was crying, screaming . . . Was there no door to this black room?

Then the blessed roundness of the door handle, which would not turn under her cold, sweating palm, until she folded a piece of her nightdress over it. And then she was going downstairs, half running, half falling, bumping down the last few steps on her bottom, in the dim light of the streetlamp through the grimy curtains . . .

The whole place rocked still in nightmare, because the creature still clung to her mind . . .

Twice she passed the kitchen door, and then she found it and broke through, and banged the light on.

Checked tablecloth; suitcase; tweed coat. Sally's eyes clutched them, as a drowning man clutches straws. The creature felt her starting to get away, struggling back to the real world outside.

But, much worse, the creature felt two pairs of eyes glaring, glaring hate. The tomcat was crouched on the old wood draining board, back arched. But the tom was not the worst. The she-cat lay curled on a pathetic heap of old rags and torn-up newspaper under the sink. And her hatred was utterly immovable. And there were five more small sharp stones now in the creature's shoe. A mild squeaking came from between the she-cat's protective legs. Little scraps of blind fur, writhing . . .

Sally's mind gave a tremendous heave and the creature's hold broke. The creature could not stand the she-cat's eyes, alien, blank, utterly rejecting.

It fled back up the stairs, right to the storeroom, and coiled itself in the dark corner, between a high shelf and the blackened ceiling.

It knew, as it lapsed into chaos, that there was one room in its house where it dared never go again.

Back in the kitchen, Sally closed the door and then the window, and lit all the rings of the gas stove. The tomcat shook itself and rubbed against her legs, wanting milk.

"Kittens," said Sally, "kittens. Oh, you *poor* thing."

At that moment there was nothing in the world she wanted more than kittens. She put on a saucepan and filled it to the brim with milk.

SHE FELT BOSS stir on her knee toward dawn. She opened her eyes and saw him on the windowsill, asking to go out.

"All right," she said reluctantly. She opened the window. She knew now that he would come back. Besides, the purring heap of cat and kittens, now installed on a heap of old curtains in an armchair, showed no sign of wanting to move. She would not be alone . . .

She left the window open. It was not a very cold night, and the room was now too hot, if anything, from the gas stove.

She was awakened at eight, by Boss's pounding savage claws on her lap. He made loud demands for breakfast.

And he was not alone. There was a black-and-white female sitting washing itself on the corner of the table; and a white-and-ginger female was curled up with the mother and kittens, busy washing all and sundry. The aunties had arrived.

"Brought the whole family, have you?" she asked Boss

sourly. "Sure there aren't a few grandmas you forgot?"

He gave a particularly savage purr, and dug his claws deeper into her legs.

"O.K.," she said. "How would some tinned meat loaf do? With sardines for starters?"

By the time they finished, the cupboard was bare. They washed, and Sally ate toast and watched them washing. She thought, I'm bonkers. Only old maids have cats like this. People will think I'm mad. The four cats regarded her with blankly friendly eyes. Somehow it gave her courage to remember the nightmare upstairs . . .

Then the cats rose, one by one. Nudged and nosed each other, stretched, began to mill around.

It reminded her of something she'd once seen—on telly somewhere.

Lionesses, setting off to hunt. That was it. Lionesses setting off to hunt.

But, for God's sake, they'd *had* their breakfast . . .

Boss went to the door and miaowed. Not the kitchen door—the door that led to the nightmare staircase. Mother joined him. And Ginger. And the black-and-white cat she'd christened Checkers.

When she did not open that door, they all turned and stared at her. Friendly; but expectant. Compelling.

My God, she thought. They're going hunting whatever is upstairs. And inviting me to join in . . .

They were the only friends she had. She went; but she picked up Boss before she opened the door. He didn't seem to mind; he settled himself comfortably in her arms, pricking his ears and looking ahead. His body was vibrating. Purr or growl deep in his throat. She could not tell.

The she-cats padded ahead, looked at the doors of the downstairs rooms, then leaped up the stairs. They nosed into everything, talking to each other in their prooky spooky language. They moved as if they were tied to each other and to her with invisible strands of elastic—passing each other, weaving from side to side like a cat's cradle, but never getting too far ahead, or too far apart.

They went from upstairs room to upstairs room, politely standing aside as she opened each door. Leaping onto dust-sheeted beds, sniffing in long-empty chamber pots.

Each of the rooms was empty—dreary, dusty, but totally empty. Sally wasn't afraid. If anything, little tingling excitements ran through her.

The cats turned to the staircase that led to the storeroom in the roof. They were closer together now, their chirrups louder, more urgent.

They went straight to the door of the narrow room, with the yellow stained-glass window which was always sunshiny.

Waited. Braced. Ears back close to the skull.

Sally took a deep breath and flung open the door.

Immediately the cold came, the clammy winding-sheet cold of the night before. The corridor, the stairs twisted and fell together like collapsing stage scenery.

She would have run; but Boss's claws, deep and sharp in her arm, were more real than the cold and the twisting—like an anchor in a storm. She stood. So did the cats, though they crouched close to the floor, huddled together.

Slowly, the cold and twisting faded.

The cats rose and shook themselves, as after a shower of rain, and stalked one by one into the storeroom.

Trembling, Sally followed.

Again the sick cold and twisting came. But it was weaker. Even Sally could tell that. And it didn't last so long.

The cats were all staring at the ceiling at the far end —at a dark gray space between the heavy brickwork of two chimneys, between the ceiling and a high wooden shelf.

Sally stared, too. But all she could see was a mass of cobwebs, black rope-like strands blowing in some draft that came through the slates of the roof.

But she knew that her enemy, the enemy who had stolen from her, was there. And for the first time, because the enemy was now so small, no longer filling the house, she could feel anger, red, healthy anger.

She looked around for a weapon. There was an old short-bristled broom leaning against the wall. She put Boss down and picked it up, and slashed savagely at the swaying cobwebs, until she had pulled every one of them down.

They clung to the broom.

But they were only cobwebs.

Boss gave a long chirrup. Cheerful, pleased, but summoning. Slowly, in obedience, the three she-cats began to back out of the door, never taking their green eyes from the space up near the ceiling.

Sally came last, and closed the door.

They retired to the kittens, in good order.

Back in the storeroom, the creature was absolutely still. It had learned the bitter limitations of its strength. It had reached the very frontier of its existence.

It grew wise.

BACK IN THE KITCHEN, there came a knock on the door.

It was Mr. Taverner. Was she all right? He thought he had heard screams in the night . . .

"It was only Jack the Ripper," said Sally with a flare of newfound spirit. "You're too late—he murdered me."

He had the grace to look woebegone. He had quite a nice lopsided smile, when he was woebegone. So she offered him a cup of coffee.

He sat down and the she-cats climbed all over him, sniffing in his ears with spiteful humor. Standing on his shoulders with their front paws on top of his head . . . He suffered politely, with his lopsided grin. "Have they moved in on you? Once you feed them, they'll never go away . . . They're a menace around Southwold, especially in the winter. I could call the SPCA for you . . . ?"

"They are *my* cats. I *like* cats."

He gave her a funny look. "They'll cost you a bomb to feed . . ."

"I know how much cats cost to feed. And don't think I can't afford to keep a hundred cats if I want to."

Again he had the grace to shut up.

Things went better for Sally after that. Mike Taverner called in quite often, and even asked her to have dinner with his mother. Mrs. Taverner proved to be not an aged burden but a smart fifty-year-old who ran a dress shop, didn't discuss hysterectomies, and watched her son's social antics with a wry, long-suffering smile.

The kittens grew; the house filled with whistling workmen; the Gas Board came finally to install the new stove.

And Sally took to sleeping on the couch of a little breakfast room just off the kitchen, where she could get a glimpse of sea in the mornings, and the cats came and went through the serving hatch.

She slept well, usually with cats coming and going off her feet all night. Sometimes they called sharply to each other, and there was a scurrying of paws, and she would waken smoothly. That noise meant the creature from the storeroom was on the prowl.

But it never tried anything, not with the cats around.

And every day Sally and the cats did their daily patrol into enemy territory. What Sally came to think of, with a nervous giggle, as the bearding of the storeroom.

But the creature never reacted. The patrols became almost a bore, and pairs of cats could be heard chasing each other up and down the first flight of stairs, on their own.

What a crazy life, Sally thought. If Mike Taverner *dreamed* what was going on, what would he say? Once, she even took him on a tour of the house, to admire the new decorations. Took him right into the storeroom. All the cats came, too.

The creature suffered a good deal from Mike's elephantine soul and great booming male voice . . .

But the boundary between victory and defeat is narrow, and usually composed of complacency.

THE LAST NIGHT started so happily. Mike was coming to dinner; well, he was better than *nothing*. Sally, in her newest dress and an apron, was putting the finishing touches to a sherry trifle. A large Scotch sirloin steak lay wrapped in a bloody package on the fridge, handy for the gas stove.

Sally had just nipped into the breakfast room to lay the table when she heard a rustling noise in the kitchen . . .

She rushed back in time to see Boss nosing at the bloody packet.

She should have picked him up firmly, but chose to shoo him away with a wild wave of her arms. Boss, panicking, made an enormous leap for the window. The sherry trifle, propelled by all the strength of his back legs, catapulted across the room and self-destructed on the tile floor in a mess of cream and glass shards a yard wide.

Sally went berserk. Threw Boss out of the back door, threw Checkers after him, and slammed the window in Mother's face, just as Mother was coming in.

That left only the kittens, eyes scarcely open, crawling and squeaking in their basket. She would have some peace for once, to get ready.

Maybe Mike was right. Too many cats. Only potty old maids had so many cats. SPCA . . . good homes.

She never noticed that the kittens had ceased to crawl and squeak and maul each other. That they grew silent and huddled together in one corner of their basket, each trying desperately to get into the middle of the heap of warm furry bodies . . .

She scraped and wiped up the trifle. Made Mike an Instant Whip instead. In a flavor she knew he didn't like. Well, he could lump it. Sitting around her kitchen all day, waiting to have his face fed. Fancy living with *that* face for forty years . . . growing bald, scratching under the armpits of his checked shirt like an ape. He'd only become interested in her seriously when he heard about her money . . . Stuff him. Better to live alone . . .

Mike was unfortunate to ring up at that point. He was bringing wine. Would Châteauneuf-du-Pape do? How smug he sounded; how sure he had her in his grasp.

He made one of his clumsy teasing jokes. She chose to take it the wrong way. Her voice grew sharp. He whined self-righteously in protest. Sally told him what she *really* thought of him. He rang off in high dudgeon, implying he would never bother her again.

Good. Good riddance to bad rubbish. Much better

living on her own in her beautiful house, without a great clumsy corny man in it . . .

But his rudeness had given her a headache. Might as well take a pill and lie down. She suddenly felt cold and really tired . . . sleep it off.

BOSS WAS CRAZY for the sirloin; Mother was very worked up about her kittens; and the window latch was old and rusted. Five minutes' work had the window open. Mother made straight for her kittens and Boss made straight for the meat. Three heaves and he had the packet open, and the kitchen filled with the rich smell of blood. Ginger and Checkers appeared out of nowhere, and Mother, satisfied her brood was safe, rapidly joined them in a baleful circle around the fridge.

They were not aware of the creature, in their excitement. It was in the breakfast room with Sally, behind a closed door and feeding quietly.

But Boss was infuriatedly aware of the other cats, as they stretched up the front of the fridge, trying to claw his prize out of his mouth. He sensed he would have no peace to enjoy a morsel. So, arching his neck magnificently to hold the steak clear of the floor, he leaped down, then up to the windowsill and out into the night.

Unfortunately, it was one of those damp nights that accent every odor; and the faintest of breezes was blowing from the north toward the town center of Southwold. Several hungry noses lifted to the fascinating new scent.

Within a minute, Boss knew he was no longer alone. Frantically he turned and twisted through his well-known alleyways. But others knew them just as well, and the scent was as great a beacon as the circling beams of Southwold's lighthouse. Even the well-fed domestic tabbies, merely out for an airing, caught it. As for the hungry, desperate ones . . .

Boss was no fool. He doubled for home. Came through the window like a rocket, leaving a rich red trail on the yellowed white paintwork, and regained the fridge. Another minute and there were ten strange cats in the room. Two minutes and there were twenty.

Boss leaped for the high shelving in desperate evasion. A whole shelf of pots and pans came down together. The noise defied description, and there were more cats coming in all the time.

Next door, the creature, startled, slipped clumsily in its feeding. Sally came screaming up out of a nightmare and ran for the warmth of her kitchen, the creature still entangled in her mind.

To the creature, the kitchenful of cats was like rolling in broken glass. Silently, it fled to the high shelf in the storeroom.

It was unfortunate for the creature that Boss had very much the same thought. The hall door was ajar. He was through it in a flash and up the stairs, the whole frantic starving mob in pursuit.

Back in the near-empty kitchen, there came a thunderous knocking on the door. It burst open to reveal Mr. Taverner in a not-very-becoming plum-colored smoking jacket. He flung his arms around Sally, demanding wildly to know what the matter was.

Sally could only point mutely upstairs.

By the time they got there, Boss, with slashing claws and hideous growls that filtered past the sirloin steak, was making his last stand in the open storeroom door.

And, confused and bewildered by so many enemies, weak from hunger and shattered by frustration, the creature was cowering up on its shelf, trying to get out into the open air through the thick brickwork of the chimneys. But it was old, old . . .

Boss, turning in desperation from the many claws dabbing at his steak, saw the same high shelf and leaped.

Thirty pairs of ravening cat eyes followed him.

The creature knew, for the first time in its ancient existence, how it felt to be prey . . .

It lost all desire to exist.

Nobody heard the slight popping noise, because of the din. But suddenly there was a vile smell, a rubbish heap, graveyard, green-water smell.

And the house was empty of anything but dust and cobwebs, wood lice and woodworm. Empty forever.

THE DEATH
OF WIZARDS

PAUL SAW IT ALL at a glance: the frail old man crossing the road; the lorry coming around the corner, down the hill, fast, nearly out of control. Not for the first time, he found himself literally of two minds. His normal human mind wanted to close its eyes and scream at the inevitable scrunch of flesh and bone. But the quick animal mind that made him a rugby player acted before he knew.

He flew across the front of the lorry as it loomed above him like a moving cliff. Grabbed the old man as he would have tackled an opponent, and threw himself at the opposite side of the road. He felt the curb drive into his backside like a blunt ax, felt the lorry's wheel tap his dangling toe as gently as a playful cat. Then the lorry was past in a flurry of dust and exhaust fumes, and gone on down the hill.

He lay there exultant, delighted with himself, as if he had just scored the winning try. The pain in his backside was receding; nothing broken, said long rugby experience. He'd even managed to fall on his back with the old boy on top, so he'd broken the old boy's fall. The old boy was struggling to get up, gasping healthily; his bones felt thin as a bird's, but he was O.K., too. Paul smelled the old man's smell—clean enough, but with the lavender sweetness of age.

"Steady on, Granddad," he said. "Let me get myself sorted out and I'll help you up." He felt a tremendously proud, caring protectiveness as he dusted the old boy down. There was nobody else around; nobody had seen what he'd done, which seemed a pity. The lorry-driver had obviously thanked God and kept going . . .

He looked around and saw the bench, set helpfully back near the top of the hill, at the edge of a small wood. "Let's go and sit down, Granddad—get our breaths back." He offered the old man his arm, but the old man said sharply, "Don't fuss—I can manage." That was Paul's first shock; it wasn't really an old gaffer's voice, ignorant or quaint or shaky. It was clear, well spoken, knew exactly what it wanted, and was used to being obeyed.

The old man sat at one end of the bench and Paul at the other, and they looked at each other. The man was *very* old. The wrinkles around his eyes and mouth were really amazing; even his wrinkles had wrinkles, as if he were a relief map of a very ancient valley. It was hard not to keep staring. But his skin was clear and healthy, his hair a splendid mane of silver, he had a beak like an eagle, and his eyes were blue, sharp, and not old at all. In fact, they made Paul jump with their sharpness.

"Well, young man, do you like what you see? Are you pleased with the fish you've caught?"

"Sorry," said Paul, and blushed; his mother had taught him it was rude to stare.

"Oh, don't apologize. You've been looking at me, and

I've been looking at you. Is the pain in your backside wearing off?"

"Yes, thanks," said Paul. Then: "How did you know I'd hurt my backside?"

"The way you fell; the way you limped. I may be old, but I'm not blind. Which rugby team do you play for?"

"School, county schoolboys, North of England." Then: "How did you know *that?*"

"Your speed, your confidence. The way you got hold of me; the way you know how to fall."

"Gosh," said Paul, deeply impressed.

"Nothing," said the old man. "You also get on well with your parents, are popular with your friends, and nobody you love has died yet, so your grandparents must also be alive—unless they died when you were a baby."

"Yes . . . but how do you know *that?*"

"By the marks on your face. Everybody's born with a blank sheet, and then life writes on it, as you get older. And yet . . . you are not *completely* happy. There is something you want you cannot have."

"God, you're amazing!" Paul's admiration was quick and generous.

"No—I've just spent a long time looking. Ninety-four years. I suppose I should thank you for saving my life . . ." Paul looked at the old man sharply; he didn't *sound* very grateful.

"Didn't you want to be saved?"

"Not particularly," said the old man. "Though I must say you did it with style. You're quite right to be proud of yourself; I haven't suffered a scratch."

"But—why didn't you want to be saved?"

"Well," said the old man, "I ache all over with arthritis, sleeping and waking. They give me painkillers, which do not kill pain; they only kill thought, which I value. And besides, I have seen all of this world I want to see. To tell you the truth, I'm bored. I'd like to be moving on to—the next thing, whatever that is."

"But there's always something new to learn . . . I'd like to know the truth about *everything* . . . Were you committing suicide?" Paul couldn't believe he'd asked that question. It popped out before he knew—like playing rugby, like saving this old man. "Sorry . . . I shouldn't have said that." He blushed again.

"No need to apologize. Why shouldn't you ask the question? But, as a matter of fact, I was *not* trying to commit suicide. I haven't endured ninety-four years in order to waste them by committing suicide. Maybe, in the hereafter, they make suicides start their lives all over again—back to square one, as you would say."

He smiled at Paul, a rather wintry smile. "No, I wasn't trying suicide; my legs had locked, that's all—I couldn't move out of the way in time, and I knew it. And I knew the lorry would certainly kill me. And I thought, at last it's over—no more taking an hour to get dressed in the morning. Now I shall *know* what happens when you die. I was really getting very curious . . . And then you came along, and gave me back my life, so brilliantly. I really must give you a present in return."

A flicker of greed lit up in Paul, in spite of how he struggled to stop it. Old people . . . especially brainy old people . . . sometimes had such marvelous things they'd collected over the years. His gran had a brass compass, over two hundred years old . . . old maps . . . dried-out flying fish. All such things he loved.

"I have a letter written by Oliver Cromwell to his wife . . ." said the old man. "How would that suit you?"

Paul looked at him sharply. The old man was smiling, teasing; but the offer was genuine.

"I couldn't take that," said Paul stoutly. "That's far too valuable."

"Or," said the old man, "do you really want me to give you what you want most in the world, and can't have? The thing that makes the corners of your mouth turn down?"

"You can't give me *that*," said Paul. "I want to be a poet. I keep sending poems to publishers, but they always send them back saying they haven't got room. I want to understand the truth about *everything*; then I would write poems they couldn't refuse . . ."

"You want to understand the truth about *everything*." The old man smiled and nodded, as if his worst suspicions had been confirmed. "What a dreadful thing it is to be young . . . no half measures. Very well, you have what you ask." He got up, stiffly; Paul saw the corners of his mouth draw in sharply with pain. Then he began tottering up the hill, toward the corner. But at the corner he stopped and turned painfully back.

"I come, sometimes, and sit on this bench," he said. "If you need me."

Then he nodded in a dignified way, and vanished around the corner.

PAUL SAT ON, dazed. After a while, a woman passed with a pram; then a whistling postman on a bicycle. It had all been so strange Paul began to wonder if any of it had ever happened—whether he hadn't had a particularly vivid daydream. Only the trembling in his legs and a low straight pain across his back remained as evidence.

And then he heard the children giggling and crashing

in the wood behind him. They seemed to be having a whale of a time—a lot of them. Funny—they should be in school. He was out of school only because he'd just taken A levels. He turned, wincing, and peered into the trees. He could see nothing, except patches of sunlit leaves, with patches of darker leaves behind; and patches of sky showing through, from the far side of the wood. Yet the noise of giggling and crashing continued. Curiosity awakened, he got up stiffly (thinking of the old man's stiffness and pain) and plunged into the wood.

Nobody there. Paths ran through the undergrowth—crazy circling paths that only children could have made, chasing each other. Old knotted ropes hung from the trees, swaying gently in the breeze; one had an old tire attached to the end of it. Some of the branches of the trees were broken; the bark of the trunks was shiny and scuffed from the soles of many small feet. The wood worked hard for its living—a well-used playground. But empty now; the children were in school, or at least had run off, hearing his approach.

He shook his head and went back to the bench. His bottom really was quite painful; as well it wasn't the rugby season . . .

The giggling and crashing started again. And again he could see nothing through the leaves. He crept up on them, very careful to be quiet. But as he entered the middle of the wood, the noise stopped suddenly; and there were only the ropes swinging gently in the breeze. He searched the whole wood very carefully. Went to the far edge and gazed out over an unbroken field of ripening wheat. Nowhere a child could hide. But at his back he heard the giggling and crashing again . . . But when he whirled, there was nothing.

He ran to the middle, among the swinging ropes. And then, making his hair stand on end, the giggling and crashing came all around him. Where no child could possibly be.

He thought for an awful moment the wood was haunted. By dead children, to whom something dreadful had happened. But the noise was so merry, and the place was so happy . . .

And then he understood: what he was hearing was the *truth* about the wood; the wood was telling him what it was *for*.

The old man had kept his promise.

He ought to have felt frightened then; but what was there to be frightened of, in happiness? And besides, he felt a poem starting to form in his head . . . He ran back to the bench and whipped out the notebook and the pen he always carried, even to rugby matches. And the poem came, like a wave.

> *The wood waits*
> *In the empty afternoon*
> *Calling to its children*
> *Like an anxious mother . . .*

His pen ran on and on, as if it had a life of its own, without pause, until the long poem was finished. And even as he wrote he was delighted with it. He knew it was far, far better than anything he'd ever done before. Oh, definitely one to send to Howard Sergeant, at *Outposts*.

He sat satisfied—blinking in the sun, contented as he had never been. Like serving an ace at tennis; like a bow that has shot its arrow straight to the mark. And his heart sang. I am going to be a poet!

But already other thoughts were crowding in, as if they were seeping up from the very planks of the bench he sat on. He knew they were an old woman's thoughts—a very tired old lady, indeed. Looking down on the town she'd been born in. Remembering how, on this very seat, she had sat with her father on the day of the carnival, waving a balloon on a stick. Thought after thought came to him. Boyfriends, marriage, children, a husband dying . . . and in between, the old woman noted how dark it was getting, and how the strength was draining out of her . . . draining, draining . . .

And then he knew, with gooseflesh running up his spine, that the old woman had sat down and died on this seat, resting after her last fatal climb up this hill . . . But it wasn't dreadful . . . there was sadness at leaving . . . but her life had been good . . . and she was looking forward to seeing her Billy again.

It finished; he felt a kind of holy awe, felt immensely privileged. Then his notebook was out again and he was scribbling, scribbling. The poem that he would later call "Old Woman Sitting":

> *I'm tired now*
> *It's good to rest*
> *The sun was this bright on the day*
> *I first went to the carnival . . .*

He finished, and again he knew it worked. His head was spinning with fatigue and joy; the sun filled his mind with a golden ecstatic mist in which living people and delivery vans passed like faint ghosts.

Then he remembered he was supposed to be going to the supermarket for his mother.

He walked down the hill like a drunken king, and halfway down got his first hint of trouble. On a corner, where the sidewalk narrowed, he came face to face with a woman carrying two heavy shopping baskets. She looked the usual kind of plump, pleasant person, with a blue floral dress, hair pulled back in a bun, and rosy middle-aged cheeks. They did what people sometimes do on narrow sidewalks, trying to get out of each other's way, stepping together to the left, then to the right, until it became a kind of absurd dance. He usually smiled at people he got into that kind of fix with. But the woman just stared at him, coldly, as if it was all his fault and he was a total idiot. And even when he got past her, he brushed against one of her baskets; and as he did, such a wave of hate and rage hit him as left him speechless. Hate against him for being young. Hate against her husband, because he drank too much and laughed with the women. Hate against the government, the unions, the blacks, the students, the Commies, the mentally handicapped . . . She stumped on up the hill; he watched her, feeling weak and sick and cold and shaken.

So he went into the town nervously, suddenly wanting to choose carefully the truths he let into himself. He soon got the trick of it. The thing only worked over short distances, up to about three yards; beyond that, there was nothing. Stood to reason, really! Otherwise, you'd go mad, feeling what the First Secretary was thinking in Moscow, or the President in Washington, or both at the same time. So he weaved through the people in the shopping precinct at high speed, rather as if he were scoring a try at rugby. Even so, he could feel flicks of their minds as he passed. Some were pleasant; but not all, by a long shot. Still, he felt in control again.

Then he thought: Suppose the supermarket's full? And I get wedged into a crowd of hot and fed-up people? But it was a quarter to two on a very hot afternoon. The office workers had gone back to work, and the mums hadn't arrived, and the place was nearly empty—easy enough to swerve around. He grabbed a basket, and flicked down the first aisle: fresh fruit. He put his hand on an orange . . .

And it happened again. He stood stock-still, as a whole life flowed down his arm out of the orange. He was a child, and the sky was full of geometric rows of black bombers from which tiny bombs fell in long, continuous streams like rain . . . Then goose-stepping soldiers were marching through ruined streets . . . Then a glimpse of barbed wire and watchtowers, and a feeling of terror such as he was never to know again, which made the sweat stream down his healthy young body, as he stood with one arm outstretched to the shelf of oranges. But it passed. He was on a ship—steep waves and feeling seasick. And then a low brown shore, and a feeling of gladness such as he was never to know again in his life. And the words shouted: *"Eretz Israel!"*

And after that it was healthy sunburned children, running, yelling, naked but for a pair of shorts. And singing and dancing, and the cool green orange groves, and thankfulness . . .

"You all right, sir?" The supermarket manager was peering at him anxiously, as if he were frightened that Paul might throw up over the fresh guavas.

"I . . . just felt a bit faint," said Paul. "I'll go out and get some fresh air." The manager took his empty basket off him, and patted him on the shoulder, in a way that gently propelled him toward the exit.

But the moment he got outside, another poem broke

over him. He sat on the metal rail by the entrance, his feet twisted together with excitement, and wrote "Old Jew Picking Oranges," which was to be the last of his three great poems.

Then he looked up and saw the manager watching him curiously through the plate-glass window. Their eyes met—embarrassing. Then the manager walked away, shaking his head, perhaps a little nostalgically, over the follies of youth.

Paul put away his notebook and went back in reluctantly, nervous as a cat now. But he went straight back to the same orange, and when he picked it up, there was nothing; its force must have been discharged into the poem, like a battery. He picked three more oranges from close around it, and got nothing there, either. The old Jew must have picked them all.

The bananas were no bother; a mild sneery grumble about the plantation foreman weighing the bunches was all they gave him. And the dried figs actually yielded a sexy daydream about a Turkish belly dancer in full action. He bought a second pack on the strength of it.

But the California tinned peaches were bad: homesickness for Mexico, loathing for a single-room shack with a leaking roof, and fear for a sick child when there was no money for the doctor; and if he missed an hour's work, the boss would not only sack him but tell the police he was a wetback . . . He dropped the peaches in the basket, feeling he'd had enough. He was growing uneasy about how long it would be before this crazy old man's gift wore off. Still, there was only the bread to get now, and he didn't reckon he'd get much nasty off English machine-baked bread . . .

He was nearly there when the girl with the loading cart came sharply around the corner and ran into him, driving him staggering back against a pile of square tins. His hands scrabbled at them, outstretched, as he fought to keep his balance . . .

There was a lowing of cattle, and the smell of blood. Blood upon blood upon blood. And a cloud of flies, and the despair of death, and wild attempts to break out, and the thud, thud, thud of the humane killer, and a gushing of blood like a toilet flushing, and the black fear of ending and never understanding.

He ran forward wildly; anything to get away from the corned-beef tins. His eyes were shut and he never looked where he was going. That was how he tripped and went face down into the open freezer full of broiler chickens . . .

He was fastened in; he could not move, he could not peck properly or stretch his wings. No day, no air, no run, no flying. And then he was hanging upside down by the legs, flapping wildly to get upright, and all the time he was moving, and the spinning razor-edged knife was coming nearer and nearer his head and neck. Then blackness.

HE CAME TO, sitting in a chair in the manager's office. Three people were staring at him.

" 'e 'ad some sort of fit," said the girl with the loading cart. But he knew she was thinking: Nice-looking wazzock—I could fancy him, if he wasn't . . . funny in the head.

"I've sent for Mrs. Soames," said the manager. "She's done a first-aid course. I've rung for the doctor." But he was thinking: Christ, that's all I needed. The week's take is down already, and now this nutter has emptied the shop . . .

"Here's Mrs. Soames now," said the second woman.

But she was thinking: Bet this kid's on drugs or glue sniffing. Most of them are, these days—don't know what the world's coming to. Now, when I was a girl . . .

And the office chair was gabbling on, in his mind, about maximizing sales and higher flow-through. Twitter, twitter, twitter, till he could have gone mad.

Mrs. Soames arrived, brisk, motherly, and efficient. She examined him, pronounced he wasn't an epileptic, since he hadn't bitten his tongue or foamed at the mouth. She forced his eyes open painfully and announced he wasn't on drugs, since his pupils were normal. She seemed very good at telling them what he wasn't, and what hadn't happened.

Paul stood up shakily, if only to stop the office chair twittering on about maximizing sales.

"I feel O.K. now," he announced. The manager cheered up visibly. "I've got your shopping," he said, pointing to Paul's wire basket lying in the corner, still full of oranges and bananas, tinned peaches and figs. "Do you want to pay for it?"

"Yeah," said Paul, reaching weakly into his back pocket and giving him three pounds. "And a shopping bag."

"Shopping bag—certainly," said the manager jovially. "We'll give you one of those on the house." And he was soon back with the change. Thinking: How soon can I get this young wally out of here? District manager could come any moment . . .

"Is that an exit?" asked Paul, pointing to a door across the office with a push-bar like the exit doors in a cinema.

"Exit, yes," said the manager. "Direct to the outside."

"I'll take it," said Paul, thankfully.

"What about the doctor?" asked Mrs. Soames, in her trained-nurse voice.

"He'll do," said the manager, thinking: Bugger the

doctor—I'll cancel him—he won't be here for hours yet.

"Bye-bye," said Paul faintly; pushed the bar and found himself in a blessedly empty back alley.

HIS MAIN CONCERN was to dodge people; but the gift of truth seemed to be getting worse. If he rested in one place more than a minute, people's feelings seemed to start oozing up out of the street through the soles of his shoes. Nasty, blurry feelings of hundreds of people who'd trodden on the place, all mixed together, like the muddly kind of feverish nightmare when you can't get things sorted out. Certainly, the world was getting more and more *unreal*. He fell to hoping sincerely he'd wake up soon.

Then he tried walking on some grass. That was better; the grass, which was long and uncut, was happy, really happy. He sat down and luxuriated in the happiness of grass, as if sinking into a warm bath. Lay back . . . and then shot upright in terror . . . And saw, fifty yards away, a metal railing, and a row of young trees, and a green gate, and a notice saying:

NO CYCLING IN THIS CEMETERY

Making his mind a blank, he ran on.

But at least he knew where he was running, now.

The old man had said, "I come, sometimes, and sit on this bench. If you need me."

He needed him.

AND HE WAS THERE—almost as if waiting for Paul, for he looked up with that wintry smile and didn't seem at all surprised.

"Have you had enough of the absolute truth?"

"Yes."

"I have seldom heard someone so certain, so quickly. What about your wish to be a poet?"

"Bugger poetry," said Paul.

"You will settle for rugby football?"

Paul's heart leaped. "Yes!"

"You want me to take back the priceless gift of truth? Which hurts you? What about the priceless gift of life you gave me? That hurts me . . . Will you take that back also?"

Paul trembled. "What do you mean?"

The old man laughed. "I am not asking you to murder me. No, we shall simply go back a little in time. I'm afraid you must lose the shopping you got for your mother, with so much effort . . ."

Paul gaped. The shopping bag full of groceries, which he'd laid on the seat, was gone. "But . . ."

The old man laughed. "I am not a thief. Feel in your pocket."

Paul felt in his hip pocket; his mum's three pounds were back. "What . . . ?"

"We are moving back in time, you and I. Soon it will be the time before the lorry came down the hill. The time before you so brilliantly saved my life. Which I did not want saved. How did you come to the place where you saved me?"

"I walked across the park, and turned right down the hill."

"Then go back to the park. Sit on a bench; bask in the sunshine; admire the sparrows. Until you hear . . . the lorry. And when it is all over, you will come out of the park and turn left *up* the hill. And go to the supermarket the other way. You have had enough truth for one day, young man. Human kind cannot bear very much reality . . ."

"That's T. S. Eliot."

"A wise man, Eliot. Nearly as wise as me." The old man laughed, almost boyishly. As if he were looking forward to a treat.

"What *are* you?"

The old man shrugged. "All I will say is that it is not wise to meddle in the death of wizards . . . Go now. I think you are a good young man—and I think you will have a happy life—as lives go."

Paul got up, reluctantly, as if he were about to commit a crime.

"Goodbye," he said, doubtfully.

"Good*bye*," said the old man, very firmly, but with a twinkle of affection.

Paul looked back once, at the park gate. The old man was sitting peacefully in the sun, head down.

HE SAT, and waited. The sun went briefly behind a cloud, and came out again. The trees swayed back and forth. There were no sparrows to observe. There was no way of telling whether time was running backwards or forwards. He was not wearing his watch; it was broken.

He jumped guiltily every time a car went past. But when the lorry came, it was unmistakable. Big, driving fast, nearly out of control. Paul thought with pity of the driver; but the driver was *asking* for it, driving that fast.

The squeal of brakes; breaking glass. Then, after about three minutes, the wail of a police siren; then an ambulance siren. Then the ambulance going away, and more police cars coming . . .

Only then did Paul dare to move.

He couldn't bear not to look. The lorry was still there, mounted up on the sidewalk, and there was a stain on the radiator grille that might have been blood or only dirt. The police were measuring the road, and there was broken glass from the lorry's headlight. He asked someone what had happened.

"Ran an old bloke down—killed instantly."

It was only when he got home from the supermarket, very late, and Mam needing the bread for Dad's sandwiches, that he thought to look in his notebook.

The three poems were still there. An old man's gift . . .

The three poems were accepted by Howard Sergeant, who said they showed real promise.

But he never wrote another one.

THE LAST DAY
OF MISS DORINDA
MOLYNEAUX

LIFE'S IRONICAL; but sometimes nice-ironical. Take the time I was struggling with all my might and main to overtake Clocky Watson in the antique trade. What I never noticed, in the middle of my exertions, was that I was becoming a very solid, prosperous citizen in the eyes of my fellow citizens.

Not, that is, until people began having a quiet word with me, putting in a quiet word for me, ringing me up and conducting rambling, ambiguous, awkward conversations that always ended up with me being invited to join something.

The Freemasons I refused; if I have one belief, it's that I must make my own way by my own bloody efforts, and my sense of humor would never let me appear in a funny little apron. The invitation to be a magistrate I put off for years; in my game the line between crook and Honest John is drawn in some very funny places (as it is in most games, if the truth be known) and I would not play the hypocrite. But I joined Rotary without a qualm, though I never did much apart from eat, drink, and gossip. My starring moment always came in their annual sale of second-hand goods in aid of the hospital fund. I think at first they hoped I'd find a long-lost Rembrandt. But in the end they put me in charge of the old lawn mowers, in the rain outside. (It always seemed to be raining.) And if I got the odd sideboard as a bargain, or a set of good Victorian chairs, I always paid more than the price they'd put on them, in their ignorance. Of course, *they* reckoned they were making my fortune . . .

But the invitation I liked best was to join the school board for Barton Road Primary. I was still unmarried at thirty-four—though not from lack of wining and dining young women—and having despaired of ever having children, I found the chance to acquire three hundred at one blow was too great a temptation.

The third meeting I attended was to appoint a new teacher. I found it amusingly boring at first. My fellow board members were not a brilliant lot, being mainly the weaker hangers-on of the local political parties. Each seemed to have a set question which he asked every candidate in turn, with an air of profound wisdom. We interviewed three worthy female mice, in tweed skirts and sweaters, and the only difference I could make between them was that one was rather tall, one rather fat, and one amazingly minute.

The fourth candidate was Miss Dorinda Molyneaux. That caused a stir, I can tell you. The Molyneaux were a county family, living five miles away at Barlborough Hall. There were five daughters, born one a year over twenty years before, while their mother was getting breeding over with so that she could return with undivided interest to riding horses, all duty done. The girls had a name for being spirited. One had run off to South

Africa with a Count Clichy, who had once tried to run our local country club. Another went far left, emigrated to America, and got involved in the Berkeley campus troubles. I looked forward with interest to what eccentricity the eldest, Miss Dorinda (or rather, to be correct, Miss Molyneaux), should display.

Miss Molyneaux's eccentricity was doing good—to the children of the underprivileged workers. For I must explain that although Barlborough is a pretty little town, it has its black spots, and most of them are centered on Barton Road.

She came in, closed the door behind her decisively, and shook hands firmly with our madam chairman, without giving her the option to shake hands or not. She then shook hands with the rest of us, with that raised eyebrow of privilege that requires introductions. She followed up the introductions with questions as to our occupations and well-being, and her general thoughts on life. She was definitely interviewing us. In all, it must have taken up nearly a quarter of an hour. And we had allowed twenty minutes for each candidate.

Then she sat down, crossed her legs, and gave us, with a smile, her undivided attention.

The first thing I noticed was how remarkably fine those legs were . . . Miss Molyneaux was a very fine young woman, indeed. Long, glossy hair below her shoulders, expensively cut to look casual. The pearls would be real, and old. A tan not acquired in English weather. A big girl, though not fat, and eyes as bold a blue as those of the first Baron Molyneaux who had crossed with William the Conqueror and stolen his bit of England.

They asked her their usual questions. Did she believe in corporal punishment? She put her head on one side, crinkling up her face in schoolgirl thought.

"I'm not *against* it. Not *really* against it. But I believe in training by kindness. I had a horse once . . ." She kindly explained her theory of animal welfare to Councillor Byerscough, who was not half as senile as he looked, and a near Communist to boot . . . I sat back, waiting for her to lose one vote after another. Pity; she was by far the brightest person we'd seen that afternoon.

But it wasn't as simple as that. I wasn't allowing for the weight of prejudice. There were four left-wingers who wouldn't have voted for her if she'd talked like Ernest Bevin and sung like Caruso. There was the headmistress, who sat with a look of spreading outrage on her face. But there were also five Tories, shopkeepers mainly, though they called themselves Independents, who were not only almost touching their forelocks to Miss Molyneaux but asking to be remembered kindly to her father. And both sides would have voted to spite the other, if the candidate had been the Queen herself.

And then there was me. I'd sat quiet, as Miss Molyneaux had swept out with a final gracious smile around the table, and hostilities had commenced. I'd sat quiet, as old battles were refought, and old wounds reopened. And in the end, deadlocked, they turned to me.

Which class, I asked gravely, might she be destined for?

"Upper year, bottom stream," said the headmistress, her eyes going remote and frosty, sensing a traitor in her camp. "Our worst problem—4C needs an experienced teacher who will keep them in hand, not someone fresh from teachers college, like . . ." She stopped herself just in time. "I can't upset the whole school system in mid-year by moving my staff about."

Why did I vote for Dorinda Molyneaux? To begin with, I fancied her. Then, I had slightly cruel curiosity about what she and 4C would do to each other. But, above all, I thought Barton Road needed a good shake-up. I longed to set a cat among the mice . . .

So she got the job, and thanked us graciously. And I earned the headmistress's undying hatred.

School-board members do not have a lot of say in the daily running of the school; but Dorinda's arrival was so spectacular that stories kept reaching me, third-hand.

The class horror (there's one in every class) moved in on her quickly. By the end of the second morning, during an altercation concerning a broken ruler, he called her a silly tart . . . Now, Dorinda might be opposed to corporal punishment, but the Molyneaux family did not get where they are today by not knowing how to cope with English peasants. And the vigor with which "Molly" Molyneaux could hurl a lacrosse ball still lived as a legend in the halls of Roedean.

The class horror, Henry Winterbottom by name, was backhanded across the ear so hard he teetered on his toes five yards before he hit the cupboard, which was rather insecurely fixed to the wall. Then he fell down, and the cupboard fell on top of him. The noise was heard as far off as the caretaker's house.

The headmistress rushed in and extricated Henry from the wreckage. Miss Molyneaux's teaching career looked doomed to early death. But blows were the coin of affection in the Winterbottom family, the only coin in an emotionally bankrupt household. And besides, the disaster had been so widespread as to bring renown on Henry's head also. Both he and Miss Molyneaux would linger in legend . . . So he uttered the gallant words, "I just opened the cupboard door and it fell on me, miss."

The headmistress, sensing she was being robbed of her

great opportunity, swiveled her eyes around the class, looking for a dissenting verdict. But the class was too firmly under Henry's thumb; and Miss Molyneaux's violence was much too treasured a possession. Not a lip moved. But Henry Winterbottom became from that day on as faithful to Miss Molyneaux as any of her many family dogs.

And that was the way it went. Miss Molyneaux was used to being firm with dogs and horses, and 4C became her foxhounds.

From 4C's point of view, she was the greatest of treasures, a genuine eccentric. Where the earnest little mice would have nagged 4C about bad handwriting, or not handing in their homework in time (death to any child's soul), Miss Molyneaux gave detailed instructions on how to groom a horse, generously brandishing a currycomb in huge strokes that carved an invisible horse out of the air.

Then there were those thrilling moments of silence, after Henry asked such questions as "Have you ever drunk champagne, miss?" Which were rewarded with the news not only that Bollinger '48 was the best champagne to buy but that Miss Molyneaux had actually consumed a whole jeroboam with a feller in a punt on the river at Cambridge, at the incredibly aristocratic hour of four in the morning.

The headmistress tried a few sneaky tricks. Classes had to be marched two-by-two to the playing field a mile away for games. It was said that many such journeys had turned the deputy headmaster's hair gray.

But Miss Molyneaux had a good eye and a vigorous disposition. She not only took over the girls' field-hockey team but joined in the boys' soccer in her flaring-blue tracksuit, laying out the school captain with a magnificent foul.

Soon the whole school was eating out of her hand, and to 4C she was a goddess. Several parents complained about requests for ponies at Christmas . . .

It was at about this time that I came back upon the scene. She nailed me at the Autumn Fair, held in aid of a school minibus.

"Their minds need broadening," she said. "No good teaching history without *showing* them. I hear you know about old things." So I turned up one afternoon with the least breakable items from my shop. And as we've learned to say now, she counted them all out and she counted them all back, heavily thumbprinted. And Henry Winterbottom got the silver saltcellar back out of Jack Hargreaves's trouser pocket before I'd even missed it. Henry gave Jack a well-aimed kidney punch by way of retribution, saying, "You can't nick off him—he's miss's *feller*, ain't he?"

Miss, who also overheard this infant dialogue, had the grace to blush, and I suddenly felt I had a chance. "We ought to take them around a stately home," I said, ever the good citizen.

"How nice," she said, with the kind of smile you give the Spanish chargé d'affaires.

"But we'd better spy out the land first," I added. "So you can make up a project. Do you know Tattersham Hall?"

"No, I don't know Tattersham," she said, suddenly sharp. "Who lives there now?" I felt I was moving into a different league.

"A lot of butterflies."

"Oh, that silkworm lot," she said ungraciously. "They

bought out Bertie Tattersham after he'd drunk himself silly, poor old sod."

The headmistress passed, giving a look that would cheerfully have crucified us both.

"You free Saturday afternoon?" said Dorinda. She was never one to wait to be asked.

I drove up to Barlborough Hall prompt on two. Dorinda was in the formal garden with two rather disreputable Pekinese called Marco and Polo; she was either teaching them to pull up weeds or instructing the flowers how to grow. Something was certainly getting it in the neck.

Marco peed on my best cavalry-twill slacks, by way of greeting.

"Not used to animals, then?" asked Dorinda brutally. "It's a sign of affection—he's marking you out as his property." Obviously, Polo felt hurt about Marco's preemptive strike on my garments; he walked up casually and buried his teeth in the tatty fur around Marco's neck. Together they rolled into some rather depressed laurels, making a sound like feeding time at the zoo.

"They're *great* friends," said Dorinda.

She looked at my Chrysler station wagon, parked on the rather thin and rutted gravel. "Is it foreign?"

"It's illegitimate," I said gravely. "Its mother was a Rolls, but they left her out one night and she was seduced by a rather common single-decker bus."

"I suppose it will get us there?"

"And your best Sheraton commode, six Chippendale dining chairs, and all your family portraits."

"Oh, yes, you're a dealer, aren't you?"

Not a propitious start, and the trip got steadily worse. We walked into the entrance hall at Tattersham, which is lined with dead and glorious foreign butterflies in celluloid boxes, which some people will pay up to four hundred pounds for.

"Yu-uk!" said Dorinda; a noise of disgust so explosive it turned every head in the room.

"I thought your lot liked dead animals?" I said.

"Only ones we've shot ourselves. Anyway, when . . . if I ever invite you for tea, you won't find a single dead animal at Barlborough. We are not a 'lot'—we're individual people, and I've never met the Duke of Edinburgh, either."

I had hoped it might be romantic in what the Tattersham people call the jungle: the old palm house, still full of palms and little tinkling power-driven waterfalls, but now alive with huge tropical butterflies that will actually settle on your hand.

"Bloody hot in here. Worse'n a Turkish bath," said Dorinda. A blue swallowtail from Malaya settled on her shoulder. "Tatty-looking thing," she observed. "Falling to pieces. Should be put out of its misery."

Then she dragged me from room to room, questioning everyone she could lay her hands on about the processes of silk farming. I left her side for a moment. It was a mistake. I heard her hoot, "You mean they have to *kill* the poor things to get the silk? Kill them by boiling them alive? Monstrous. Should be abolished. I'd rather wear nylon knickers, now I know."

I got her away from the blushing curator with, as the R.A.F. used to say, maximum boost.

"Not bringing the kids here," she announced, as we tumbled down the front steps. "Nothing but a bloody slaughterhouse. What's that?" She stopped abruptly, so that I banged into her, which was not unpleasant.

"That's Tattersham Church."

"But it's three miles from the village."

"But very close to the Hall. The gentry could walk there without even getting wet. The villagers could walk it in an hour—nothing to peasants."

The blue frost of her eyes traveled slowly up and down my face.

"I wasn't aware there was a peasants' union, Mr. Ashden," she said at last, "and I wasn't aware you'd appointed yourself shop steward. I suppose your father was a dockworker or something, and you're not going to allow me to forget it. I suppose you left school at twelve, and worked polishing the gentry's boots for two shillings a week, and a half day off every fortnight."

"My father," I said, "is a bank manager in Cottesden, and I took my degree in history at Durham."

"More the petit-bourgeois union, then?"

"Do you want to see the church?"

It might have been the sudden frost in the May of our relationship, but I shuddered as we approached that church. It wasn't the sort of church I like. It might have been medieval once, but it had been badly got at during the Gothic Revival. The worst thing they'd done was to re-case the outside in some pale, marble-like stone, as smooth and nasty as a marshmallow. The years are not kind to that sort of stone; green algae had gathered in every crevice and ledge, and dribbled its pale greenness down the walls. It looked like a hollowed-out tombstone, with windows.

The door was open. In fact, from the rusted lock and the porchful of dead leaves, I guessed nobody ever bothered to close it; the nearest village was three miles away, and there was no fear of vandals. All the notices flapping on the notice board were yellow and held on with pins that had deteriorated into blobs of rust. The vicar, the Reverend Ernest Lacey, lived five miles away, at Tettesden: if it was still the same vicar.

We pushed on, through the inner door. Inside, purple-and-blue windows, in the black darkness. We stood for a moment, unable to see even our feet.

Then the family tombs began to loom toward us out of the darkness. They reared up to left and right, the whole length of the wall, a flowering of white marble pillars and marble faces lying on gilt cushions, trophy of shield and sword and trumpet, and potbellied exulting cherub with dust piled in his navel. They crowded inward across the black-and-white tiled floor, like a crowd at a road accident, bare white marble arms outflung plead-ingly in frozen futile gestures; white marble eyes seeing nothing but seeming to know a great deal. Between them, the space for the living, a few short box pews, seemed to cower and shrink. Even if that church was packed, the dead would surely outnumber the living.

IN THE FAMILY VAULT UNDER THE ALTAR
ARE DEPOSITED THE REMAINS OF
JOHN ANSTEY ESQUIRE
SECOND SON OF THE LATE CHRISTOPHER
ANSTEY ESQUIRE
AND ONE OF HIS MAJESTY'S COMMISSIONERS
FOR
AUDITING PUBLIC ACCOUNTS
WHO DEPARTED THIS LIFE THE 25TH NOVEMBER
1810

So many wanting to be remembered, and so few coming to remember them. It struck me that the ignored dead might get angry, like tigers in a zoo that have been left hungry for too long.

"Oh, that's *beautiful*," breathed Dorinda. She was staring at a grille that bordered the altar—a thing that the blue window behind reduced to a skeleton, but which on closer inspection still disclosed a lick of gilt. I went up and fingered it. Very fine wrought-iron work, of curiously individual design. It closed off a pointed arch, and seemed to my bemused gaze to be almost woven out of odd-shaped distorted crosses, overlapping and weaving through each other.

"It is by Tijou?" whispered Dorinda, awed for once.

"Too late for Tijou—Tijou's your 1680s—St. Paul's. This is more your 1760s. Still, a good piece of blacksmithing."

"Peasant! But the children could make rubbings of the patterns on it—they could copy out the words on the tombs, and draw the cherubs. And Henry would love to draw all those spears and shields."

"And there's a couple of monumental brasses, I'll bet." I pulled back a faded red carpet, unpleasantly damp to my fingers, to reveal a six-foot knight and his lady, engraved flat in brass, inlaid in the black-and-white marble of the floor.

"Oh, this would make a *lovely* project—we could have an exhibition in the school auditorium. But how can we get them here?"

She turned to me, flushed with enthusiasm, mouth open. I wanted to kiss her, but settled for saying, "Well, the school's getting the minibus soon. Can you drive it?"

"Of course."

"And if I bring my illegitimate Rolls, I can pack twelve into that."

"Will it be safe?"

"Never lost a grandfather clock yet, and they're worth money."

"Oh, let's *do* it, Geoff!"

One part of me was elated; she'd never called me Geoff before. But the other half of me, the antique dealer, was doubtful.

This church felt wrong. I do not say this lightly. Dealers are undertakers of a sort. When a man dies, the undertaker comes for his body, and quite often the dealer comes for the rest. How often I have been left alone to break up the home a man has built up over fifty years, and sell the pieces where I can. As I break up the home, I know the man. I have known a cracked teapot yield enough evidence of adultery to satisfy ten divorce-court judges. I learn that he was mean from his boots; that trapped forever inside the sepia photographs are seven of his children. From his diary, that he believed in God or the Devil or Carter's Little Liver Pills. I deal in dead men's clocks, pipes, swords, and velvet breeches. And passing through my hands, they give off joy and loneliness, fear and optimism. I have known more evil in a set of false teeth than in any so-called haunted house in England.

And this church felt wrong . . . I tried to temporize. "It's . . . not a good example of the style. I have a friend, a vicar, with the most beautiful church. He's studied it for years. He'll explain everything to the kids . . . It's got bells they can ring . . ."

She set her chin stubbornly. "No. *I* found this. If you won't help me, I'll come on my own. Hire a bus . . ."

I disliked the idea of her and the kids being here alone even more. So, against my better judgment, I said "O.K."

Then she said, suddenly more sensitive than I'd known her, "You don't like the place, do you, Geoff?"

"It feels wrong."

"We're not going to *feel* it; we're going to draw it." And the brave invulnerable smile came back, like a highwayman putting on his mask. I think, in that moment, I fell in love with her.

And knowing that, I still didn't stop the awful thing that happened.

"COR, SIR, THERE ain't half a niff down there," said Henry Winterbottom, sticking his nose through the gilded grille. "What is it, the bog?"

"Clot," said Jack Hargreaves. "That's the crip. Dracula's down there." He started chewing avidly at Henry's filthy neck, until Henry gave him a punch that sent him rattling against the ironwork.

"Yer mean . . . bodies?" Henry's eyes glowed with what might have been described as an unearthly light. "Bodies all rotting, with their eyes falling out an' the flesh hanging off their bones, an' *skulls*."

"Can we go down an' get one out of the coffin, sir?" asked Jack Hargreaves.

"No," I said firmly.

"Aw, sir, *please*. We wouldn't do it no harm. We'd put it back, after."

"It's unhygienic, shows no respect for the dead, and besides, the grille's locked," I said.

"Oh, yeah," said Jack Hargreaves, rather professionally. "Reckon you could pick that lock, Winterbottom?"

"Try me."

But I shooed them on and got them distracted in brass-rubbing a knight in armor, to the sound of tearing rubbing paper, and cries of "Stupid bastard" and *"You did that."*

I prowled on; I couldn't keep still in that place. It

wasn't just the cold. I thought I'd come prepared for that, with a quilted parka and three sweaters. No, I kept having, not delusions, not even fears, but odd little anxieties . . . preoccupations. I had the conviction the walls weren't vertical . . . or was it the floor that seemed to slope down toward the middle of the nave? Certainly the floor was hollow; no one could walk on it and listen to the echo of his footsteps without realizing that. Then . . . the windows didn't seem to be letting in as much light as they should. I kept going outside to check if the sky was getting cloudy, but it was still bright and sunny, thank God, and I went back feeling the better for it.

Then I stared at the cross in a side chapel. It just looked like two bits of wood nailed together. I mean, it *was* just two bits of wood nailed together; but though I'm not a religious sort, I tend to see any cross as something more than two bits of wood nailed together.

And that smell. Or niff, as Henry would have it. It wasn't strong, but it was everywhere; you never got it out of your nostrils. The only thing I can liken it to was when I got in a new lavatory bowl at the shop; it had to be left for the sealant to dry overnight, so the builder stuffed wet paper down the hole, but the biting black smell of the sewer filled my shop and dreams all night.

For a while, till lunch, the children made things better. There's an atomic bomb of enthusiasm in a lively class of thirty-five let loose from school for the day. I could almost feel their vitality invading every part of the dark affronted silence. But, little by little, the silence absorbed it . . . Lunchtime was still happy, with the children asking what the big house was for. But they were curiously reluctant to get back to work afterwards, and then the grumbles started.

"Miss, this tape won't stick!"

"Sir, me pencil's broken again."

Dorinda was a tower, a fury of strength, coursing around the church non-stop. I began to realize just how hard a good primary teacher can work. But the complaints began to overtake even her speed. Soon, in spite of both our efforts, only half the children were working; the rest were standing around in little dispirited groups.

Then there was a god-awful scream from the chancel —one of the younger girls screaming, on and on. Dorinda ran, I ran. The child was standing tearing at her cheeks with her fingers, eyes shut and a noise issuing from her open mouth like a demented steam whistle.

"It's a spider, miss. Behind that man's head." They pointed to the recumbent effigy of the tenth Lord Tattersham, who had a smirk of dying satisfaction on his face, and who appeared to have been carved from some singularly pale and nasty cheddar cheese.

"Garn, only a spider . . ." Henry flicked with his hand behind the tenth lord's ear and the spider dropped to the floor. We all gaped; it was impressively huge. Henry raised his hobnailed boot . . .

"No," I said. "It's just an ordinary spider—just got rather old and big—a grandspider, maybe!"

There was a thin and nervous titter; then I picked up the spider and let it run up my parka. "They're very useful," I said. "If it wasn't for them, the flies of the world would poison us all." I carried the spider out, saying encouragingly to him, "Come on, Eustace." It seemed important just then to dispel fear, discourage killing. When I got back, most of them were working, and the cheerful noise was back.

"Thanks," said Dorinda. "You wouldn't make a bad teacher, you know."

"Thanks," I said. "But I *am* a good dealer. Eustace'll

fetch a pound for somebody's stuffed spider collection."
She looked as if she half believed me, then turned away
laughing. That was good, too. Though I thought there
was something a little shaky in her laugh.

I went to check my pile of gear by the door. Cameras,
gadget bag. But also my first-aid kit and two big flashlights. I had come prepared for a siege. Two large ther-
mos flasks of coffee; a box of chocolate bars. I hadn't the
slightest idea what I was expecting, but nothing good.

A memorial on the wall caught my eye.

TO THE MEMORY OF THOMAS DORE
AN HONOURED AND PAINEFUL
SCHOOLEMASTER
LAY PREACHER AND BENEFACTOR OF THIS
PARISH.
HE PUBLICKLY REBUKED VICE AND
DISCRETELY PRACTISED VIRTUE
AND LEFT HIS INTIRE ESTATE
TO BUY TRACTS FOR THE POOR.
THIS MONUMENT WAS ERECTED BY
PUBLICK SUBSCRIPTION
AMONG HIS GRIEVING FRIENDS AND
PUPILS
MDCCCX
BLESSED ARE THEY THAT REST IN THE
LORD

There was the crash of a drawing board, the tinkle of
paper clips, and a wail of "Oh, miss, he's tore it!"

"Thomas Dore, where art thou," I muttered. "We could
do with some reinforcements."

But there was no crack of thunder in response, no

rending of the tomb, only echoing cries of "Henry's took my eraser, sir."

I did my utmost; I whizzed up and down with my flashgun and camera, taking pictures of everybody working; I gave out coffee, then followed up with a round of chocolate bars. But more and more, in my rounds, I came across a scatter of work abandoned. And more and more I found children gathered miserably in the shelter of the porch, on any excuse: a stone in the shoe; need for the toilet; feeling faint, feeling sick. I ferried many across to the toilets in the house. Their eyes caught the butterflies in the entrance hall. The demands to go to the toilet reached epidemic proportions as word of the butterflies got back; one would have thought cholera or dysentery was raging.

In the end, I made a bargain with them. If they'd go back and finish their work and clear up nicely, I'd fix a quick trip around the butterflies.

"That's bribery," hissed Dorinda in the live-silkworm room.

"Do you want to put on a good exhibition or not?" I hissed back, reaching forward just in time to stop Henry from stuffing three live silkworms into an empty cigarette packet (though all the display cabinets appeared locked and sealed) . . .

I must admit I was glad to see Tattersham Church fading back into the dusk in my rearview mirror as I herded the minibus toward home like an anxious sheepdog. I was just grateful that nothing really bad had happened . . . even though the minibus ahead seemed full of the fluttering shapes of swallowtail butterflies.

They tumbled out of the cars happily enough in the schoolyard. In fact, they'd sung the first two lines of old pop songs over and over, all the way home, a sure sign of well-being.

"Where's he taking you tonight, miss?" inquired Jack Hargreaves, loudly.

"What do you mean?" bridled Dorinda.

"'e's taking you to the flicks, ain't he? Your feller? I mean, 'e's not stingy . . . they've got Elvis on at the Roxy."

"It's a cowboy film, miss—*Love Me Tender*."

"Oh, it's lovely, miss—he gets killed in the end," chorused the girls.

"It's dead wet," chorused the boys.

"Let me run you home," I said to her tactfully, as she was about to explode.

When I dropped her off, I said, "What about old Elvis, then?"

She invited me to a horse race at Meersden on Saturday; and it poured all afternoon. I can't think of a worse punishment than that.

THERE THE WHOLE THING might have died. But it rained all Sunday as well, and I spent the time in my little darkroom, developing the photographs I'd taken in the church. They'd come out remarkably sharp, for flash, and I blew them up to 10 × 8, to console her. They'd look quite nice around the classroom walls . . . The one thing I couldn't make out was a face that appeared in one, peering around one of the tombs. It wasn't my face, and it certainly wasn't Dorinda's. Far too ugly. And, as it had a bald head, it certainly wasn't one of the children's.

It was well back in the harsh shadows thrown by the flash, watching two of the girls rubbing a brass-lettered tablet set in the floor. The girls were very intent (or pretending to be very intent) on what they were doing, and were obviously quite unaware of being watched. The face didn't look like a real person's, somehow; I might have put it down as the face of an effigy from one of the tombs, except that the eyes were dark and alive and watching. It worried at my mind all the time I was printing and developing. I kept on going across to the print where it was hanging up to dry, and staring at the face; I think I was trying to reason it out of existence, as a trick of the flash on a piece of crumbling stonework. As a projection of my own eye and mind. But it looked . . . it looked, let's face it, hungry and evil. I didn't like the thought that I was making it up out of my own imagination; I've always had a down-to-earth, trouble-free imagination.

Anyway, I ran down to the school with the photographs on the Wednesday and the kids were pleased to see me, and so was Dorinda—and so, by a miracle, was the headmistress. The kids had been busy, working from what they'd done in the church, and the lively results were hanging all over the walls. It appeared that as soon as they'd got back into the classroom, they'd come back to rambunctious life and produced the best stuff ever seen. So good that an inspector had been summoned. I was introduced to him: a pushy young man who went wild over my photographs and said it was seldom that a school-board member took such an interest, and who went on about having the whole exhibition set up in the foyer at County Hall. I wondered whether he was just angling to get a date with Dorinda, but his enthusiasm seemed genuine enough and had sent the headmistress into seventh heaven.

I pointed out the strange watching head in the photograph. Dorinda insisted it was a trick of the light. But Jack Hargreaves said, "Yeah, sir, he was there. An old bloke. He didn't say nothing. Just hung around in the shadders, watching the girls, dirty old sod. I thought 'e was the caretaker."

The headmistress gave Dorinda a very funny look, and Dorinda went a bit pale. The inspector changed the subject rather quickly, and went back to his praise of the drawings of cross-eyed cherubs and the very fine picture of a tomb that Henry was busy on. It had a mournful draped lady on top, in the Regency style, and the inscription:

TO THE MEMORY OF MARY CRAIG
A WOMAN OF EXEMPLARY PIETY AND
DISCRETION
WHO WAS CALLED HENCE AT THE EARLY AGE OF
29
YET HAVING IN AN EMINENT DEGREE ATTAINED
THAT

"You'll have to hurry and finish this," said the inspector.

"Can't, sir—this is as far as we copied. We had to rush at the end."

"Pity," said the inspector. "It certainly can't be hung up in County Hall in that unfinished state."

I saw a look pass from Henry to Jack Hargreaves; I thought it was a look of pure disgust. How wrong I was, I was only to discover later.

ON MONDAY MORNING at the shop, the phone rang, sounding like trouble. It was the headmistress, and even over the phone I could tell she was tight-lipped and shaking with fury.

"You'd better get down here straight away, Mr. Ashden. I knew this church business would lead to nothing but trouble. I feel I must call a meeting of the board, but I think you are entitled to be consulted first."

I covered the mile to school in record time. The headmistress was waiting just inside the entrance, and pounced immediately. She *was* tight-lipped and shaking. She led me to the hall where Dorinda's exhibition had been hung before going to County Hall. She gestured with a quivering hand at the big central exhibit. It was Henry and Jack Hargreaves's drawing of the Regency tomb; the draped lady on top still looked like a wilting lettuce leaf, but the inscription had been completed:

TO THE MEMORY OF MARY CRAIG

A WOMAN OF EXEMPLARY PIETY AND

DISCRETION

WHO WAS CALLED HENCE AT THE EARLY AGE OF

29

YET HAVING IN AN EMINENT DEGREE ATTAINED

THAT MATURITY

WHICH CONSISTETH NOT IN LENGTH OF DAYS

DIED MCCLXXX

Unfortunately, other words had been scrawled over this chaste message, huge words in a wild hand. Words like "whore" and "strumpet" and "doxy."

"That," said the headmistress, "is what comes of ill-advised expeditions." She led me to her office. The inspector was there, rather white around the gills in the face of such massive female wrath. And Dorinda, who if anything looked rather red in the face, and defiant.

"Have you faced the lads . . . with this?" I asked.

"Certainly not."

"Can I see them?" I asked, as calmly as I could. "I think it might stop us making fools of ourselves."

"What *do* you mean, Mr. Ashden?"

"I mean these are not words commonly found in the twentieth-century child's vocabulary."

The inspector nodded; he was no fool. The headmistress picked up that nod, and Henry was duly summoned.

"Henry," I said. "Suppose I was to send you out for a strumpet . . . where would you go to get one?"

Henry looked at our assembled faces warily—too old a hand not to smell trouble coming a mile off. But then a look of genuine bafflement came over his face. "Music shop?" he offered.

"That's a *trumpet*, Henry."

"Cake shop?" A flicker of a grin crossed his face.

"That's *crumpet*, Henry."

"Dunno, sir." His face was utterly still again.

"So, Henry, what would you call . . . a woman . . . who took money for going with men?"

Henry's face froze in a look of pure horror. Never had such words been uttered in this holy of holies.

"You may answer, Henry," said the headmistress, without moving her lips at all.

"A . . . tart, miss. On the game. Or a scrubber." The whites were showing all around his eyes.

"So if you didn't know what a strumpet was, Henry, why did you write it on your picture of the tomb?"

"'Cos it was on the tomb when Jack an' I got there, Saturday afternoon, sir. We didn't know whether to copy it or not, but we thought it must be official."

I beat the inspector to our cars by a full ten yards . . .

"NEVER IN MY FORTY YEARS as a servant of God have I known such a thing," boomed the Reverend Ernest Lacey.

"One opens one's church to schools for the benefit of the community as a whole, and *this* happens. Children today . . ."

"Can you suggest," I said, "how children today could possibly have reached up that high? I mean, is there a ladder available that they could have used?"

The young police sergeant whom Lacey had brought with him nodded thoughtfully.

"There is no ladder," said the Reverend Lacey. "They must have brought one with them."

"On their bicycles?"

"That's an adult's work, sir," said the sergeant. "You can tell by the sweep of their arm, in the lettering." He stood up on a pew, and stretched up. "Big fellow—almost as big as me. That's adults, Reverend."

"Disgusting."

"Henry," I said, "was that bald man here again, when you came?"

"Yeah," said Henry, very chastened. "He was hanging about, peeping at us. Didn't say nothing. I thought he might stop us, but he didn't say nothing. He's only really interested in girls . . . He was a rum 'un, though." Henry blushed delightfully, and stopped.

"Why, Henry?"

"Can I whisper, sir?" He drew close. "Jack Hargreaves reckoned he were only wearing a shirt . . . a raggy shirt, all dirty. Reckon he was one o' *them*, sir."

"One of what, Henry?" asked the headmistress in dire tones.

"An escaped lunatic, miss," said Henry, dissimulating. "A nut."

"Nut or not," said the sergeant, "if it's adults, it's a crime. Now, if you'll pardon me, Reverend, I'll take evidence. Then you can get the place cleaned up." He went to the tomb and began to scrape some of the black paint of the vile lettering off with a knife, into a little envelope. I noticed the paint could not have been dry; it came off the white marble too easily. I saw the sergeant wrinkle his nose.

We left him and drove back to school, the headmistress emitting sighs all the way, like a dragon cooling down after breathing fire; and Dorinda making subtle little self-righteous noises that seemed to be demanding an apology from her superior.

MY SHOP BELL rang while I was brewing coffee. It turned out to be the young uniformed sergeant from the church. I offered him a cup; he drifted around my shop looking at things.

"It's all paid for, sergeant," I said, half sharply, half a joke.

"That's all right, sir," he said soothingly. "I'm into old things a bit myself. That's a nice Viennese regulator . . . The trade price is twenty pounds, I see."

I raised my eyebrows. "Nineteen to you, sergeant. Or is that bribing a policeman in the course of his duties?"

Surprisingly, he laughed, and got out a checkbook. "I'm afraid I'm not the usual sort of police sergeant; I've got A levels. It worries my superintendent. He doesn't think I'm quite human. First he sent me off to Bramshill College to get rid of me, and now he keeps me at headquarters for dealing with the nobs, and anything funny that crops up, like this church business."

"There have been developments, then?"

"Oh, yes. Of a sort. We know he's got a key to the church."

I gave a grunt of surprise.

"The vicar got a woman in to clean up, then he locked

the church; thought he had the only key. A week later he went to look around, and the joker had been at it again. And three times since, in the last fortnight. I've been spending a few sleepless nights in that vestry . . . but nothing happens while I'm around. Then the first night I'm not, it happens again."

"I don't envy you," I said. "It's a nasty building. I don't think I'd spend a night alone there for a superintendent's wages."

"I wasn't alone, sir," he said with a wry grin. "Local bobby was with me."

"What does he think?"

"Hasn't a clue. He's new—came last year from Stropping. I'm afraid village bobbies aren't what they were. I'd like you to come and see the place again, sir, if you will. I'd like your professional opinion."

"It wasn't those kids, you know."

"I know it's not kids."

As we went, I slipped the pictures I'd taken in church into my pocket. Or rather, one of them.

I looked at the interior of the church aghast. Every tomb seemed to have been vandalized.

WILLIAM TRENTON
VICAR OF THIS PARISH FOR FORTY YEARS
AND AN INDUSTRIOUS HARBINGER OF CHURCH
MUSICK
THE SWEETNESS OF HIS HARMONIES CHARMED
THE EAR
AND THE MILDNESS OF HIS MANNERS THE
HEART
DIED MDCCCV

That one carried, scrawled in furious letters:

THEEFE. EXTORTIONER. GIVE BACK THE TITHES
YOU RUINED JACK BURTON FOR

And on the tomb of a lady of Invincible Virtue and
Great Condescension:

SHE PLAYED THE HARLOT WITH HER OWN SON

I walked from one to the other.

"Nasty," I said. "But not brainless. It's almost as if he
knew all about them. A mad local historian?"

"It's funny you should say that. I've checked the church
records. There was a farmer called John Wilberforce
Burton—died in 1783. Dispossessed of his land—killed
himself—not buried in sacred ground. And the lady he
made that comment on, she had a son who never married.
She outlived him. The comments are all *relevant*. Almost
like he'd known them personally."

"Has every one been got at?"

"He's left the Victorian ones alone . . . and the
schoolmaster, Dore."

"Oh, the pillar of virtue, yes. Well, he would, wouldn't
he?"

"Funny thing is . . ." The sergeant paused in embarrassment. ". . . I had a writing expert in—a graphologist.
Superintendent went mad about the expense of getting
him over from Muncaster. I got all the kids in that class
to scribble stuff down for me. He went over them—that's
how I know it wasn't the kids—but he did say one funny
thing. Apparently the writing's very old-fashioned. It
seems that every century makes its own kind of mark . . ."
He ground to a halt.

"You mean, like the young Georgian gents who carved
their names so elegantly on the pews at Newhurst during

the long sermons . . ." And I ground to a halt, too. We looked at each other in the gloom of the nave, then shrugged, as men do, and changed the subject. How different Dorinda's story might have been if we hadn't.

I pulled out my photograph. The one with the bald head, watching the little girls brass-rubbing. I suppose now we'd got onto daft topics, I wasn't afraid to raise the matter.

"What do you make of that, sergeant?"

"Oh, this is the famous photograph? I'd meant to ask you about that. Only I reckoned the lads were making up a tale, to get out of trouble. Rum-looking bloke, if it *is* a bloke . . . hard to tell . . . could be a lump of marble . . . statue's hand or something . . ."

"Let's line it up from where I took it."

We looked. There was nothing on any of the tombs where the head appeared in my photograph.

"Could be anything. Maybe one of the kids left a packet of sandwiches on a ledge. It looks crumpled . . . crumpled and yet . . . bloated . . . bit like a turnip lantern. Could even be the head of another kid."

"A *bald* kid?"

"Could be a trick of the flash, making him look bald. If he's real, I wouldn't fancy meeting him up an alley on a dark night."

We both laughed uneasily. Then he said: "Do you mind if I hang on to this? I'll get some copies made. Somebody in the district might recognize him. Somebody who's been to Madame Tussaud's wax museum maybe." We laughed uneasily again.

And there we left it.

I MUST SAY the official opening of our exhibition at County Hall was quite a do. That was in the days when money was no object; the catering was elegant, and the whisky flowed like water. The exhibition looked great; they'd borrowed my negatives and blown them up to a yard square and very sharp, and the kids looked far keener and more industrious than they really had been. But their work was good, and beautifully mounted; good mounting can make a thing look worth a million dollars.

You must remember that was also in the days before kids were taken out of school a lot; I think the county was trying to encourage projects in the elementary grades. There were a lot of teachers there that evening, and a lot of inspectors and organizers and advisers, and a lot of councillors who'd mainly come for the whisky (which they drank at incredible speed, never batting an eyelid; they must have had a lot of practice). Form 4C were there as well, brought by the headmistress from Barlborough on a bus, with four other teachers as reinforcements. The children looked incredibly clean: I didn't recognize them till they spoke.

Dorinda, I remember, came straight from home in her white Mini. She looked so happy and excited. There was such a press of people around her, complimenting her, or just touching their forelocks and asking to be remembered to her father, that I couldn't get near. But I remember to this day how happy she looked . . .

Working around the exhibits, I came face to face with my police sergeant, every inch the gent in natty tweed; Mike Watkins as I knew him now, from his name on the check.

"How's your Vienna regulator doing?"

"Fine. That's about all that is."

"Not caught your mad local historian, then?"

"Nobody recognized the photograph. Though I got

some damned funny looks. You know, what strikes me is the way it all started after 4C had been to the church."

"It wasn't them!"

"I know it wasn't. But things started happening immediately after . . . like they'd *disturbed* something. Something pretty nasty. I've got one new piece of evidence."

All the time, we'd been moving around the exhibition. Now something old and beautiful and shiny caught my dealer's eye, among all the cross-eyed cherubs and dim brass rubbings. A padlock, thin and elegant, and polished with Brasso half out of its life.

"Hang on," I said. We went across together. The notice under the padlock, rather wildly written, read:

A MEDIEEVIL LOCK. ON LOAN FROM
TATTERSHAM CHURCH FROM THE CRIP
(DRACULA) DONE UP BY J. HARGREAVES
AND H. WINTERBOTTOM

The lock was not medieevil, or even medieval. It was elegantly Georgian, with an interlacing pattern of crosses—the lock from the grille of the vault under the altar.

An awful premonition gripped me.

"What's your nasty piece of evidence?" I asked. He shuffled uncomfortably.

"Well, you remember I scraped some of the black paint off that first tomb that was vandalized? I sent it to forensics, and they couldn't make head nor tail of it, so they sent it on to the Home Office. Lucky I'd scraped off plenty."

"Well?" I asked sharply.

"Well, old Sir Bernard Spilsbury got to the bottom of it. It wasn't paint at all—it's the decomposed remains of tissue. Animal or human, they can't really tell . . . it's so old."

"How old?"

He gulped. "They reckon . . . centuries old . . ."

"Oh, my God, the lock . . . the crypt. Somebody who knew the owners of the tombs personally . . . It's crazy, sergeant. If we say anything, they'll throw us in the nut-house."

He became very constabulary, the way even the best ones can. "I have evidence, sir, that party or parties unknown have entered the crypt and violated the cadavers, and are using their remains to write graffiti on the tombs. All of which are crimes."

As from another world, the voice broke in on us: from the cozy world of pretty girls handing around drinks and art advisers plotting, and councillors knocking back whisky.

"Ladies and gentlemen, in honor of this unique occasion, the chairman of the county council, Councillor Neil Fogarty, will present certificates of merit to each child who took part."

It went quite smoothly until the name Hargreaves, J., was uttered. No Hargreaves, J., came forward.

"I'm certain he was on the bus," said the headmistress, testily.

"Perhaps he's gone to the . . ."

"Carry on," said the headmistress.

They carried on, until they came to the name Winterbottom, H. Not only was he missing also, but a thorough search of the cloakrooms and corridors had revealed no trace of Hargreaves, J., either.

"Where are they?" hissed Dorinda, realistically taking the class monitor on one side and shaking the life out of her.

Eventually, there were tears. And the appalling admission that the two had slipped away from the bus, having asked to stop for the bathroom at Tattersham. The whole class had got off: Jack and Henry had deliberately not got back on. Others had answered their names on the roll call. Jack and Henry had brought sandwiches and flashlights. They were going to lie in wait in the church for the bald-headed man who wrote the dirty words.

The next second, Dorinda was running for her car; and the sergeant and I were pounding down the corridors of County Hall behind her.

WE NEARLY CAUGHT UP with her in the parking lot; she drove off from under our very noses.

"We'll take my car," I shouted. Which we did, and by putting my foot down on the turnpike, I nearly overtook her at Selmerby. But at that point she took to the little winding lanes that she'd known on horseback since a child.

"We've lost her, sir," said Sergeant Watkins. "Drop me at the next phone booth and I'll summon help straight to the church."

But I couldn't bear to stop. One thing kept ringing through my head: Henry Winterbottom saying that whatever the thing was, it didn't bother *boys*. It was the little *girls* it was interested in.

In the end, Sergeant Watkins took the law into his own hands (as he had every right to do), and jumped out as I slowed down at a crossroads. At least he had the courtesy to slam the door, so I didn't even have to stop. But the minutes ticked away; I took a wrong turning and got lost. And still the minutes ticked away.

It was half an hour before I pulled up by Tattersham Church. The white Mini was parked by the porch. No light on in the church, or in the big house; but in the moonlight, the church door gaped wide. Henry's skill with a lock had worked again.

I ran through the inner door; into pitch darkness.

"Dorinda?"

There was a kind of mindless animal sob.

"Dorinda, for God's sake!" I shouted.

Then I heard a slithering noise, somewhere among the box pews; I was just beginning to see the outline of the windows now, but nothing else.

Then Henry's voice came, quavering: "Careful, sir. We're in the corner, here. Watch it, he's prowling around."

"He'd better not prowl around me," I shouted, "or I'll break him in half."

"Watch it, sir. He's all slippery . . . pongy . . . he sort of falls apart when you touch him."

Oh, God, the lights. Where were the lights? I realized I'd never known.

"Where are the lights, Henry?" I was moving toward him, slowly, stealthily. Listening for the slithering that was moving between us.

Dorinda began to sob again, softly, mindlessly.

"The lights don't work, sir," quavered Henry. "They must have cut them off."

My outward-groping hand came into contact with something upright, round, and hard. I knew what it was; one of the churchwardens' staffs that are set upright at the end of the back pews. I got it loose, and felt for the top—a heavy brass bishop's miter; it would make a good club. I felt a little better, and moved on. The sound of Dorinda's sobbing, the boys' heavy breathing, came nearer. So did the slithering. And I could smell him now—the smell that had always been in this church, but a thousand times stronger. The smell of death; I had smelled it, plunging into the bowels of a crashed bomber in the war.

I could smell him, I could hear him; but I hit him because I *felt* him: a sudden drop in temperature on the right-hand side of my face as he came at me—as if he drew the warmth out of the surrounding air . . .

I had never struck a blow like it before, and I hope never to strike one like it again. It would have killed a man; but I could never have brought myself to hit a living man that hard. It had all the fear in me, all the rage, all the hate. And I could tell from the feel of it that the churchwarden's staff hit him where his neck joined his shoulders. It felt like hitting a rotten marrow, with bone splintering inside. Cold drops splashed my face. But there was no shudder, no gasp of pain or groan; it was hitting a dead thing, and instinctively I gave up hope.

The next second, the staff was snatched from my hands so fiercely that I lost all use of my fingers. And the second after that, I was flung against the pews with such force that the seat back, like a horizontal ax, drove all the air from my lungs, and I thought my back was broken. But I had felt the large hands that flung me—cold as ice, even through my trench coat. I lay on the floor and listened to the slithering go past me toward the corner where Dorinda was.

I don't know how I got back to my feet, but as I did so, a sound came to me from the sane world outside: the wail of a police-car siren. The windows of the church lit up from without, with the cold blue light of car headlights. And I saw him. Or it.

For, sensing the flare of light, it turned, and I saw it across the tops of the box pews. A bald head, with blank black eyes which shone in the light. A broad chest, with what might have been a growth of black hair. And around the head and shoulders, not a ragged shirt, as Henry had said. But the green rags of a shroud . . .

Now there was a second police-car siren. Old Watkins must have had them homing in by radio from every point of the compass.

For a long moment the creature paused, like a badger brought to bay in its own wood. Then it seemed to sense that there would be no end to the lights and the noise, and the men, with whom it had little quarrel. Men who could run it to earth and destroy and demolish and block it off forever. Though the unreadable expression on the bald face never changed, I knew that it despaired.

The next second, it was limping at great speed across the nave, toward the altar. I heard the grille to the vault clang, and it was gone.

Seconds later, the beam of a flashlight cut across the nave from the porch. There was a fumbling, and all the lights went on; Sergeant Watkins must have known where the master switch was. And then the place was full of caps and blue uniforms.

"Where?" asked Mike Watkins. I nodded toward the grille that led to the vault. He walked across, took something from his pocket, and clicked it into place on the grille. He gave me a certain look, and I nodded. There are some things that are best not entered in policemen's notebooks, if only for the sake of chief constables and the judiciary.

"How did you get the lock?" I asked him.

"I confiscated it as material evidence," he said ruefully. "But it's better back where it is. I don't think we'll have any more bother, do you?"

I shook my head; but I rattled the old Georgian lock gently, just to make sure.

There was a gaggle of blue uniforms in the far corner, but it was parting; someone was being led out.

Dorinda was as white as a sheet, silent, eyes looking nowhere—all the signs of deep shock. But at least she was putting one foot in front of the other.

"I've radioed for an ambulance," said Sergeant Watkins. The boys followed Dorinda out, with that same white, glazed look on their faces. Except Henry, who summoned up enough energy for a ghost of a grin and said, "Cor, sir, you didn't 'arf fetch him one . . ."

I went to the hospital with Dorinda in the ambulance; the boys went in the police car.

Halfway there, she opened her eyes and knew me. "Geoff . . . thanks."

But it wasn't the Dorinda Molyneaux I'd known. The unshakable confidence had gone; the certainty that there was a practical answer for everything.

"I never realized . . ." She closed her eyes and was silent, then continued: "I thought if you were decent . . . and kept the rules . . . God wouldn't let things like that . . . happen to you."

I didn't ask what had happened to her. I just said, "God lets road accidents happen to decent people every day. Why should that kind of thing be so different?"

"Yes," she said, with the sadness you expect from an old, old woman. "Yes." She reached out and grabbed my hand, and played with the knuckles. "I like you—you're *warm.*" She went on holding my hand till we got to the hospital.

Mike Watkins joined me in the waiting room—with his notebook.

"I suppose you're after the name and address of the accused," I said, with a weak attempt at humor.

"Only for my own interest."

"Must have been old Anstey, the Public Auditor. It was the Anstey vault."

"Well, I'm not going down again to look—not for a superintendent's wages. But I don't reckon it was Anstey. Anstey's memorial was desecrated, too. And I've seen a painting of him, in old age—a thin, elegant old gent, with lots of frizzy gray hair."

"What I saw hadn't got gray hair." I shuddered at the memory. "Who d'you reckon it was, then?"

"The only memorial that wasn't desecrated was Thomas Dore's."

"The honoured and paineful schoolemaster and bene-factor of this parish . . ."

"Still publickly rebuking vice . . ."

"And discretely practising virtue . . . God, I feel sick. I'd like to blow the place to smithereens and him with it."

"Nasty thing, repressed sex," said Sergeant Watkins. "We were shown a lot of that at Bramshill College. Prefer a pint of beer and a game of darts, meself. Don't fret, Geoff. He won't get loose again. I'll have a word with the vicar. He'll believe us . . . Nobody else would."

I took good care of Dorinda after that. Eventually, she got so she could walk into a church again—if I held her hand tight. She did that just before we got married. Which was the last day of Miss Dorinda Molyneaux.

NOTES ON
FIRST PUBLICATION

"Rachel and the Angel" first published in *Rachel and the Angel and Other Stories* (London, 1986; New York, 1987). Reprinted here by permission of Pan Macmillan Children's Books, a division of Pan Macmillan Ltd.

"Graveyard Shift" has not appeared previously.

"A Walk on the Wild Side" first published in *The Haunting of Chas McGill and Other Stories* (London & New York, 1983), reprinted in *A Walk on the Wild Side* (London, 1989). Reprinted here by permission of Methuen Children's Books, a subsidiary of Reed International Books.

"The Making of Me" first published in *Echoes of War* (London, 1989; New York, 1991).

"The Night Out" first published in *Love You, Hate You, Just Don't Know*, Josie Karavasil, comp. (London, 1980), reprinted in *The Haunting of Chas McGill and Other Stories*.

"The Woolworth Spectacles" first published in *Antique Dust* (London & New York, 1989).

"A Nose Against the Glass" first published in *Rachel and the Angel and Other Stories*. Reprinted here by permission of Pan Macmillan Children's Books.

"Gifts from the Sea" first published in *Echoes of War*.

"The Creatures in the House" first published in *You Can't Keep Out the Darkness*, Peggy Woodford, comp. (London, 1980), reprinted in *The Haunting of Chas McGill and Other Stories* and *A Walk on the Wild Side*.

"The Death of Wizards" first published in *Rachel and the Angel and Other Stories*. Reprinted here by permission of Pan Macmillan Children's Books.

"The Last Day of Miss Dorinda Molyneaux" first published in *Antique Dust*.